3-21

W9-BXY-995

# Riverwatcher

# Riverwatcher

## Ronald Weber

Skyhorse Publishing

All Rights Reserved. No part of this book may be reproduced in any manner without the express written consent of the publisher, except in the case of brief excerpts in critical reviews or articles. All inquiries should be addressed to Skyhorse Publishing, 307 West 36th Street, 11th Floor, New York, NY 10018.

Skyhorse Publishing books may be purchased in bulk at special discounts for sales promotion, corporate gifts, fund-raising, or educational purposes. Special editions can also be created to specifications. For details, contact the Special Sales Department, Skyhorse Publishing, 307 West 36th Street, 11th Floor, New York, NY 10018 or info@skyhorsepublishing.com.

Skyhorse® and Skyhorse Publishing® are registered trademarks of Skyhorse Publishing, Inc.®, a Delaware corporation.

Visit our website at www.skyhorsepublishing.com

10 9 8 7 6 5 4 3 2 1

Library of Congress Cataloging-in-Publication Data is available on file.

ISBN 978-1-62087-810-1

Printed in the United States of America

*For Mary Ames*

# 1

THE SIREN OF an EMS ambulance sliced through the July morning just as Mercy Virdon turned into a parking space across from the Six-Grain Bakery. Ordinarily, she didn't stop at the bakery on a weekday, when the regulars hanging out would be eager to corner her. There was always something, meaning some complaint, and usually about things—"The Brown Drake hatch was a washout this year, Mercy"—the manager of Michigan's Department of Natural Resources office in Ossning could do nothing about. Ordinarily, stopping at the bakery wasn't worth the grief, even if the place had the best coffee in town.

She listened to the siren long enough to realize it was fading—the ambulance on its way out of Ossning—before switching her attention to the other cars and trucks parked along the street. She was going inside the bakery regardless, but knowing who the owners were would give her advance warning of what to expect. She had lived in Ossning too long, it occurred to her, if she knew who owned the vehicles you saw every day on the streets—too long, too, if you knew exactly what their owners would say when you ran into them. She was musing about that, experiencing a tinge of melancholy despite the perfection of the morning, when she saw a green Land Rover she recognized all too well.

It was in the process of pulling from the curb into the street, the driver peering straight ahead, unconcerned with the possibility of oncoming traffic. The vehicle was Verlyn Kelso's, the driver Verlyn himself. Not that it could be anyone else. Verlyn wouldn't let Jan near the vehicle, let alone Kit. One of the two must have been pressed into operating the cash register at the fly shop of the Kabin Kamp if Verlyn was in town on a July morning. There was always a fishing guide or two in the shop, tying flies or watching someone tying flies, but Verlyn drew the line when it came to guides at the cash register. Oddly, Verlyn had turned into a hard-nosed businessman, which anyone married to him, as Mercy had been, wouldn't have expected. Perpetual delinquent seemed more likely.

But she didn't want to think about that—or Verlyn's odd appearance in town on a weekday morning. It was the morning itself she wanted to hold fast. When Mercy left Fitzgerald at the A-frame at Walther Bridge he was loading his Grand Cherokee for a morning of fishing on the mainstream above Danish Landing. A report had come in about tricos up there—early in the season for their appearance, but the report had come from an occasionally reliable source—and Fitzgerald, propelled along on an adrenalin rush, meant to check it out.

She didn't mind leaving him at the A-frame and heading off to work dressed in her summer uniform. She didn't mind a bit until, halfway into Ossning on the North Downriver Road, she abruptly switched off a Patsy Cline CD and gave full attention to the quality of the air wafting through her open window. It was unusually sweet. She had an impulse to close her eyes, feel the air wash across her face, weave through the unruly mound of her hair—which wouldn't be wise even though the Suburban was the only vehicle on the road. Better, she should turn off on one of the gravel roads that led to the river, park at a landing, enjoy air and sun.

But that wouldn't do, either. It wouldn't look right if anyone came along and saw an on-duty DNR officer idly basking in morning light. She could claim to be working—some people thought that was what her job amounted to anyway, *looking* at the river, *thinking* about it—but would know she wasn't. She wasn't earning her pay as a public servant, which meant getting to the office on time and meeting her appointments and attending meetings and shuffling through the stream of paper. She had joined the DNR, long ago, because she liked outdoor work, and had risen to the point where she had little reason to be outdoors. Some serious irony there.

She could, though, ease into her workday and the demands of her conscience by stopping at the Six-Grain Bakery for a mug of coffee and a chat with Bonnie Pym. She and Bonnie could commiserate together about being cooped up inside on a July day, prisoners of work. Together they could glimpse through the windows of the bakery the sunlight in the maples along the street, sigh, describe all the places they would rather be, bemoan the fate of indoor workers everywhere. Bonnie was your woman if it was sympathy you were after, even though getting to her meant negotiating the minefield of the bakery complainers.

*    *    *

"THOUGHT YOU'D BE busier."

Mercy had taken one of the tables for two, hoping to limit access to the DNR, before she realized there were only a few customers in the bakery, all as solitary as she, hunched over coffee and morning newspapers. Bonnie had left the counter to one of the younger girls and sat on the edge of the chair across from Mercy.

"Earlier we were."

"I'll have to remember that."

"Weather's the thing," Bonnie said. "Real nice out, people come early, don't lounge around so much."

"I suppose."

Something in Mercy's tone alerted Bonnie. She leaned forward across the table, eyes narrowed. "Feeling poorly?"

"On a day like this?"

Bonnie waited.

"Work blues, maybe. You ever think," Mercy asked, "of doing something else?"

"You kidding? When don't I. You, too?"

"Now and then."

"You've got the best job of any girl around."

"There's a new woman doctor in town."

"Yeah, well, that's a whole other planet."

"I suppose."

"I'd like to marry a rich, great-looking guy," Bonnie said, "then not do a thing."

"You shouldn't have given up so quickly on Fitzgerald."

Bonnie lifted two mauve-nailed fingers to her lips, then held them in the air as if a cigarette still dangled between them. "It was the other way around."

Mercy smiled. "He's not so great looking, anyway."

"Easy for you to say," Bonnie said, and smiled back.

"What I'd like to do today is what he's doing, fishing the mainstream. All day, just fishing it."

"Maybe he won't catch anything."

"Fishing it and then hanging out at Verlyn's fly shop and swapping lies with the guides. What a life."

"Yeah, well, that's what he gets for winning the lottery."

"Fitzgerald's one of the idle rich, Bonnie. I've always known that but, day like this, I *really* do. You know what I mean?"

"You're feeling poorly because he's rich and you're going to work."

"You've got a way," Mercy said, "of getting to the heart of things. But he's not exactly rich. Just comfortably off."

"There's a difference?"

*       *       *

BONNIE REFILLED THE coffee of the other customers in the bakery, finally worked her way back to Mercy's table. Mercy put a hand over her mug.

"Had enough before I came in."

"You just wanted to see little ol' me?"

"As a matter of fact," Mercy said, "I've got a question. How come Verlyn was in here?"

Bonnie replaced the coffee pot behind the counter, then came back to the table, settled again on the edge of the chair across from Mercy. "Same deal," she said. "See little ol' me."

"Why?"

"Now why'd you think?"

"Seriously?"

"Verlyn in town this time of year, big spenders staying at the lodge? Doesn't that seem serious?"

Mercy said, "I wondered when I saw the Rover."

"Actually, there probably aren't so many at the lodge just now. Sort of quiet, end of July, before the August rush. So that's part of the reason Verlyn was in."

"And you're the other."

Bonnie grinned, leaned across the table. "Between you and me, I think there must be trouble with Jan. He's been coming in nearly every day, chatting me up. All it's amounted to so far."

"No quiet evening over in Traverse City?"

"Nope."

"Or down and dirty at the Keg O'Nails?"

"Not yet."

"Lord, Bonnie."

"Hey, don't get me wrong." Bonnie leaned back in her chair and with a swishing sound crossed her legs beneath her nylon uniform. "It's a way of killing time, is all. I wouldn't go across the street with Verlyn."

"Does he know that?"

Bonnie shrugged. "With him it's hard to tell. There's sort of a look in his eyes."

"Nothing new about that."

"You'd know."

"Tell me about it," Mercy said.

*       *       *

IT WAS NEARLY ten o'clock when she reached the office. Surprisingly, her mood had improved. She was still missing out on the day, boxed in by bureaucratic walls and fluorescent lighting, but Bonnie had gotten her mind off herself and onto Verlyn. More specifically, onto Jan. Were there problems with wife number two?

Tiny, soft-voiced, *sweet* Jan was thought to be just what Verlyn needed after his riotous mismatch with Mercy. Everyone said so, including Jan herself. Jan's style as a wife was simply to be everything Mercy hadn't been. Dressed in a prim, pressed safari outfit—her idiotic idea of what one wore in the north country—she ran the lodge of Kelso's Kabin Kamp with smooth efficiency, leaving Verlyn free to manage the fly shop and organize the guides. Free as well to carry on as boorishly as ever, with never a glowering look, let alone a harsh word, from his loving spouse.

Mercy wasn't fooled, though everyone else might be. Jan was younger than Verlyn—a good ten years, Mercy thought, a difference she had meant to establish from birth records but hadn't gotten around to—and stood in line to inherit the Kabin Kamp when Verlyn met his maker. That might be a long way off, but, financial opportunities in the north country being what they were, Jan could wait. When the time came, Mercy knew what would emerge from the dainty butterfly: merry widow, rich bitch.

Which you couldn't wholly begrudge her, not after putting up with Verlyn now nearly as long as Mercy had. But Mercy meant to be around, when the time came, to be certain Kit, her son with Verlyn, got his fair share of the Kabin Kamp. If the lodge went to Jan, the fly shop could go to him—which Verlyn might be thinking as well, now that he allowed Kit to work around the place. The possibility caught Mercy by surprise: she and Verlyn for once on the same page about something.

But that wasn't what was on her mind. It was Jan—and possible trouble in the marriage. It wasn't surprising, the trouble, if that was what it really was. In the long run, Verlyn wouldn't be able to tolerate perpetual peace any more than perpetual discord. He wasn't made for *any* kind of long run—which, it occurred to Mercy, maybe she wasn't, either. But if there was trouble in the marriage, it could mean a third was in the offing, Verlyn requiring a wife to help with the Kabin Kamp now that slavery was abolished, and that meant Mercy would have to recalculate everything in regard to Kit's place in the line of inheritance. Thinking about it that way, she would just as soon see Jan remain in the picture.

Mercy smiled to herself, which caused the secretary standing before her in the outer office, Fern Lax, to tilt her head with a quizzical look.

"You ever find yourself thinking some crazy thing," Mercy tried to explain, "you thought you'd never think in a million years?"

"No."

You wanted secretaries for order, not empathy. Fern Lax fit the bill exactly. Mercy smiled again, asked if there were any messages.

"I was trying to tell you. You're supposed to call the sheriff's office."

"Any indication what for?"

"Elsie didn't say."

When Mercy phoned from her office, Elsie, Willard Stroud's wife and secretary, said the sheriff wanted a DNR representative out at Rainbow Run campground first thing. "Said to tell you personally," Elsie added, "but you weren't in."

"I was a little late this morning. What's up out there to involve the sheriff?"

"Something big."

"Kids raising hell again?"

"No," Elsie said, but didn't elaborate.

"All right," Mercy said. "Tell him I'm on my way."

# 2

CALVIN McCANN PAUSED, an ear angled to the side, concentrating on the sound.

The siren was coming from just upriver, from the road across the Borchard at Walther Bridge, but he couldn't tell if it was a sheriff's patrol car or an emergency vehicle. Verlyn claimed he could tell from the sound alone, but Calvin didn't believe him. Verlyn blew a lot of hot air. On the other hand, close as he was, the road running right past the Kabin Kamp, maybe he could.

Calvin turned back to the woman standing in thigh-high current beside him and at the moment casting an olive Woolly Bugger to attractive water along a downed cedar. It didn't seem entirely right thinking of her as a woman since, Verlyn had told him, she had just turned seventeen and was still in high school in Dublin, Ohio. On the other hand, looking at her, noting the way she filled out her waders, Calvin had no trouble thinking of her as a woman. Verlyn might have sharp ears, but he himself had the eyes of a hawk.

"That's good," Calvin said to her, "but try casting up tighter. Hit close against the log, toss in a little slack so the fly drifts down, then retrieve quick across the current."

She smiled back at him as she began her backcast.

Her name was Gwendolyn Underwood, which struck him as odd, the Gwendolyn part. It sounded like the name of a middle-aged woman. But maybe her father, Graham Underwood, wanted another G name and couldn't think of anything better. Gina would have been a possibility. Or Gray, short for grayling. Calvin could have suggested that as a name, telling Graham Underwood how grayling had jammed the Borchard before the white pine was cut and sunlight raised the water temperature, and that was the beginning of the end for the grayling. But Verlyn said Graham Underwood, a big-time executive of some sort down in Ohio, wasn't the type you suggested things to, let alone a name for his only child. You only took his money and did what he wanted.

What he wanted at the moment was expert fly-fishing instruction for Gwendolyn, which was where Calvin came in. Verlyn had taken him aside and said that was all she was supposed to get. "What do you take me for?" Calvin said. "You know what," Verlyn said. He recounted what Calvin already knew, that Graham Underwood spent two weeks at the Kabin Kamp every June with a group of cronies from Ohio, fishing during the day and at night tossing back single-malt Scotch and swapping lies around the stone fireplace in the lodge. In itself that wasn't unusual. Most of the fishermen who came back to the Kabin Kamp year after year were cut from the same mold. What set Graham Underwood apart was that he spent money like a Greek shipping magnate. He bought flies by the fistful in the fly shop and loaded up with more gear than a dozen men could use in a lifetime, including a new Sage rod every other season, just to try something different.

Verlyn treated fishermen like that with kid gloves, which in Graham Underwood's case meant guiding him himself on afternoon float trips on the South Branch of the Borchard. Ordinarily, Verlyn didn't guide anymore, knowing it was better for someone other than the owner of the Kabin Kamp to be the target of abuse when the client's day on the water was a bust. But Graham Underwood wanted the headman for his guide, and it wasn't easy saying no to someone who had recently bought a Sage from you. So Verlyn floated him through some runs on the South Branch that he and Calvin maintained as semisecret, keeping Graham Underwood happy with fat brookies and an occasional trophy brown. Deep-secret runs were another matter, Verlyn holding to some standards.

This season Graham Underwood made a second trip to the Kabin Kamp with his daughter in tow. She was of an age to learn the basics of fly fishing, but he was smart enough to know she wouldn't learn as quickly or as well if her father were the teacher. He picked out equipment for her in the fly shop—waders, vest, rod, all the trimmings—but Gwendolyn chose her teacher, Calvin. "She's got good taste," Calvin said when he learned. "She hasn't met you yet," Verlyn said, "only heard about you." "What I meant," Calvin said, "is she didn't choose you."

Each morning after she had breakfast in the lodge, Calvin got together with Gwendolyn in the fly shop. They did some practice casting together in the mowed area across from the shop, where customers tried out new rods, then Gwendolyn pulled on her waders, and they got in the river and fished downstream together to a canoe landing. It wasn't a favorite stretch of the mainstream as far as Calvin was concerned—too many cabins visible among the spruce and pine, too many canoes bearing down on you from the liveries in Ossning—but the level streambed made for easy wading, and there were no overhanging trees to cause problems with backcasts.

"Keep in sight," Verlyn had said, giving the main reason for fishing the stretch of water below the Kabin Kamp. "In sight of who?" Calvin asked. Verlyn didn't answer, the reason being that Calvin already knew the answer. Some fishermen who stayed at the Kabin Kamp, older types especially with bum knees or bad backs, talked about fishing more than they actually fished. When they did venture in the water, it was usually the stretch from the lodge to the canoe landing, the fish therein the most fished-over fish in the Borchard. When he wasn't floating the South Branch with Verlyn, Graham Underwood could be one of the fishermen on the stretch of water, keeping an eye on his daughter and the guide. "No taking off in the truck," Verlyn said, giving Calvin his instructions. "No fishing the South Branch. No showing her beaver ponds in the pine barrens. Stay visible." Calvin shrugged and said, "You know me, boss." "That's the point," Verlyn said.

More and more, Verlyn sounded like a regular old fogy. There were times still, off with Calvin for private fishing, when he was himself, meaning as he was when he and Calvin, young guys, camped all summer on the South Branch, called themselves blood brothers, generally thumbed their noses at what passed for commonplace life. Then

Verlyn inherited Kelso's Kabin Kamp when his dad died, and began the process of becoming a regular old fogy.

When Calvin had laid out for Fitzgerald the reason for Verlyn's decline, Fitzgerald had nodded and quoted Thoreau, which was like him to do: "I see young men, my townsmen, whose misfortune it is to have inherited farms, houses, barns, cattle, and farming tools; for these are more easily acquired than got rid of. Better if they had been born in the open pasture and suckled by a wolf, that they might have seen with clearer eyes what field they were called to labor in." "That's good," Calvin told him, "except Verlyn didn't inherit a farm." "You're too literal," Fitzgerald said. "Naw," Calvin explained, "you got to keep things straight, is all."

What was straight now, he noticed, was Gwendolyn's line, a fish on. She was leaning forward, the rod bent in a tight arc, looking like she might get pulled into the water. Calvin moved close beside her, just to her left side, told her not to force the fish. "Just keep a tight line."

Gwendolyn's mouth was open, her eyes wide under a long-billed blue hat, the pony-tailed hair dangling below a shimmering chestnut brown in the sun. *The things you notice*, Calvin thought.

"You're doing good," he said to her. "Soon as you can, run in the line. Hold the fish on the reel. Take your time."

The fish probably wasn't big, but it was good enough for a first one on a fly. All her life she would remember it, forever hook it in her dreams. He didn't want her to lose it. You had to see your first fish, remove the hook from the jaw, release the miracle of it back to the river. He pulled his landing net from the clip at the back of his vest, held it ready.

Suddenly, the fish came out of the water, in a spray of foam danced for an instant on its tail—a rainbow, strong, fourteen inches maybe. Just as instantly Calvin knew what came next: limp line, straightened rod, deflated heart. "Naw," he said when Gwendolyn turned to him with stricken eyes, "nothing you could have done." He tried for a tone he didn't feel. "Think of it like a long release. Best kind there is. You didn't have to put a finger on the fish. We come back tomorrow, we'll hook that guy again."

Gwendolyn kept looking at him, but the appearance of her eyes had changed. Anger flared back at him. "That's baloney, Calvin."

Calvin nodded. "You're right."

"So why'd you say it?"

Calvin waited a moment before he asked, "Anybody ever call you Gwen?"

"Not at home. At school."

Calvin nodded again. "Tell you what, Gwen. Let's wade on past the canoe landing. There's a logjam I know, down there around a bend, where a big brown holes up. You can't get a cast in where he's at, but that Woolly Bugger might tempt him to come out."

"You're not just saying that?"

"He does come out, smacks your fly, you'll think you've gone to heaven."

*　　*　　*

FITZGERALD HAD SPOTTED a few tricos in the air but none on the water, and no fish were feeding. He sat on a downed log on the edge of the stream, tying on an Adams Wulff as an attractor with a Pheasant Tail nymph on a dropper, hearing the whine of a siren coming from downstream. The sound was a long way off, but it cut into his attention.

His mind had been emptied of everything except the feel of sun on his skin, the flat sheen of the water above a stretch of riffles, and the deadly silent accuracy of jays and swallows inhaling tricos in the languid air. He always told himself, going off for a morning of fishing rather than remaining saddled to his desk, that he would spend the downtime when the fish weren't hitting to think about his novel. He could work out plot details, form sentences in his head, even write a few things down in the spiral notebook he dutifully kept in a shirt pocket. He kept telling himself that, yet never did a thing.

In *Walden* Thoreau tells of night fishing on the pond from a boat, drifting in a gentle breeze and thinking large thoughts, then suddenly getting a strike and feeling jolted from "vast and cosmogonal themes" to a linkup once again with nature. That was the way it ought to be,

Fitzgerald agreed, but wasn't with him. Nature steadily held the upper hand when he went fishing, fish active or not. Maybe that was why, later in life, Thoreau gave up fishing: so he could concentrate solely—Fitzgerald had looked up the definition of *cosmogonal*—on theories of the universe. If so, it was unfortunate. He preferred a Thoreau united with the pond and its "mysterious nocturnal fishes."

The siren was probably coming from a vehicle crossing the river at Walther Bridge. The next bridge downstream was too far for the sound to carry. Fitzgerald moved from the downed log into the current, water tightening around his legs. He planned to wade upstream a ways, holding to the middle of the stream, floating the attractor and the nymph along wood piles, giving the tricos time to turn on. He'd go as far as a gray-shingled cabin set back in the pines, two hundred river yards or so, and if there was still no feeding activity, give up for the day, head back to the A-frame, saddle himself at his desk.

Maybe he would.

The siren coming from Walther Bridge had carried Mercy into his thoughts. They had left the A-frame together that morning, but Mercy had been heading off to work. Most people did. Someone who was working drove the vehicle crossing the bridge with its siren on. That was how people lived, by working. Yet here he was, wading a fine stretch of the Borchard on a fine morning, birds and insects and unseen trout his only company, not doing anything that could be called work. "What should be man's morning work in this world?" Thoreau asked in *Walden*, the assumption being there ought to be some.

Fitzgerald had worked before, for a newspaper, and might again. Technically, he was on indefinite leave of absence from the *Detroit Free Press*. Winning a modest state lottery had given him enough money to temporarily support the kind of life he was leading, which meant renting the big A-frame at Walther Bridge and reading Thoreau and writing a novel and fishing the Borchard through all the seasons. And having Mercy Virdon as a live-in partner—Mercy who had a job and a schedule to keep and, given the way the rest of the world was set up, a normal life. On certain mornings Mercy's example caused Fitzgerald to work up a decent sense of guilt.

Not that Mercy indicated in any way that he should. She kept telling him he was lucky, *damn* lucky, and should take full advantage. She would if she had won the lottery. She would spend her days fishing the river and tromping the woods studying the wildlife and, the weather lousy, staying inside listening to CDs and reading books and tying flies that were works of art. She wouldn't have *any* problem with that kind of life.

He knew Mercy meant what she said, but knew, too, she would never win a lottery because, a basic problem, she never bought a ticket. When he asked her about that, she tossed a hand in the air and said, "Because lightening never strikes twice," meaning because he had already won a lottery. "But it does," he said, "all the time." "So why don't you keep buying tickets?" "Because I'm not greedy," he told her, "except for you."

Deep down, Mercy didn't want to win a lottery. Winning would upset her life, complicate it at least, and she was content with it the way it was. She had the only job she ever wanted in the only town she ever wanted to live in. She didn't have a husband, but she had a son, Kit, and now she had Fitzgerald. There was that much of her life that hadn't been perfect, that much that was lacking, until he showed up on the Borchard and rented the house at Walther Bridge and fell in love with her. Thinking about it that way, you could say, ticket or no, Mercy *had* won a lottery.

Fitzgerald reacted a heartbeat too slow, setting the hook into nothing, when a fish hit the Adams just after it settled on the water. He was casting mechanically, thinking of Mercy, expecting nothing on the dry fly and little if anything on the nymph. He drew in the line, dried the Adams with false casts, dropped it again onto the same stretch of water. He needed to center his attention—the fish was probably small but a start for the day—and that meant forgetting Mercy, emptying his mind.

When he came to the gray-shingled cabin, he would turn around, switch to a pair of Matuka streamers, wade downstream to where he had parked the Cherokee. Then he would head back for the A-frame, pick up a bottle of Valpolicella, drive into Ossning for cheese at Glen's and fresh bread at the Six-Grain Bakery, show up at the DNR office at lunch time, and tell Mercy it was too nice a day not to have a picnic.

They would drive to the town park on the East Branch of the Borchard, and there Fitzgerald would tell her what had just occurred to him: She had won a lottery, so to speak, when he showed up in her life. He could picture the way her eyes would flash when he said that, and he would tell her she was probably as Irish as he was.

Then he would ask her, again, to marry him.

\*　　　\*　　　\*

KIT WAS STANDING outside the fly shop, having a smoke, when an EMS ambulance raced by on the bridge road, siren blasting the air. Two sheriff's patrol cars had crossed the bridge just before, blue lights revolving but no sirens, which was all that was needed considering the fact that there wasn't another vehicle on the road. It was Kit's view that some guys got into emergency work just so they could turn on sirens as they raced through the woods.

There was probably an accident on the South Downriver Road, a madman hauling logs driving up the rear end of a tourist out seeing the sights, which amounted to nothing more than flat vistas of jack pine. They would have to scrape the tourist off the asphalt, which was a job Kit wouldn't care to do, though maybe guys who liked sirens didn't mind.

From the fly shop he passed through a stand of white birch to the water's edge, sat on one of the lodge's peeled-log benches, flipped the stub of his cigarette into the river. A tiny trout rose to it, turned away. He lit a fresh cigarette and leaned back against the bench, worried.

It wasn't the way he should be feeling since, that morning, he had been doing the next best thing to fishing, which was running the fly shop while Verlyn was in town, none of the guides even around, tying flies and telling lies the way guides do when they aren't guiding. Today they weren't all guiding since the lodge was only half full, so they must be out fishing on their own, which was another thing guides did when they weren't guiding. And why, long term, it was the life Kit had in mind for himself.

In the meantime, he was satisfied working in the fly shop. Before, Verlyn had only let him help out the maids in the lodge and mow grass, mightily pissed off, as was Mercy, when he dropped out of Central Michigan. Verlyn hadn't even *started* college, yet now he thought going to school the greatest thing in the world. Mercy was another matter, having two college degrees, which was something Kit could barely imagine. But it was Verlyn who owned the fly shop and assigned the guides, not Mercy, so it was Verlyn he had to deal with day to day.

He had done the "peon" work around the lodge and pretty much kept his mouth shut, and eventually Verlyn had let him stock shelves in the fly shop and now and then run the cash register. He was moving up— but he wasn't giving in, not entirely. Verlyn called cigarettes "cancer sticks," which was why Kit smoked, going outdoors on his break time and lighting up in full view of Verlyn watching through the window of the shop. When he was a young guy, Verlyn probably smoked his head off, as everybody did back then, but now people who smoked drove him as wild as canoeists who littered the river or fishermen who kept the trout they caught.

Calvin was worse. You couldn't even smoke outside when you were around him, Calvin saying how he had read in some article that secondary smoke was worse outside than in, which was clearly bull. But you couldn't talk Calvin out of anything, which was why, if you ignored smoking and the fact Calvin didn't touch alcohol and a few other batty things about him, Kit liked him so much. Calvin—a modified Calvin but still the top guide on the Borchard—was his model.

Right now, Calvin was on the stretch of water below the Kabin Kamp, fishing with Gwendolyn Underwood, and she was the reason Kit was worried. Gwendolyn was pretty enough, so you wouldn't mind spending the day with her, guide fee or not, but Kit considered her too young for anything more. His taste ran to older women, at least over twenty-one. He wasn't twenty-one himself, but he was certain he looked like he was. When he stopped in at the Keg O'Nails, the manager, Deke Musso, never asked his age. Gwendolyn Underwood, on the other hand, wouldn't get past the door. She still had the look of a kid.

You could tell Calvin was lapping it up, the way Gwendolyn paid attention to everything he said, even the bull, and looked at him with wide eyes. Calvin was an expert when it came to the Borchard and fishing, but he was as old as Gwendolyn's father. He didn't look like her father, though, which might be the point as far as Gwendolyn was concerned. Calvin had a gray beard and gray hair in a pony-tail that hung out below the big Western Stetson he always wore on the river and usually a leather vest over his blue-denim shirts and duck boots on his feet whether it was wet or not. Calvin probably looked exotic to Gwendolyn, whereas to Kit he just looked like Calvin.

So Calvin would be lapping it up out there on the river with Gwendolyn, but Kit was pretty sure he wouldn't try anything on her. Calvin already had a string of women in Ossning and God knew how many tucked away in New Zealand when he was down there guiding in winter. And Kit had heard Verlyn make a point of telling Calvin to keep his hands off as far as Gwendolyn was concerned, her father being a hotshot businessman who kept coming to the Kabin Kamp year after year. Verlyn didn't want Calvin doing anything to rock the boat. Calvin had acted the smart ass, but you could tell he understood. Calvin had his head on pretty straight when it came to mixing business with pleasure.

About Verlyn, on the other hand, Kit wasn't so sure. He talked a good line to Calvin, and he certainly knew Gwendolyn was business since he personally guided her father on the South Branch. What had Kit worrying was what happened to Verlyn's eyes every time Gwendolyn came in the fly shop, going from their usual look, hard cash-register eyes, to glazed-over high school eyes, meaning eyes filled to the brim with impossible longing.

Kit didn't get it. Unlike Calvin, Verlyn had only one woman, but the woman was Jan, and Jan was still pretty sharp looking. So why did Verlyn get that look in the eyes around a kid like Gwendolyn Underwood? This morning, after Calvin and Gwendolyn had gone out on the lawn to work on her casting, Verlyn had abruptly put Kit in charge of the fly shop, went out to the Land Rover, shot off to town. He never went into Ossning during the fishing season when the fly shop was busy, but he had done just that nearly every morning since Gwendolyn and her father arrived at the Kabin Kamp.

Kit flipped another stub of cigarette into the river, watched it ride the current a few seconds before a trout—probably the same one, trout being none too intelligent—rose to take a look. He would have to make Verlyn a priority, watching out for him so he didn't do something stupid, make a fool of himself where Gwendolyn was concerned, and thereby harm the Kabin Kamp's reputation with someone like Graham Underwood. Business hotshots like that had hotshot friends, and word could get around.

Verlyn kept yakking to anyone would listen that a fishing lodge was a fragile thing as far as business went, and the slightest thing could send it down the tubes. He had the quality of the fishing on the Borchard in mind when he said that, but it could apply as well to messing around with a customer's daughter.

Kit got up slowly from the peeled-log bench, began making his way back through the stand of white birch to the fly shop. He had the feeling he was dragging a weight of concern behind him, which didn't seem entirely fair since he wasn't even an apprentice yet in the guide business. But that was the point: Someone had to keep an eye on Verlyn so he didn't foul up a future that, if Kit played his cards right, might come his way.

# 3

A SHERIFF'S PATROL car blocked the road into Rainbow Run. When Mercy pulled up beside it, Zack Cox got out of the car and came over to her open window.

"About time."

"For what?"

The deputy pushed back his broad-brimmed hat, drew a hand across his forehead. "We got us a long day here."

"C'mon, Zack. Quit stalling."

"Willard's been tryin' to get you."

"I know. But I'm here now. What's up?"

"Campground's sealed off. Nobody in or out 'til we get things figured out."

"But about what?"

"Willard said to send you in. Second loop, all the way back. Said you'd know where."

Mercy stared at him.

"Yup," Zack said. "Afraid so."

\*       \*       \*

AN EMS AMBULANCE was there, stopped in the middle of the loop road. In front of it she could see another patrol car and Willard Stroud's unmarked car, both parked just behind the blue Ford pickup. Mercy pulled her Suburban to the side, quickly got out, began half-running up the packed-dirt path to the campsite obscured by pines. Willard Stroud met her partway. When she saw his face, she knew there was nothing to ask.

Stroud led her back down the path to his car. When they reached it, he leaned against the side, tilted his face to the sun, closed his eyes. "Don't suppose you have a smoke," he said to her.

"You know I don't."

"We're hunting for footprints before everything's all messed up. Probably is already, ambulance boys clomping around." Stroud opened his eyes, looked at her. "Footprints are a waste of time, my experience. But you have to hunt anyway."

"He's dead?" she asked even though she knew it was pointless.

"Before we got here."

"Oh, Lord."

"We're waiting on Slocum Byrd before the boys move the body. I'm guessing he's been dead a while."

"How?"

"Looks like a shotgun was blasted through the tent. He was on the cot, maybe reading. You know how he was. He had one of those battery lanterns with neon tubes, still on, pretty faint, when we went inside. If it was night when it happened, that battery strong, the tent would have been lit up like a church. He was a sitting duck."

Mercy raised a hand. "Charlie was *murdered*?"

"You think it could be something else, shotgun blasted through the tent? It's why we're hunting for footprints."

"But no one would murder Charlie."

Slowly, Stroud shook his head. "No one should, you mean."

*    *    *

STROUD ASKED MERCY to wait in her Suburban while the medical examiner did his preliminary work and the body of Charlie Orr was removed to the ambulance. When he came back to her, Stroud opened the front passenger door, got inside.

"I was about right. Slocum thinks he's been dead six, eight hours, give or take, so it happened sometime between midnight and first light.

But Slocum says, the look of things, there was more than one shotgun blast. Maybe a double barrel."

"Good Lord."

Stroud looked at her closely. "You going to be all right?"

"Of course I am."

"I got you out here—you probably figured it out."

"Because we're in a state forest campground, and the Ossning field office of which I'm the director has immediate responsibility."

"That's part of the reason. I'm closing off the campground for a while. There were three campsites occupied last night, besides Charlie's and the campground hosts'. I want to keep those folks in here. And I don't want new folks coming in. We agreed on that?"

"You think Charlie was murdered by a camper?"

"You've got to start somewhere, is all. But it's possible. Someone who knew he was camped here."

"Plenty of people knew."

Stroud nodded. "Another reason I wanted to talk. You knew Charlie."

"So did you."

"But you knew his situation out here, how he got here, what the arrangement was with the DNR. If he wasn't killed by one of the campers, we might have to start looking into that."

"The campground hosts can tell you some."

"They're the ones in the big fifth-wheeler?"

"Burt and Billie Berry."

"She found him."

"Billie did?"

"Probably her footprints we're going to find. We had a little talk when I got here, but she wasn't all that coherent. Couldn't seem to remember Charlie's name. Kept calling him the Odd Fellow."

*    *    *

AFTER THE AMBULANCE left for Ossning and his deputies were finished examining the murder scene, Stroud led Mercy up the path to the campsite. They stood together on the edge of the clearing, silent, looking across at the white tent. Stroud pointed in the direction of the shredded sidewall, the side through which the shotgun blasts had obviously come, and Mercy nodded. Then Stroud said, "I haven't been out here in a while. There's a few questions, if you're all right."

"I'm fine," Mercy said.

"The tent's the same? The one he always had here?"

"Of course it is. Charlie wouldn't change anything, not as long as it still worked. He found it at some military surplus store way back when. It was a bear to put up, old wall tent, all that heavy canvas, no shock-cord poles. Once up, though, it could handle anything."

"Except this," Stroud said.

"You know what I mean—the weather. Charlie saw it all from that tent. At first he didn't have any heat, except for a wood fire outside. Then Verlyn or Calvin or somebody like that told him about those little propane outfits you can use both for cooking and heating, and Charlie got himself one. He was snug as a bug in there, heavy old tent with the propane going."

"He cooked inside?"

"Mostly outside on a wood fire. Mostly beans and rice. And peanut butter sandwiches. Charlie lived on peanut butter. He'd go over to the Kabin Kamp now and then for a real meal or into town, but mostly he stayed out here, eating beans and rice and peanut butter sandwiches. He wasn't what you'd call a gourmet."

"Everything else about the campsite the same, then? The way it was before? Nothing changed?"

"Why do you want to know?"

"Take your time."

"I think so," Mercy said when she finished looking, "the same. Charlie might have been in the military himself the way he kept his camp. Neat as a pin."

"Take a look inside."

"The tent?"

"I could tell you, you'd rather."

"Why don't you?"

"The tent fly was closed when we got here. No sign the inside was entered. There's books, fly tying material, trunk with clothing, couple bottles of whiskey, one unopened, some money in traveler's checks, writing paper, personal items, fishing stuff—but not as much of that as you'd think."

"Charlie went light. He thought most fishermen had too much of everything. He'd refined things down. Just a couple rods, a couple lines, not that many flies. He reminded me some of my uncle Louis. Louis was a golf nut, but he'd refined things down to playing with a single club, a two iron. He wasn't bad, either."

"I remember Louis."

"The point is it's normal that Charlie didn't have much equipment around."

"Reading lantern beside the cot, radio, propane heater-cooker you mentioned, flashlights, toilet articles. About it."

"All normal."

"So no outward indication Charlie's routine was any different? Or he had any visitors that might have stayed?"

Mercy shook her head. "I saw him maybe a week or so ago. Not here but out on the river, night fishing the South Branch. He was just the same. But nobody ever *stayed* with him. He had plenty of visitors, but you always knew he wasn't looking for permanent company. There was always a line you didn't cross. He was tucked away at the end of the campground, away from other sites as far as he could get, by himself. You know that as well as I do."

"I thought so," Stroud agreed, "but I wanted to check."

"So where are we? What do we do now?"

"I want you to talk to the host couple—that's one thing—before I do. Tell them the campground's closed, nobody in or out, that your office and my office are working together on this. We're in agreement. Then find out why the woman—"

"Billie Berry."

"—was down here, this end of the campground, early in the morning. After that, go back to work. I'll let you know what develops."

"That's working together?"

"In a murder investigation, it is. But I may need more help, especially if I have to get into past stuff about Charlie."

"You said that before."

"You have to figure, first off, that what happened—it's due to something recent."

"So you talk to everyone in the campground."

"If that doesn't work, you spread out, anyone who had contact with Charlie in the last few days. You keep going back, spreading the net wider. The wider the net gets, the problem is, the bigger the holes for things to slip through. So I don't want to get into past stuff unless I have to."

"All right," Mercy said. "I'll stop and see Burt and Billie, then I'll go to work. But I expect to hear from you soon."

"Soon enough," Stroud said.

\*　　　\*　　　\*

"THERE'S ONE OTHER thing," Mercy said when they got back to their vehicles. "The Parks and Recreation people in Lansing are going to be looking over our combined shoulders on this. Bad publicity—a killing in a state campground. They'll want us talking to the media, pointing out how extraordinary that is, soothing the public. We ought to make sure we're telling the same story."

"Hmm," Stroud mused.

"Michigan campgrounds *are* safe, as a matter of fact, but we've got to make people believe that. It might be a good idea to have a news conference, the two of us together, say the same thing to all the media types at once."

"Not until I've got more information."

"I meant that. In a day or two. In the meantime, we have to get out a statement: just the straight facts and that we're working together and that nobody has to be afraid of the campgrounds. What I'm thinking is we might get Fitzgerald to help. He knows how to deal with the media."

"Hmm."

"I know you told him not to do any writing behind your back. But he'd be working with us on this. Okay?"

"Let me think about it."

"Think quick." Mercy dipped her head, turned away. "I can't believe I'm doing this. Charlie's dead, and I'm worrying about how to soothe the public. It's obscene."

"I know what you're saying," Stroud said.

# 4

---

"**H**EY, SUGAR," BONNIE Pym called out from behind the counter
when Fitzgerald stopped at the Six-Grain Bakery for Italian
bread. He was going to tell her about the picnic lunch he was planning, cheese and wine to go with the fresh bread, when he realized that
though Bonnie's greeting was the same, there was a hollow quality to
the words.

"Something wrong?"

"Plenty."

Bonnie came around the counter, took his arm, led him back to the
entrance door. "Mercy's hunting for you. She's been calling around."

"Now she's found me."

"She wants you to stop at her office."

"What I planned. I thought we'd have a picnic at the town park."

"I don't think so."

When he looked at Bonnie closely Fitzgerald could see that her
makeup was smudged about the eyes, which wasn't like Bonnie. It
looked for all the world as if she had been crying, which wasn't like
Bonnie, either. Bonnie was always primed to face the world. "Tell me,"
he said to her.

"I think she'd rather herself."

"Mercy?"

"Nice day like this," Bonnie said, "gone to nothing in an instant.
Makes you think."

*    *    *

WHEN FITZGERALD GOT to the DNR building, Fern Lax waved him inside Mercy's office without a word, closed the door behind him. Mercy was on the telephone. She looked at him, then swiveled around in her chair, back to him, facing the window that looked out on a wall of Norway spruce, rich green in soft sun. When she finished the conversation and turned back to him, he could see she wasn't in much better shape than Bonnie Pym had been.

"Tell me."

"Charlie Orr's dead."

Fitzgerald looked back at her.

"Last night sometime. In his tent."

"Heart?"

"Willard Stroud thinks he was murdered. Charlie was probably on his cot, reading, a light on, and someone shot him through the tent wall. Billie Berry, one of the campground hosts, found him. I just got back from there."

"Nothing could be done?"

"Stroud had an emergency crew out, but it was way too late. Slocum Byrd thinks Charlie was dead several hours before he was found."

"Out on the river," Fitzgerald said, "I heard the siren." Then he said, "*Murdered*?"

"Shotgun—and more than one shot. What else could it be?" Mercy stopped. "Why'd you say 'heart'?"

"Charlie had a heart attack, way back. That was when he started coming up here all summer, staying in the tent. It was a fairly mild attack, but I suppose it brought intimations of mortality. You have to start doing what you want to do."

"I didn't know about that."

"You probably did. You've just forgotten."

"I wish to God it had been his heart."

"If anything."

"Yes," Mercy said, and abruptly turned away, giving him her back.

*     *     *

SHE DIDN'T FEEL like lunch, but a walk in the town park was better than staying in the office, the two of them trying not to look at one another. She told Fern Lax she would be back in an hour or so in case the sheriff's office called again. Or if Burt or Billie Berry called.

In the park, walking the pine-chip path along the placid East Branch, Mercy explained that she had been on the phone with Willard Stroud when Fitzgerald came to the office. "Something he hadn't got around to asking me at Rainbow Run. Only three campsites were occupied last night. He wanted to know if that was unusual."

"Occupied in addition to Charlie's site?"

Mercy nodded. "And the host couple's. I told him it was more or less normal, given the time of year and the nature of the campground. The end of July can be pretty slow before the August rush."

"And the trico hatch."

"That brings in the fishermen—and usually only fishermen camp at Rainbow Run. That used to be the case, anyway. In the old days."

"Before my time," Fitzgerald said. "You had to have a fishing license to camp, right?"

"Before my time, too. But that was the deal: fishermen only. Imagine trying to pull that off these days. You'd have civil-liberties types all over you. Back then, the campground was pretty primitive: couple outhouses, water pump, no designated campsites, no fees. All you needed was a license in your possession, not that anyone probably ever checked. You could camp right on the edge of the river, roll out of your tent and go fishing, which was good along that stretch of water. There weren't any canoe liveries in Ossning then and not as many cabins along the mainstream. The river was pretty much entirely for fishermen."

"The way God intended."

"Then the park service came in and redesigned the campground, moving everything back from the river, putting in the loop roads and the campsites, improving the facilities. Rainbow Run became a regular fee-required state forest campground, open to anyone. I understand there was some grumbling from fishermen, but they didn't have much of a leg to stand on. Canoeists wanted to use the campground, just plain campers and families, all sorts of folks—you couldn't restrict it to one group. And you couldn't have campsites anywhere people wanted. There was some erosion of the riverbank, too much danger of fires. The campground had to be laid out and run in a professional manner. And that's what happened."

"Start with perfection," Fitzgerald said, "aspire to progress. The American way."

"The Ossning field office is in charge, which is why Stroud called me out there. Day to day I don't get much involved personally, and neither does Stroud. I talk with the host couple a few times during the summer, but our enforcement and maintenance people run the show. Stroud has a deputy drive through the campground on a regular basis, keeping an eye out. High school kids from town out partying are about the only problem we've had."

"Recently?"

"A few years ago. Stroud started arresting kids for underage drinking, hauling them before a judge. That did the trick."

"They party somewhere else, you mean."

"I suppose."

"And no other problems out there?"

"Nothing big that I can remember. Fern is checking the files to make sure."

"What's Stroud think?"

"About who killed Charlie?" Mercy stopped walking, turned away, looked out at the river. "You should see the size of the chubs in here. Kids catch them. You wouldn't believe how big."

Fitzgerald said, "I brought a bottle of wine from home. I was going to pick up bread and cheese, but I didn't get that far. We could go back to the Cherokee, pull the cork."

"I'm working."

"I know."

Mercy turned back to him, took his arm, reversed direction on the pine-chip path. "What difference does it make?"

*    *    *

BUT ONCE BACK in the Cherokee, she didn't want the wine. She just wanted to sit a while longer and look out at the river before she went back to the office.

"Wine's better with food," Fitzgerald said.

"It's not that. It's just—"

"Charlie."

"No one should die like that. It's not fair."

"It's not." Then Fitzgerald said, "Charlie didn't care for wine. He was a whiskey man. When I first met him up here, he always had a flask in his fly vest, cheap stuff, Heaven Hill or something. One day I stopped at his campsite with a bottle of Irish, John Jameson, and we tried it out. Charlie said it was okay, which was his way, never too much immediate enthusiasm. But after that, I noticed he always bought good Irish whiskey for his flask."

"Charlie wasn't a drinker."

"I didn't mean that. He just liked a nip now and then. And he liked to puff away on a pipe on the river, keeping the mosquitoes off. Charlie enjoyed life's little pleasures."

"He lived the way he wanted. You can't say that about many people."

"Thoreau comes to mind."

"What?"

"You're right," Fitzgerald said. "Charlie was pretty unique. I'm going to miss him."

"Lord," Mercy said, "so am I."

They were silent inside the Cherokee, watching the slow slide of the river beyond, before Fitzgerald said, "Couldn't you take the rest of the day off? We could drive somewhere. Over to Traverse City, check out the bookstore, maybe just park and look at the bay. Do something."

Mercy shook her head. "I didn't answer you before. Stroud's got Rainbow Run closed off, nobody in or out. He had me tell the host couple, letting them know the DNR and his office are together on this. Billie Berry was still too torn up to talk, so I'm going back out this afternoon. In the meantime, Stroud is checking all the campers. They're all suspects because of proximity. Then I suppose he'll try to find anyone who might have seen Charlie on the river last night."

"Was he fishing last night?"

"Surprising if he wasn't. After that he'll have to look into Charlie's past—family problems, that sort of thing. It was odd when Stroud told me that, how he'd have to check out the past. I never thought of Charlie having any other life than up here. I don't know a thing about it. I mean, was he married? Are there children? All I know is he lived in Big Rapids."

"He was married," Fitzgerald said. "He mentioned his wife now and then."

"Children?"

Fitzgerald shrugged.

"So Stroud's starting with the campground. That's where you come in."

"Me?"

"The tourism people in Lansing will be worried witless that citizens won't think Michigan campgrounds are safe. So I told Stroud we should get out a statement saying this is a one-in-a-million thing. Then we should probably hold a news conference, making the same point. Maybe you could help us some."

"Stroud agrees?"

"He said he'd think about it. But he'll agree once he starts hearing from downstate. Murder in a state forest campground is serious business."

"Charlie's murder is."

"Of course. But I have a job to do, and one side of it—like it or not—is PR."

"You know I'll help in any way I can."

"This started out to be such a nice day," Mercy said after a moment, "I wished I could be out fishing. Now look what's happened."

"When I stopped at the bakery, Bonnie said it makes you think."

"Oh, no, Fitzgerald," Mercy said. "Don't start on that."

# 5

THE BIG BROWN's hiding spot was a wonder of the river that most people, slipping past in a canoe or even wading that stretch of water, never noticed. You had to take your time, search every piece of the bank with your casts before you noticed.

Calvin couldn't remember when he had first noticed, but he remembered vividly the first time the big brown came out of the hiding spot and smacked his streamer. He had held his breath as if that would keep the fish from breaking off the tippet or throwing the hook. He wanted to see that fish. When he finally got it to the net, he measured with the span of his thumb and little finger doubled, calculating eighteen inches, and when he cupped a hand under the belly, it felt solid as a log.

He remembered releasing the fish, feeling the electric movement as it shot from his hand, imagining the return to its hiding spot. The fish would sink deep in the current, hold there, aware of the hurt where the hook had pierced its jaw, realizing . . . Realizing what? That it had made a mistake yet lived to feed another day? Another wonder was that you could catch fish through the years, hold them in your hands, yet draw a total blank when it came to knowing anything of their world.

"See it?" he said to Gwendolyn Underwood and pointed with the tip of his rod. "The spot cut into the bank? Tell me what you notice."

"It's small."

"That's part of it. The cut's maybe three feet across. What else?"

"The current swirls around."

"It's an eddy. So what would happen if you dropped a dry fly in there?"

"It would go in circles."

"Like in a whirlpool, right. So how about a wet one?"

"You'd get tangled. There's branches or something in there. You can see just in front of the cut."

"So you've got a three-foot cut with the current rotating and the whole thing fenced off beneath the surface with woody debris. And inside there, snug as a bug, is a fat brown trout. What's your strategy?"

Gwendolyn looked at him with large dark eyes. "Fish somewhere else?"

"That's not a strategy. The brown's got to eat, and he's not getting enough holed up in there. He's got to come out, but he's not going to risk that in daylight. It's daylight now, and we want to hook him. So what do we do?"

"What you said before? Try a Woolly Bugger?"

Calvin nodded. "All you can do. Bugger with no added weight. Cast up tight to the woody debris, real tight, see if you can tempt him to eat the fly. Get the right angle so the fly swims the length of the wood."

"It's only three feet."

"All you need. And luck."

"I'll try," Gwendolyn said, and lifted her rod for a backcast.

"One other thing. You get too close to the wood or get too deep, find yourself hung up, you'll have to break off. The water between here and there is over our waders."

"Oh, swell."

"Makes it interesting," Calvin said, "problems like that."

*       *       *

"Go tell him," Verlyn said.

"He's downriver with Gwendolyn Underwood."

"I know where he is. Put on waders, go tell him. I don't want him hearing from somebody else."

"How's he going to hear when he's on the river?"

"Dammit," Verlyn said. "*Tell* him."

Kit shrugged. Whatever Verlyn was doing in town every morning, running off in a rush, was working. He came back in a better mood and picked up where he'd left off in the fly shop, running the cash register and chatting up the customers. This morning was like that until one of Willard Stroud's deputies came in the shop and explained why, earlier, an ambulance had roared past on the bridge road. An old guy who camped all summer at Rainbow Run had been shot to death through the tent wall while he was inside for the night.

Kit knew him, Charlie Orr. You couldn't be around the river any amount of time and not know. He came in the shop now and then, but he wasn't a big spender, a few spools of tippet material being about all, and he didn't hang around half the day swapping lies with the guides. Kit didn't pay much attention to him. Now and then he saw Charlie Orr fishing on the river, the South Branch ordinarily and usually when it was getting dark, and nodded in recognition, but that was the extent of it. What was there to talk about with an old guy like that?

Verlyn and Calvin seemed to find plenty, which probably showed they were getting old themselves. Kit knew they fished with Charlie Orr some nights, and some nights they went to his camp and sat around, telling fish stories. So it was understandable that Verlyn would be interested when the deputy told what had happened at Rainbow Run, but it didn't follow that he would be all worked up. It was like Charlie Orr's death was a death in the family.

Since he was first with the news, the deputy was full of himself and inched out the story, Verlyn locked in on every word. When the deputy mentioned that Willard Stroud had called Mercy Virdon out to the campground, you could tell Verlyn meant to call her himself, getting more dope on what had happened. Verlyn told the deputy a reward should be offered to help get Charlie Orr's killer, but the deputy said it was too early in the investigation for something like that. For all he knew, the sheriff might have pinpointed the killer already. Verlyn seemed to think that unlikely, which figured since he had a low opinion of Stroud's ability and said that Charlie's friends on the river would put up the money for the reward if the sheriff didn't have the killer within twenty-four hours.

"Dead or alive," Verlyn said. "That kind of reward."

It was after the deputy left the shop that Verlyn told Kit to get on waders and go downriver and let Calvin know about Charlie Orr. "He'll want to quit fishing," Verlyn added as Kit was heading out the door. "He'll want to come back here."

"What for?"

Verlyn ignored him. "Stroud's a waste of time. Tell Calvin we'll get together with Mercy. She'll know what's up."

"The guy's dead," Kit said. "There's nothing you and Calvin can do."

"Get your rear in gear."

"Okay," Kit said, "but what about Gwendolyn if Calvin wants to come back here?"

"Fish with her."

"Take over for Calvin, you mean?" Kit cocked his head and gave Verlyn a sly smile. But Verlyn didn't seem to notice. Whatever feeling had been stirred up by the presence at the Kabin Kamp of Gwendolyn Underwood had been overridden by the news of Charlie Orr's death.

*     *     *

CALVIN WASN'T WHERE he was supposed to be, downstream between the lodge and the canoe landing. He had taken Gwendolyn farther down, beyond a tight bend in the river, ignoring Verlyn's instructions.

That was among the things Kit liked about Calvin. Technically speaking, Verlyn was Calvin's boss since he assigned the guides from the fly shop and guiding was how Calvin made his living, but that didn't stop Calvin from doing what he felt like doing. Calvin wasn't anybody's *peon*. He was the only one around, in fact, Mercy excepted, who gave Verlyn the needle now and then. As far as Calvin was concerned, Verlyn was just someone he had been around since they were both kids growing up in the north woods.

Kit waded down the center of the river, moving quickly along the level bottom while out of habit checking trout cover along the banks. If he had known Calvin and Gwendolyn were so far down, he would have taken a canoe, though there would be a problem hauling it back upstream. Kit knew some portage routes overland to the Kabin Kamp,

38

but they led through private property, and Verlyn was a stickler for respecting property rights along the river. Calvin wasn't, which was another reason Kit liked him.

All property along the river, Calvin maintained, ought to be public. Kit pointed out that Calvin's cabin was on the South Branch of the river, but Calvin said he would put his money where his mouth was. He would turn over his property to the state the minute Verlyn turned over the Kabin Kamp. The two properties weren't of equal value, and Kit considered his own future wrapped up in the future of the Kabin Kamp, but he favored open access to the river anyway. He followed Calvin's example and tore down every no-trespassing sign he ran into.

Ahead he spotted Calvin and Gwendolyn, the two of them facing the bank just below a stretch of riffle water. Gwendolyn was casting, and Calvin was beside her, looking twice her size and pointing to where she should drop the fly. Gwendolyn kept shaking her head from side to side, giving the impression she couldn't get it right, but she kept on casting to where Calvin was pointing. When Kit got closer, he decided to call out, not wanting to come up behind the two of them without warning.

"Hey, Calvin."

The big Stetson swiveled around, ponytail swinging beneath, and Calvin lifted his sunglasses so he could see better. When he noticed who it was, he called back, "Hey, Kit," and turned to face the spot where Gwendolyn was casting. When Kit came up beside him, Calvin said, "Stay put. Gwen's got a fish in there."

Gwen? Kit looked at him but Calvin was intent on where Gwendolyn was placing her fly. "What fish?"

"Big brown. He holds in that little cut. I've got him a couple times."

Kit watched Gwendolyn make a few more casts, decided she was wasting her time as far as hooking any big brown went. "Listen," he said to Calvin, "I've got something to tell you."

"How come you're not fishing?"

"I didn't come down to fish."

"You've got a rod."

"Listen," Kit said. "Verlyn sent me."

Calvin probably thought that meant Verlyn was checking up on him. He didn't shift his eyes from the bank. "You hear the siren before?" Kit said. "He wanted you to know what happened. Charlie Orr got killed."

Calvin turned his head slowly, and Kit could feel his eyes behind the sunglasses looking back. "The ambulance was going to Rainbow Run, but it was too late. Charlie was dead already. Somebody last night blasted a shotgun through his tent while he was in there."

Calvin said evenly, "How do you know?"

"One of Stroud's deputies stopped at the shop, told Verlyn. Verlyn said to come down, tell you."

"Zack Cox?"

"What?"

"Which deputy stopped?"

"I don't know his name. It wasn't Zack. The older one—beard, big belly, out of shape. What's it matter?"

"It doesn't," Calvin said.

"Stroud had Mercy out to the campground. Verlyn said you two could talk to her. She'll know more."

"That's good."

"You want to head on in," Kit said, "it's okay. I'll fish with Gwendolyn a while, bring her back to the lodge."

Calvin nodded. He started moving downstream, circling around the area where Gwendolyn was fishing, heading toward the bank. He meant to go the quick way, overland, through private property. Halfway to the bank, he stopped and looked back at Kit.

"They know who did it?"

Kit shook his head. "Stroud's working on it. Verlyn said something about getting up a reward."

"That's good."

"For the killer dead or alive."

"Preferably dead," Calvin said. "Save the state the cost of housing the creep."

*     *     *

Kit watched until Calvin stepped out of the river and moved into a wall of pine. He turned to Gwendolyn, looking back at him with wide eyes beneath a long-billed blue cap. "Bad news, huh?"

"He's an old guy who spends all summer at the campground at Rainbow Run. He's been doing it for years. All the fishermen know him." He stopped and corrected himself. "Knew him."

"To get shot at night inside your tent. That's horrible."

"There are a lot of nut cases around, even up here. You never know when you'll cross paths." It seemed a worldly-wise thing to say, but Kit didn't like the sound of the words when they came out of his mouth. He sounded like an older brother instructing a kid sister. He glanced quickly at Gwendolyn. She wasn't that much of a kid.

"You knew him, too?"

"Not as much as Verlyn and Calvin. They fished with him at night over on the South Branch and hung around his camp. Mercy, too."

"Who's Mercy?"

"My mom. She runs the DNR field office in town. She fishes a lot, too."

Kit could feel Gwendolyn looking at him, her head tilted to the side. "I don't have things straight, I guess. I know Verlyn's your dad. But he's married to Jan."

"Before," Kit explained, "he was married to Mercy. Now Mercy's living with a guy in a big place just up from the bridge, other side of the river. He's a newspaperman who won a state lottery."

"Wow," Gwendolyn said.

"I don't live with either Mercy or Verlyn. I'm on my own since I dropped out of college. Verlyn lets me use one of the back rooms of the lodge. That's because Mercy got on his case. Before that I camped at Danish Landing."

"Wow," Gwendolyn said again.

"It was a good place to camp, good fishing along there, but Mercy got uptight about it, my being alone. I wouldn't mind going back, matter of fact, but now Mercy will really be uptight."

"Because of the dead man?"

"Things happen. You can't live your life worrying about everything that might." Kit stopped himself. He realized he was contradicting himself as far as worldly-wise instruction went. "You want to catch some fish," he said, "let's go downstream a little more. There's a place you can hook some brook trout. They aren't big—maybe eight inchers—but brookies are neat."

Gwendolyn pointed with her rod to the cut where she had been casting. "Calvin said the brown in there is a monster."

"Yeah, well, that's Calvin. He's got hiding places like that up and down the river. Half of them, you want to know, are probably in his imagination. The other half only he can figure out how to hook the fish." When Kit glanced at her again, seeing how she had taken the remark, he found Gwendolyn smiling at him. "He's a good guy, though. Best guide on the river."

Gwendolyn kept smiling at him, which was puzzling. He didn't know how to take it. Was she agreeing with him or making fun of him or what? He tried to figure out the meaning by saying, "We could go back to the lodge, you'd rather."

"I'd rather fish for brookies," Gwendolyn said.

"It's a long walk back up," Kit said, still not sure, "wading against the current."

"I don't mind."

"Or we could take a shortcut through the woods, cutting across some private property. We could do that if you wouldn't let on to Verlyn. He's got a thing about private property."

Gwendolyn didn't hesitate, which caused Kit to smile back at her. "Let's catch some brookies," she said, "take the shortcut back."

# 6

W HEN MERCY VIRDON arrived, Billie Berry told Burt he wouldn't
need to stay at her side. He could wait outside, getting himself
some fresh air. Mercy said that wasn't necessary, that he could be present while they talked, but Billie said Burt had been cooped up with her
in the fifth-wheeler, comforting her, ever since she had discovered the
Odd Fellow.

"I'm better now," Billie said the moment the door closed behind Burt.

"Are you really?" Mercy asked her.

"When you came before, I felt so—"

"Of course you did." Mercy had taken both her hands, was peering
into her eyes. Billie had to steel herself inside to prevent tears from
welling up once again. "It was horrible for you finding Charlie that way."

Billie waited until Mercy released her hands. She asked then if Mercy
would like something, iced tea or lemonade, and Mercy said no, she
wouldn't be staying long.

"Willard Stroud will need a formal statement, Billie. But that can
probably wait until tomorrow. In the meantime, he needs some preliminary information. You know how men think—that it's easier talking to
another woman."

"It is."

"Law of averages," Mercy said, and smiled at her. "Some things they
get right."

They sat together at the dining table at the end of the galley kitchen.
Through the window at the side, Billie could see Burt talking with the
sheriff's deputy beside the patrol car parked at the entrance to the first

loop road. When she turned from the window, she realized Mercy was waiting for her, blue eyes looking back beneath a mound of gray-streaked hair. "Please," she told her. "Ask anything you want."

"A small thing is what you called Charlie. Odd Fellow. Stroud wondered about that."

"It's foolish." Billie resisted an impulse to look away, to look at her hands folded together on the table, to look anywhere other than back into Mercy's eyes. "Burt and I make up names for people—for the campers—that seem to fit them. It's a way of passing time. I know it's foolish."

"I don't think so," Mercy said. "The name was certainly right for Charlie."

"We never used it—not to him. It was just between ourselves. The first day we came as the host couple, Burt found a man already here, staying alone in a tent at the end of the second loop. That seemed odd. We didn't know his real name, so Burt called him the Odd Fellow. The name slipped out when I was talking to the sheriff."

"So it started with Burt—what you called Charlie. But you two eventually learned his name."

"He introduced himself to us. After a day or two, he did. He was so polite and pleasant. But it was strange, in a way. We were the host couple, the first for the campground, but he'd been camping here for years. It was as if he was the real host. Burt didn't know what to make of it."

"I remember," Mercy said. "Burt came into the office, and someone told him the situation. Charlie had been coming to Rainbow Run since it was a no-fee, fisherman-only campground. He was an institution here, someone all the other fishermen knew, so when the campground was reorganized, Charlie was sort of grandfathered in by my predecessor, Cliff Klem. Charlie wasn't held to the two-week camping limit. He could camp all summer—and hold off on the daily fee and write a check at the end of the season. The only other thing was he had to move to a regular campsite. He couldn't keep camping back in the wild along the river."

"Burt was concerned."

"Of course he was. Charlie was an exception to the new rules. But Burt came around, as I recall, once he understood. Charlie could be a big help, given that he knew everything about the campground. And about fishing the river."

"Yes," Billie said, but she knew, the moment she said it, something was wrong. Her tone was.

"Charlie was always generous with fishing information."

"Yes," Billie said again, but her tone still wasn't right. From the look in her eyes, she knew that Mercy had noticed. "He was more my friend than Burt's," she tried to explain. But putting it that way made it seem that she and Burt disagreed about the Odd Fellow, and that wasn't so. Yet there was something, still and all. Some . . . difference. She talked with the Odd Fellow about matters other than fishing or the campground, and Burt never did. She considered the Odd Fellow a friend, and she knew Burt didn't. Didn't exactly. There was that difference.

"I don't mean he and Burt didn't get along."

"Of course you don't."

"That there was ever any unpleasantness. It's just—"

"Sure," Mercy said, "it's the way you said. You were closer to Charlie than Burt was. Charlie could be a good friend. He had a lot of interests."

"Yes," Billie said.

"Was there anything in particular the two of you shared?"

Billie peered at her hands. She wanted Mercy to understand, another woman, and she did. You could tell. But what she had to grasp next was more difficult to put into words, since Billie didn't fully grasp it herself. "He always had books," she began.

"You can say that again. The ladies at the library in town, they all knew Charlie. That's what you talked about, books?"

"Not really. It's just that he was usually reading when I came to see him. That's what I meant. I didn't know what the books were about. He'd close the one he was reading when I came."

Mercy said, "That's something else the sheriff wondered about. You came to Charlie's campsite early this morning. Was there a particular reason for that?"

"No."

Mercy waited for her.

"I mean, I came every morning. Almost every morning. He was always sitting in a camp chair, with a fire going if it was cool out, smoking his pipe, drinking coffee, reading. He always looked like he'd been up a while, waiting for me. We had coffee together and had a conversation."

"Why in the morning?"

"It was a good time for both of us, I suppose. Burt sleeps late, so I'm quiet in the trailer. It's a good time to get out, to walk. There aren't chores yet in the campground. There—"

Billie stopped herself. She wasn't being entirely honest. She and the Odd Fellow—she and Charlie Orr—were both morning people, early morning people. That was the only explanation. They were both at their best then, the most alive and alert, qualities they had recognized in one another from the beginning. Billie had wondered, though, how he could be a morning person since he fished late each night. Burt did as well, but he wanted nothing to do with mornings except sleep through them. She herself went to bed early each night, usually just after Burt went out to fish, and had a good rest. That Charlie Orr could fish late and still be a morning person was one of the things, she had known, that would remain a mystery about him.

"So most every morning you walked from here to the second loop and had coffee with Charlie."

"I brought my own."

"You had coffee and you talked. And that's what you were planning on this morning, going to see Charlie while Burt slept in. Is that right?"

"Yes."

"And there wasn't anything unusual about the morning."

Billie shook her head. "There was a cleaned trout in the refrigerator, one Burt had caught. I put it in a plastic bag and arranged the bag in the freezer with the others while I was waiting for the coffee to brew. After that I poured a mug and left."

"And there wasn't anything special you wanted to talk with Charlie about? Or he wanted to talk with you about? It was just—conversation?"

"Yes."

"As far as you were concerned, it was a morning like every other?"

"Yes."

"Until you found him."

Instantly, tears rose into Billie's eyes, and this time she couldn't force them back. She lowered her face into her hands, her shoulders trembling. Mercy reached across the table, touched her arm, massaged it, trying to help. But nothing could. She had to let the tears flow.

*　　　*　　　*

WHEN SHE EMERGED from the bathroom, water splashed on her face, Billie knew how awful she must look, eyes red and swollen, hair in disarray—not the way a campground host should look in front of a supervisor. She was going to apologize, say how foolish it was to keep crying, but Mercy stopped her before she could say anything.

"There's no reason to put you through this. Stroud can wait."

"Really," Billie said, "I'm fine now."

"No, that's enough."

Through the window, Billie could see Burt still talking with the deputy sheriff. She blew her nose into a Kleenex, tried to smile, said to Mercy, "I wish you'd stay. It's better if you do."

"You're certain?"

"Yes."

"Only long enough for a couple more questions. Stroud will want to know if you noticed anything, anything at all different, when you walked to Charlie's campsite. This morning when you went there. Did anything catch your attention?"

Billie had already thought about that. In her mind she had gone over everything again and again, discussed everything with Burt, every possible detail. She shook her head.

"Nothing with the other campers?"

"I only saw Ordinary People. Another name," she said when she could see that Mercy was confused. "A young man with a family in a new tent camper—in twenty-four. That's the campsite number. He was trying to start a fire. His real name is Phillip."

"Did you speak with him?"

"I would have on the way back. I usually did—talk to others—on the way back."

"Did Phillip happen to notice you?"

"He might have. I don't know."

Mercy was quiet for a while, simply looking back at her across the table. Finally she asked if Billie felt she could describe what she saw when she reached Charlie Orr's campsite.

"Yes," Billie said, "I can." She had noticed something—something strange—right away. Odd Fellow wasn't there, beside the campfire. And there wasn't any fire. She could always smell it when she reached the loop road. But there wasn't any, and the fly of his tent wasn't open. She thought he must still be sleeping, though that wasn't like him, not in early morning. So she hesitated. She didn't want to just walk up to the tent. But it seemed so strange, and she went closer—went under the tarpaulin strung over his picnic table—and that's when she noticed a faint glow of light coming from inside the tent. She didn't want to go any closer, not if he was still in there.

Billie stopped, trying to read the expression on Mercy's face. "I thought it wouldn't be right. I might startle him. I would feel so foolish."

"Of course," Mercy said. "He was usually outside when you arrived. Ready for you. So you started to leave?"

But she hadn't been able to. It was so strange. She just stood there, under the tarpaulin, until she noticed the angle of the tent. It leaned to the side—as if one of the support ropes had come loose. From the inside he would have noticed, would have come out and done something. But it was so—so still inside. So quiet. Finally she had moved off to the side, all the while looking at the tent, then saw in the sagging wall a perfect pattern of holes. She had stared at them. Only seconds might have passed, but it seemed to be a long time, staring at them, before the holes registered in her mind. A long, terrible time.

"And then," she told Mercy, "I threw the coffee mug in the air and began running back to Burt. I was screaming, and he made me stop. Made me tell him what was wrong. Made me say I was sure what I'd seen. Then he called 911 on our cell phone."

Mercy waited, very still, before she said, "And what you had seen were the shotgun holes in the tent wall?"

"Yes."

"You never looked inside the tent?"

"The fly was closed."

"You never opened the fly and looked inside?"

"Oh, no. No."

"The holes told you—"

"And the quiet."

"They told you—"

"That he was probably dead inside."

Mercy patted Billie's hand. "One more question. Did you or Burt hear any gunshots last night?"

"After I went to bed, all I heard was Burt come back late in the truck. I heard him rummaging around the kitchen before he came to bed. He didn't say anything that I remember. This morning, afterward, going over everything in our minds, he said he'd heard noise in the night that sounded like firecrackers."

"Firecrackers," Mercy repeated.

"It's not unusual. It's still July, and campers have them left over."

"Did Burt tell Stroud about this?"

"One of the deputies, he did. It could have been the gun he heard, couldn't it?"

"But Burt isn't sure what the sound was?"

"No, he said it could have even been a dream."

*　　　*　　　*

WHEN HE SAW Mercy Virdon leave the fifth-wheeler, Burt Berry came over to her vehicle and waited by the door. "You get what you needed from Billie?" he asked when Mercy arrived.

"Willard Stroud will want more. I'll try to hold him off a bit. She isn't in good shape."

"Not so good," Burt agreed. "She's never stumbled into something like this."

"Who has?"

"That's so."

Mercy said, "Billie said you heard firecrackers last night."

"Maybe I did. Sort of an explosion. Firecrackers were the only things I could think of."

"What time?"

"After midnight, all I could say."

"You didn't do anything?"

"Well, no. I wasn't sure I heard 'em for one thing. Another is it happens sort of regular, firecrackers going off here. You get used to it."

"So Billie said. But firecrackers that late at night?"

"People sit up around a campfire, drink beer, get themselves a little snockered. You know how it goes."

"As a matter of fact," Mercy said stiffly, "I don't. Besides, fireworks are illegal on state land. There's a sign posted on the bulletin board at the entrance. You *know* that."

"That's so," Burt said, and looked away.

"You've got to crack down, Burt. Fireworks could set off a fire out here."

"That's so."

"If campers won't follow the rules, call our office. *We'll* crack down." Mercy stopped abruptly. It wasn't the time to be lecturing Burt about his duties. "So," she began again, "you heard what sounded like firecrackers, but you weren't sure."

"Knowing what I know now," Burt said, "I'd of got up, checked around. Maybe I'd of run into whoever did it. Other hand, maybe it's luck I didn't, somebody with a shotgun shooting up tents."

"He only shot up one," Mercy corrected him.

"Makes you wonder why he picked it. Except maybe he didn't. Could be he wanted to shoot up something, and it was the first he came to. The campground sign out on the Downriver Road—idiots come by, shoot it up all the time. You wonder whether they pick the sign or they're just shootin' anything around."

"Random violence," Mercy said.

Burt nodded. "That's the name for it."

"And that's why, after what Billie saw this morning, you didn't go down to Charlie's tent to see for yourself?"

"Didn't think it wise. Billie's seen that shot-up sign. She knows what bullet holes look like."

"So you did the sensible thing and called 911."

Burt nodded. "Only time I ever tried that number."

*     *     *

WHEN WILLARD STROUD saw the Suburban, he left Zack Cox and moved from the campsite to the edge of the loop road, waiting for Mercy. When she stopped, he opened the passenger door, got in beside her.

"Don't suppose you brought any smokes."

"Information," Mercy said. "I've been talking to Billie and Burt. The deputy up there said you were still here."

"Finishing up."

"And?"

"If you mean did we find anything new, no."

"You didn't tell me before about Burt hearing firecrackers in the night."

"I didn't know before he told one of my boys."

"Fireworks are illegal on state land. There's a sign posted at the entrance."

"Lots of things are illegal. They still happen."

"All right," Mercy said. "So what do you think?"

"Your man Berry may have heard the shotgun blasts that killed Charlie. The other campers are being interviewed. We'll find out what they heard. But what's it amount to? All it does, someone else heard, is help narrow down the time of the shooting."

"Billie didn't hear anything. All she remembers is Burt coming to bed. He was out night-fishing."

Stroud said, "What else she say?"

He listened as Mercy went over the conversation. When she finished, he asked her to tell him one thing more. "You the one that picked those people to run the campground?"

"The parks division in Lansing does. That's who would-be hosts apply to. I have a veto if I want to use it. Rainbow Run is the only camping area on the Borchard of enough size to qualify for a host couple."

"So you know their backgrounds."

"Not beyond what the application says. They've been here a half-dozen summers, so I've gathered a little more."

"And?"

Mercy stared at him. "For God's sake, Stroud. You suspect Billie and Burt?"

"Just tell me."

"They're sort of professional campground hosts. Up here in summer, somewhere in Florida in winter. Retired, children grown. They're nomads. They live year-around in the trailer."

"Why?"

"Why are they nomads?"

"Campground hosts. Why do that?"

"Free camping in nice places. That's the only payoff. And it's something to do, an activity, and it gets them involved with the campers. Some people are like that. Congenial."

"You had any trouble with them?"

Mercy shook her head. "I have to do a performance review after each season. Couple of sentences for Lansing. I keep saying the same thing: Burt and Billie are perfect for the job."

"Except they allow fireworks in the campground."

"That's something we've got to work on. Otherwise, I meant."

"All right," Stroud said, "now tell me this. What she said about talking every morning with Charlie. What do you make of that?"

Mercy tipped her head to the side. "You're a shrewd old dog, Stroud."

"I heard what you didn't say."

"Billie was probably half in love with Charlie, if you want to know. She said it was morning coffee and conversation, but it was more than that. More she doesn't recognize herself. But so what? *I* was half in love with Charlie. As Billie saw him, he probably seemed a hundred-and-eighty degrees removed from Burt. Every summer he was here, camped in the same place, willing to have coffee with her and talk. She didn't have to live with Charlie, which might not have been a walk in the park, a man who camped in a tent all summer and read books all day and went fishing all night. Charlie's life was one she could dip into, so to speak, and that gave her pleasure. She and Charlie had a friendship."

"You said it was love."

"*Half*-love. But for a woman there's no certain line between the two. Men never understand that." Mercy smiled thinly. "Like me to continue?"

"My experience," Stroud said, "love's a motive for murder."

"Oh, come on."

Stroud changed course. "What do you know about the husband?"

"You told me to talk to Billie."

"I'll get around to him. Background I'm asking for."

"I don't know much. Burt's a fisherman, so hosting at Rainbow Run is ideal for him. He's always a little careful around me, wanting to look good, wanting Billie to. But that's okay. It's a damn nice trait, as a matter of fact."

"He do any hunting?"

"I've no idea. He and Billie leave for Florida about when bird season begins, but he might. Why?"

"I'm wondering if he has shotguns around."

"Let's say he does. That would put him in the same company with nearly every other functioning male in Tamarack County. I wouldn't say that's much to go on."

"All right," Stroud said. "Husband and wife, they get along?"

"They must, working together, living bunched up in a trailer. I can't imagine it. Fitzgerald and I'd be at each other's throat."

Stroud let himself smile. "I wondered why he got himself that big place."

"Very funny. When I was leaving," Mercy said, "Burt mentioned something—random violence, somebody shooting at Charlie's tent for no reason at all. When we talked before, you didn't suggest that."

"It's a possibility, always is, but think what's involved. Anybody drove in the campground late, they'd come right past the hosts' trailer. But they didn't hear anything except maybe firecrackers. *He* did. The only other way in is off the river or overland off Downriver Road, a hike through the woods either way. And lugging a shotgun. It could happen that way, but you'd have to figure, coming that way, Charlie had been singled out. It doesn't figure to be random violence. It is, we've got no hope. But a jealous husband isn't random."

"Jealous because she had coffee and talk with someone they called the Odd Fellow?"

"It's a possibility."

"Well, I think it's a stretch."

"Your opinion has been noted."

# 7

"HEY, STRANGER," SANDY Wink called out when Fitzgerald came from the lobby into the lounge of the Borchard Hotel. He waved to her, then waited a moment, eyes adjusting to dim lighting, before taking one of the high stools at the bar. Beyond the bar a pair of waitresses were setting tables in the dining room for the lunch crowd.

Sandy positioned herself in front of him, absently ran multi-ringed fingers through frizzy yellow hair. "I'd figure you've been avoiding me, I didn't know better."

"You do, though," Fitzgerald said.

"Weather, huh? Too good to spend in bars."

"That's so, actually. I've been fishing, eating, sleeping, fishing again. Heck of a life."

"Weather too good for writing your book, too?"

"Ah, Sandy," Fitzgerald said, "you know how to wound a guy. Now round up a mug of coffee, assuming it's strong."

When she came back with the coffee, Sandy braced both hands against the bar and leaned forward, her conspiratorial stance. "So how come you're in now? It's perfect out."

Fitzgerald encircled the mug with his hands. "You've heard?"

"It's all over town."

"That's why. Dark bar and strong coffee. Bad mood."

"He never came in," Sandy said, "but I knew about him. People talked about an old guy camping at Rainbow Run."

"Charlie liked a nip," Fitzgerald said, "but he wasn't a bar type. And he wasn't so old. Late sixties, maybe. But it was hard to tell. He was one of those people who reach a certain age, don't seem to get any older. He always looked the way he did when I first met him."

"Way back?"

"I was working on the paper in Detroit, coming up here on weekends, fishing all the time, sleeping in my car. About the first people I met were Calvin McCann and Verlyn Kelso. Through them I got to know Charlie. We'd fish together all night, then go up to his campsite and make breakfast. Charlie wasn't much of a cook, so Calvin or Verlyn would bring a big iron skillet and we'd mix potatoes, eggs, onions, ham, cook it all together. Charlie would eat like a trooper, but when he was alone all he'd make himself was beans and rice and peanut butter sandwiches."

"You never grilled a trout?"

"Those days, we could have. It was before catch and release came on the mainstream and the South Branch. But Charlie was way ahead of his time. He never kept fish, and neither did Calvin or Verlyn. I didn't have to worry. Hardly ever caught any."

"He was a good fisherman, huh?"

"About the best, as far as I was concerned. Calvin and Verlyn were good, but they'd always been good. They assumed you knew more than you did. Charlie was patient with me. I learned a lot from him. It was important with Charlie to do things right on the river. But I always had the feeling, fishing with him, that it didn't matter if we caught anything. Being out on the water mattered, getting late, canoeists gone and most other fishermen—wading out there in that spooky time before full dark when it cools down and you can't see much but you feel the current against your legs and you sense in your bones the complete indifference of nature. You get a hint of where you fit in the order of things."

"Gee."

"I always felt Charlie knew where he fit. He was a wise and humble man."

"Gee."

Fitzgerald smiled. "Ask a simple question, get an inflated answer."

"Hey, it's okay. You should hear the stuff gets said in here." Then Sandy asked, "Stroud thinks it's murder, huh?"

"Last I heard."

"What a shame, nice man like that."

"What a shame," Fitzgerald repeated.

When the phone rang down the bar, Sandy excused herself and went to answer it. When she came back, she said the call was from Mercy.

"I forgot to say," Fitzgerald said. "We're meeting here."

Sandy shook her head. "Change of plans. Says she's tied up. She'll see you at the sheriff's office. It's about the murder, huh?"

"Expect so."

"Maybe Stroud caught the madman who did it."

"Let's hope."

"You don't sound hopeful."

"Told you," Fitzgerald said. "Bad mood."

*    *    *

FITZGERALD DROVE THE three-block main drag of Ossning and pulled into the parking area of the city-county building. Backed into one of the handicapped-parking spaces near the entrance was the white van of a television station in Traverse City.

When he came through the glass door into the sheriff's office, Fitzgerald took a look at Elsie and stopped in his tracks. Winter and summer Elsie wore pastel-colored sweatshirts with glittering appliqué on the front. "Best ever," he told her. "Thought the last I saw was. This beats it."

"Ha," Elsie said. "You say that to every girl in the building."

"Only the good-lookers."

"Ha."

Fitzgerald dipped his head in the direction of the closed door behind Elsie. "Boss in?"

"Thinking."

"If it's okay, I'll wait. Mercy's coming over."

"He knows," Elsie said. "Said to go in."

Inside, Fitzgerald closed the door behind him and took a chair in front of the sheriff's desk. "Don't encourage her," Stroud said without looking up from some papers.

"I didn't think you could hear."

"Didn't. I know how you operate."

Fitzgerald smiled and said, "Mercy's tied up with something."

"She called, told Elsie." Stroud glanced up with tired eyes. "Seems the state park people downstate had a cow when she told them she was getting out a statement about Charlie. Told her any statements would come from Lansing. She argued that she knew about Rainbow Run, but they said they knew about the parks in general. They had statistics proving how safe they were and to mind her own business."

"Something tells me that didn't sit well with Mercy."

"You'd know. You've got to live with her. Anyway, we've got no statement on our hands."

"I saw a TV van outside."

Stroud rubbed his eyes, said, "News conference. There's still that. I want to say what I've got to say once, not dribble it out to every reporter who calls."

"Good idea."

"What I thought. Except I only got two people down in the conference room. Newspaper and TV from Traverse City. And Gus Thayer. Gus already put out a story, bare bones, for the AP."

"That's the way it is these day, all the news organizations cutting back on staff. It's all bottom line. They'll use what Gus sends over the wire and copy what the Traverse City people put out."

"You'd figure Detroit would be interested, killing in a state campground."

"You'd figure," Fitzgerald agreed. "So you don't have any need for me?"

Stroud raised a hand, held Fitzgerald in the chair. "Maybe I do. Come down to the news conference. Soon as Mercy shows up, we'll get started."

*        *        *

THE REPORTER FOR the *Traverse City Record-Eagle* turned out to be a bearded intern on summer vacation from Kalamazoo College. The TV reporter from WGTU was a rail-thin blonde who looked no older than the intern. Only Gus Thayer of the weekly *Ossning Call*, with a bristling crew cut, thick-rimmed glasses, and a craggy, middle-aged face, seemed an honest-to-god journalist. Fitzgerald, examining the three from the side, realized he had never before thought that way about Gus.

The three were lined up on hard chairs before a folding table, Stroud and Mercy behind it. The TV reporter asked if they could get started since she had another assignment in Gaylord, and when Stroud said all right, she nodded to a jeans-and-tee-shirt cameraman and he switched on a hard blue-white light. Stroud and Mercy leaned forward, eyes narrowed, trying to ignore it.

"Sheriff Stroud," the TV reporter said, "would you begin?"

You sit up there, Fitzgerald thought, pinned by the light, and you believe they are making a videotape of what you are saying. They are. But they aren't going to use it, not the way you are saying it. You are saying it the way you have worked it out, talking from prepared copy or notes, one thing leading logically to another—what you believe is a careful, considered statement. But what you will see on the tube that evening, assuming they use anything at all, are snippets, bits and pieces lifted from the tape with the reporter's narrative overlaid. Your face will be there, and some of your words, but you will hardly recognize either one. You will be on TV, but you won't be happy.

With newspaper accounts, it is only marginally better. There is more length and usually more coherence, and there isn't the intrusive appearance of attractive young reporters trying to act like genuine reporters. There is the same picking and choosing that often as not selects what you thought were, when you talked about them, minor matters and passages put in quote marks that, even when accurate, don't read like anything you think you said. You are in the paper but only less unhappy.

Even experienced news sources, the types who gave news conferences all the time, rarely understood how the game worked. They wanted conduits, and what they got were filters. You want the former, Fitzgerald used to say when he was working the political beat for the *Free Press*, take out an ad. You want it for free, you get me. But understanding that, if you were on Stroud and Mercy's side of the table, didn't make it easier to take. Disappointment was built into the game. If he couldn't help with a statement about the safety of Michigan camp-grounds, maybe he could try, later, to help Stroud and Mercy through the raw edges of their disappointment.

"The Tamarack County medical examiner," Stroud was saying, "says Mr. Orr died as the result of wounds to the head and upper torso—two shotgun shells, .16 gauge, fired at close range from outside his tent. Preliminary time of death was between midnight and six o'clock. At the present moment we have no motive for the shooting, and no arrests have been made. We're in the process of interviewing campers in Rainbow Run who may have heard or seen something. Individual sites are set back from the interior road and shielded by pines—so we might not get much visual information. And we're trying to locate others who may have come in contact with Mr. Orr. We believe he was fishing on the South Branch of the Borchard River prior to returning, sometime during the night, to Rainbow Run. It was his practice to fish late into the night.

"The body was found by Mrs. Billie Berry while she walked the camp-ground road at approximately seven-thirty. Mrs. Berry and her hus-band are campground hosts at Rainbow Run. A 911 call was made from the Berrys' mobile home, and an emergency vehicle was dispatched to the campground. Nothing could be done for Mr. Orr. We're treating his death as murder. That's all the information I have for now."

Stroud turned to Mercy, introduced her as the manager of the DNR field office in Ossning, said she would say a few words.

"Only that a statement will be issued by the parks department in Lansing pointing out the exceptional nature of an incident like this in Michigan campgrounds. It will be sent to news organizations around the region."

Mercy looked back at Stroud, and Stroud said, "Questions?"

Gus Thayer waved his hand like a kid in school. "You didn't say," he said to Mercy, "that Charlie had this sweetheart deal. He didn't pay to camp."

"That's incorrect," Mercy said. "Mr. Orr did pay, though not in the usual manner. At the end of the season, he sent the DNR a listing of the nights he had spent in Rainbow Run and a check to cover the full amount. This special arrangement was an acknowledgement of his years of camping there that went back to a time when it wasn't a fee-required campground."

"Any others get the same treatment?"

Mercy's lips tightened, but her voice remained even. "Not that I know. But if you mean at state campgrounds in general, you'd have to ask Lansing."

Gus turned his attention to Stroud. "Maybe that's why he was shot. Some camper was teed off about Charlie getting favored handling by the DNR."

Stroud glared at Gus across the table but didn't reply.

"You looking into that?"

"We're looking into everything."

Following Gus's lead, the intern with the *Record-Eagle* waved his hand. "Was theft involved?"

"We don't believe so," Stroud said. "We believe nothing was taken from the campsite, nor was the tent entered. But it's too early to say definitively that theft wasn't the motive."

"If it wasn't," the intern said, "what was?"

"As I said, at the moment we don't know."

"Could be a thrill killing," Gus Thayer said. "Kids from town used to horse around out there."

"Correct," Mercy said. "*Used* to. There have been no recent incidents. The campground is regularly patrolled both by the sheriff's office and DNR enforcement officers."

"Yeah," Gus said, "and look what happened."

The intern raised his hand again and asked if the murder weapon had been found.

"Not as yet."

"That mean," Gus Thayer asked, "you found a shotgun but don't know if it's the right one?"

Stroud stared at Gus before he said, "I'm not prepared to comment on that."

"I hear there was a break-in at a river place. Not too far from Rainbow Run. I hear a shotgun may be missing."

"I said," Stroud said stiffly, "I wasn't prepared to comment."

"The shotgun could be the murder weapon."

"Let's move on," Stroud said. When no questions followed, he said hopefully, "If that's all—"

The TV reporter stood, light from the camera swinging to her, enveloping her. She went through the motions of consulting a notebook before she looked up at Stroud. "WGTU has learned that a reward will be offered. Could you comment on that, Sheriff Stroud?"

Stroud glanced at Mercy, who shrugged, before turning back to the TV reporter. "Where'd you hear that?"

"WGTU has learned that money is being raised by fishing companions of Mr. Orr. Apparently, Mr. Orr had a great many friends who are deeply concerned that the murderer be apprehended. All information from the public is to be directed to your office."

"Who told you so?" Stroud persisted.

"That Mr. Orr had many friends?"

"About a reward."

The TV reporter smiled serenely. "WGTU stands behind its sources."

"You'd know what she's saying," Gus Thayer piped up, "if you had a talk now and then with your deputies. Verlyn's passing a hat out at the Kabin Kamp."

# 8

"DON'T KNOW WHICH one gripes me more," Stroud said after the news conference ended and he had guided Mercy and Fitzgerald to his office. "Gus or Verlyn."

"I nominate Gus," Mercy said, "playing to the camera like that."

"I wouldn't worry," Fitzgerald said. "He'll end up on the cutting-room floor. All you'll see is Ms. WGTU."

"Lord," Mercy said, "normal-sized women must look like blimps on TV. That one's anorexic, I'll bet you anything."

"Gus I deal with later," Stroud said, "and whichever deputy's been blabbing to him. Verlyn is first off. He's got no business getting up a reward."

"I don't know," Mercy said. "It might be a good idea."

"Awful idea. We get flooded with calls, we have to sort out the crazies, we track down what seems promising. Takes all our time."

"But that's it. You might get something promising."

"We already have. What I'm going to tell you," Stroud said, "stays in this room. We checked out the three occupied campsites at Rainbow Run. One is a young couple with kids trying out a new tent camper. They never saw Charlie, didn't know anybody was even camping back at the end of the loop, but they may have heard something in the night. One of the kids was up, crying, and they heard this noise but were too sleepy to pay much attention. It might have been what Burt Berry heard, but they can't swear to it. An older couple in a travel trailer didn't hear a thing. They come up every year from Indiana. They'd talked with Charlie in the past but not this year—and last night was just like every other night. They say they sleep like logs when they get out in the woods. That leaves Only Orvis."

"Who?"

"What the Berrys called the other camper. Seems he's solo, fishes at night, fancy equipment. We haven't talked to him yet."

"Why not?"

"Best reason there is. Can't find him."

*      *      *

STROUD CALLED OUT to Elsie, and they waited until she brought in coffee in Styrofoam cups. He told her to close the door on the way out of the office.

"Well?" Mercy said.

"We've got an understanding?"

"Oh, for goodness sake, Stroud."

"The guy registered at the campground, so we've got his name and home address. Alec Proffit, Norwich, Vermont. Now why would someone from Vermont come all the way to Michigan to fish?"

"Better fishing?" Mercy said.

"Long drive, there to here."

"Maybe he flew, rented a vehicle. We'll know the plate on his car from his campground registration."

"It's a Vermont plate on a gray Toyota Land Cruiser. So we know what we're hunting for. We know something else. We took a look at the guy's campsite. Lot of gear there, so you'd think he hasn't taken off for good."

"That's legal, going through his belongings?"

"Legal enough when we found one of those spiral notebooks. Stenographer's notebook. Just a single thing in it." Stroud paused, looked from Mercy to Fitzgerald, held Fitzgerald's gaze. "Bunch of notes about Charlie."

"Good Lord," Mercy said.

"Looks like he was watching Charlie, shadowing him. He's got in there about Charlie going out fishing at night. He went to the same area, over on the South Branch, fished himself but kept an eye on where Charlie was. No indication he ever talked with him. Just made these notes."

"But why would he?"

Stroud kept looking at Fitzgerald. "That's what I'm wondering."

Fitzgerald said, "I had a feeling this was getting around to me."

"Not too surprising. You notice the notebook that TV girl used during the news conference? Dead ringer for the one in Alec Proffit's tent."

Fitzgerald stroked his chin, looked at the framed topographical map of Tamarack County on the wall behind Stroud, sipped coffee. Finally he said, "You think he's a journalist."

"You're quick," Stroud said.

"Anybody can buy a notebook like that. But let's say you're right—the missing guy's a journalist of some sort. A background check will tell for sure."

"We've got the state police running one. And we've got out the alert about his vehicle."

"The next question is why a journalist would be interested in some-body camped all summer in Rainbow Run. You might make a story out of that, I suppose, but it doesn't sound very exciting. Charlie was unique but not that unique. And you wouldn't come all the way from Vermont for a story like that."

Stroud leaned back in his chair, nodded his agreement. "There's something else in the notes. This fellow did more than keep track of Charlie up here. He went down to Big Rapids, snooped around, found out Charlie's wife is a school librarian, retired. Has a bunch of Big Rapids addresses jotted down. Charlie was retired from the post office. I didn't know he was from Big Rapids."

"He mentioned it," Fitzgerald said. "But I never heard him talk about the post office. I didn't know what he'd retired from."

"Early retirement—one of those management shifts. He took the opportunity, got out. This Alec Proffit, he wasn't just interested in Charlie as a fisherman. It's more than that. No reason to go down to Big Rapids if it wasn't."

"But *what* more?" Mercy said.

"You see why I didn't bring it up at the news conference?"

"Of course. But what's the next step?"

"Keep seeing if we can locate this Proffit." Stroud paused, looked from Mercy to Fitzgerald. "And try to figure out why he was shadowing Charlie."

"How?" Mercy asked.

"What I think the sheriff's getting around to," Fitzgerald said to her, "is this isn't free coffee."

*    *    *

STROUD'S PLAN FOR Mercy was that she should drive down to Big Rapids, pay a call on Charlie's wife. It would be an official call, as a DNR supervisor of the campground in which Charlie died, offering her condolences. She could also offer her services with funeral arrangements. The state police had notified Charlie's wife of his death, but the body wouldn't be released until Slocum Byrd was finished with his examination. Mercy might act as a go-between, helping Charlie's wife make decisions at a painful time. Stroud didn't know if there were children, adults now, helping her as well.

Mercy's real task would be to learn what she could about Alec Proffit. Had he spoken with Charlie's wife? Had he spoken with post-office authorities in the town? What *had* he done in Big Rapids? Stroud could send a deputy down there, but Mercy going would rock the boat less in the event Alec Proffit wasn't involved in Charlie's death. Stroud didn't want the investigation to get ahead of itself. He didn't want to give any indication Proffit was a person of interest until more information was in hand.

"You mean I'm more subtle," Mercy grinned at him, "than your ham-handed deputies?"

"What I mean is I thought you'd want to help. We're working together on this, we said. While you're at it down there, you could try to get a feel for Charlie's family situation—wife first of all, relatives, children if there are any, friends. We may have to move the investigation in that direction."

"Proffit seems a better bet."

"Maybe. But there's a rule of thumb: Don't count your chickens 'til they're hatched."

"Highly original. All right," Mercy said. "I'll phone from the office, see if I can call on her sometime tomorrow."

"Let me know right away what you learn."

"You know how I follow orders."

"Why I mentioned it," Stroud said.

Stroud's plan for Fitzgerald was that he would look into the possibility Alec Proffit was a journalist. He could call someone he knew at the *Free Press*, get the ball rolling. There must be some data bank of journalists the paper had access to. Stroud could have the state police run the same kind of check, but for the time being he preferred to limit their help to matters of criminal background. He didn't want the state police looking into anything about journalists, stirring up that nest of potential trouble. Imagine something like that getting back to a fool like Gus Thayer.

"Okay," Fitzgerald said at once.

Stroud looked at him closely.

"The paper will help. No problem."

"You're gathering information, is all."

"I won't write anything, if that's what you mean. We still have a deal: I ever do, I'll let you know in advance."

"All right," Stroud said.

"Oh, come on," Mercy said. "We're all doing this for Charlie. That's the whole point."

"It is," Fitzgerald said.

Stroud nodded and asked, "You want more coffee?"

"No," Mercy said, "but what's that business Gus had about a break-in and a shotgun? "

"Another thing to chew Gus out about, bringing that up. Caretaker of one of the places down from Rainbow Run, where you come into the river along Dunkellin Road, he discovered a break-in and called the office. He checks the place once a week, so there's no certainty when it happened. He thinks only one thing might have been taken—shotgun from a gun cabinet. He doesn't know what gauge."

"Doesn't the owner know?"

"You know the area I'm talking about, all log places, look like motels they're so big? Those places are closed up most of the time, owners gone. This case, the owner's off fishing in Montana, you can believe that. Has a place on the Borchard yet goes off, middle of summer, to Montana. I don't understand rich people."

Mercy said, "You ought to talk more to Fitzgerald."

"He means the filthy rich," Fitzgerald said. "So it may have been the shotgun that killed Charlie, but there's no way of knowing until the owner returns."

Stroud tossed a hand in the air. "All he can tell us is the gauge of the gun, assuming he can remember. If it's a .16 gauge, stolen within the rough time period of Charlie's death, there might be a connection."

"But it won't matter," Mercy said, "if you don't find the gun. All you'll have is a possibility."

"We're checking the area around Charlie's campsite, tramping through the woods. We find anything, all that jack pine, it'll be dumb luck."

"There's one thing," Fitzgerald said. "The break-in at an empty house—that might suggest knowledge of the river. Someone had been around enough to notice the house wasn't being used. He wasn't a stranger to the river."

"Maybe," Stroud said. "On the other hand, maybe he was a stranger who stumbled on an empty place."

"More dumb luck," Mercy said. Then she said, "Let's *do* something, *talk* about it later."

# 9

"TACKY," JAN SAID after Verlyn placed the sign near the fly shop's display of tippet spools. She took the sign down and replaced it with a piece of white cardboard neatly lettered with a red marker in sweeping cursive.

"Can't be *red*," Verlyn told her. "Charlie's dead."

Jan turned the piece of cardboard over and redid the sign with a black marker. "Better?"

"Except it looks like a woman wrote it." The message itself, though, was still exactly to the point: CHARLIE ORR REWARD FUND. SEE VERLYN OR CALVIN.

"You'll have to start a separate bank account," Jan pointed out, "to keep track of the money. You'll have to account for every penny."

"I got it."

"And there's what the reward goes for. You'll have to specify. It could go just for information."

"I got that, too."

"Or the information would have to lead to the arrest and conviction of the killer."

"Quiet day in the lodge?" Verlyn said. "Nothing worth doing in there?"

Jan bit her lip, gave Calvin a wan smile, turned on her heel. Calvin watched until she was gone from the shop. "Mellow out," he told Verlyn. "She's trying to be helpful."

"We don't need any help. We've got a sign, we take the money that comes in, we hand it over to Stroud. Let him decide what it goes for."

"Right," Calvin agreed.

"I told Graham Underwood about Charlie before you came upriver. Put him in for five hundred, he said."

Calvin winced. "I'll do a couple hundred soon as I get my checkbook from the cabin."

"Reward of a few grand, information will roll in. Stroud's getting his job done for him."

"Right," Calvin said. He was sitting on the high stool at the tying bench that occupied the center of the shop but hadn't clamped a hook in the vise, beginning something. Usually he didn't hang around the fly shop without tying, working automatically, talking with Verlyn or with customers if they wanted to talk to him, keeping busy. Some days, bad weather or no guide trip scheduled, he would finish a half-dozen flies before he knew it. Today, with the news about Charlie Orr, he didn't feel like starting even one.

"I've got a call in to Mercy," Verlyn said. "Fern Lax said she was tied up with Stroud, some kind of news conference. Fitzgerald's over there, too."

"So maybe Stroud's got it solved already."

"Not unless a guy walked in the door and confessed."

Calvin said, "You got somebody in mind?"

"I was speaking in general. I've been thinking, going over names, trying to make a list. No problem if I'd been the one camping in Rainbow Run. List as long as your arm. Same for you."

"Naw," Calvin said. "A few women I've dumped, is all."

"With Charlie I can't come up with a single name. There's some probably thought he had a screw loose, living in a tent. Hell, I thought he had a screw loose."

"Naw. Eccentric, is all."

"But that's no reason to shoot him."

Calvin nodded, stroked his beard, looked beyond Verlyn at the sign beside the tippet spools. "You'd need a good reason."

"That's what I'm saying. There isn't one."

"Maybe there is."

"Well?" Verlyn said when Calvin didn't continue.

"I'd rather not say."

"Dammit, Calvin. You're getting into a bad habit. You start something, then clam up. You don't want to tell, don't start."

"All right," Calvin said.

"But you did start. So tell."

"You'll be pissed off when I do."

"*Tell.*"

"After the kid came downriver to get me, it popped into my head.
Seeing him did it."

"Kit?" Verlyn snapped.

"Not the kid himself. That old stuff. What he got himself into."

*    *    *

"WE TURN HERE," Kit said when they reached a small clearing in the
jack pines with a shallow rivulet crossing it. "We follow this down to
the mainstream, walk upriver the rest of the way. Verlyn goes bonkers
otherwise."

"Keep the peace," Gwendolyn Underwood said. "I understand."

She wasn't, Kit had decided, the spoiled rich brat you would expect.
She didn't have any hesitation about hiking back through the woods to
the Kabin Kamp, and she'd had a ball getting brookies to strike a Para-
chute Adams in a stretch of water that allowed long, smooth drifts. She
wasn't quick enough setting the hook, but she was getting better—and
she didn't get down on herself when she missed a strike. She just made
another cast, concentrating all the harder. Kit had to tell her when it
was time to head back to the lodge for lunch.

"Couldn't we stay," Gwendolyn had said, "while they're hitting?"

"Your dad will wonder where you are."

"He knows I'm with Calvin."

"Except you're not. And he expects you back for lunch."

The jack pines closed in again, and they walked along the rivulet,
single file, Kit leading the way, rods held pointing behind them. When
they reached the mainstream, Kit told Gwendolyn to be careful, there
was muck they had to get through to reach the streambed, and she
moved up beside him and put a hand on his arm, steadying herself. The

grip of her fingers was amazingly strong for someone so slender.

"That's the only bad part," Kit said when they reached firm footing, "following the stream back to the river."

"It wasn't so bad," Gwendolyn said.

"There's some places, you don't know your way, you sink in past your knees. You need help getting out."

"You know a lot about the river."

"I should," Kit said, "growing up here."

"Couldn't you be my guide?"

Surprised, Kit turned, looked into large eyes beneath the blue cap, realized with more surprise that Gwendolyn was still gripping his arm. "Calvin is."

"But couldn't I ask your dad for you?"

"You could," Kit said after a moment's consideration. "But you'll have to play it by ear, be sort of tactful. Verlyn and Calvin, guys that age, can be touchy as hell. And about nothing."

"Yeah."

"You might say it's because of what happened to Charlie Orr. Calvin feeling the way he does about it. You understand, Gwen?"

"Yeah," she repeated, and seemed not to notice that he had shortened her name.

*       *       *

BEFORE CALVIN COULD explain, Jan came into the fly shop and announced that fresh coffee was ready. For Calvin there was tea.

"We're busy in here," Verlyn told her.

Jan looked around the shop, seeing no one else there, but held her tongue.

"I could stand a mug," Calvin said.

Jan gave Verlyn another look. "Honey?"

"Bring it," Verlyn said, "you're gonna keep asking."

Calvin waited until Jan had brought two big mugs, then left again for the lodge before he asked Verlyn why he was being so rough on a wife who was going out of her way to be a sweetheart.

"None of your business."

"That's so," Calvin agreed.

"The one smart thing you ever did," Verlyn said, "was not get yourself married."

"I figured it wouldn't work with being a guide, going to New Zealand, things I do. You got a different situation. You need somebody to run the lodge. Who's gonna do that except a wife? You learned with Mercy."

"I learned a lot with Mercy. All bad."

"Funny thing," Calvin said. "She says the same about you. But it doesn't figure—everything bad yet you two end up with Kit. He's a good kid."

"Okay," Verlyn said. "You've had a slug of tea. Now get off the dime."

"It's not about Jan."

"Dammit, Calvin."

"Coming upriver I was thinking who'd want to shoot Charlie, harmless guy like that, and came up blank. There's no reason, which means shooting him is senseless. Now you think about that a while, senseless crimes, and you ask yourself what's going on. Going on these days. It's always the same thing. You read about it all the time in the papers. You with me?"

"No."

"Like I say, Kit's a good kid. But he had this trouble at school."

Verlyn leaned across the glass-topped counter beside the cash register, stared at Calvin sitting at the tying bench. "Kit got busted at Central Michigan, one time, for smoking pot. You're talking about that?"

"You hear about senseless crimes, eventually you learn drugs are behind them. In the past it was booze, now it's drugs. Kit telling me about Charlie, that made me realize."

Verlyn kept staring at him. "Some drugged-out crazy shot Charlie? That what you're thinking? Drugged-out crazies don't hang around the Borchard for trout."

"Charlie was shot in the campground."

"What's the difference? Some drugged-out crazy went into Rainbow Run and blew Charlie away for the hell of it? You're losing it, Calvin."

"You're forgetting something."

"What?"

"Charlie smoked pot himself."

Verlyn thought for a while before he said, "That was way back. Everyone smoked a little on the river then. Kept the bugs off at night."

"I didn't," Calvin said.

"You were weird then, too. So way back Charlie smoked pot on the river like everyone but you. So what?"

"How do you know it was only way back? Charlie still smoked a pipe on the river. Not many guys do that anymore. How do you know he wasn't loading it up with pot?"

"I'd have smelled it, is why. You don't think I'd remember the smell?"

"I don't know," Calvin said. "Old guys like you don't remember so good."

"You're the same age," Verlyn said, "and you don't have any mind to remember with. In the old days, night fishing, pitch black on the river, you could locate Charlie by the smell of his pot. He could locate me the same way. It's a long time since I smelled pot on the river."

Calvin said, "Maybe old guys don't smell so good, either."

"Okay," Verlyn said, "even if Charlie was still smoking pot, what's that got to do with his getting shot?"

"For his stash. Somebody was after it."

Verlyn suddenly reddened, looked like he was about to leap the counter. "You're thinking *Kit*?"

"Naw," Calvin said. "Mellow out. Kit wouldn't do that. But he might know who around here needed drugs bad enough."

"Pot's not like that. You don't kill for it, unless you're a dealer and another dealer moves on your territory."

"Maybe you'd kill," Calvin said, "you need it bad enough. You're up in the woods, you're craving some pot, you run across an old guy who's got some—" When Verlyn didn't respond Calvin asked, "Or maybe Charlie got mixed up with some dealer. You see what I'm getting at?"

"I'm trying not to," Verlyn said.

*     *     *

"I GOT HER back," Kit said when he came in the fly shop in his waders.

"She's having lunch with her dad."

"She hook that big one?" Calvin asked.

"We went down, fooled around for brookies. She got some strikes."

"She's coming along."

"Yeah." Kit looked at the sign on the wall about the reward fund for Charlie Orr, then looked at Verlyn. "She might say something about me guiding her in the morning. It wasn't my idea. She thinks Calvin may be too busted up because of Charlie."

"All right," Verlyn said.

Kit kept looking at him, astonished. Then he shrugged and looked again at the sign. "Any takers?"

"Gwendolyn's old man," Calvin told him. "And me when I get my checkbook."

"Put me in for twenty-five," Kit said, "if you're takin' that small."

"It adds up," Calvin said.

When no one said any more Kit shrugged again, said he would be back after he had a smoke and got out of his waders. Verlyn watched from the window as he passed around the shop and moved through the stand of white birch to the river's edge. "Talk to him," he said to Calvin.

"How come you don't?"

"I talk to him, we both end up yelling. You might drag something out."

"That's so," Calvin said. Then he was looking at the sign Kit had been looking at. "The kid could end up with the reward."

"What?"

"Depending on what he says. Your kid, though, member of the family and all, it wouldn't look good. Jan might get upset."

"Dammit to all hell," Verlyn said. "*Talk* to him."

# 10

THEONA ORR WASN'T at all the way Mercy had envisioned her when they spoke on the phone, settling arrangements to meet that afternoon. The woman facing her now seemed older than Charlie, elderly almost, with snow-white hair, colorless skin, and a tiny, fragile-looking body. It was her voice, though, that was most surprising. On the telephone it had seemed only prim, but in person it was direct and decisive—and, it struck Mercy, wholly resistant to any suggestion of grief. Although Mercy had made clear her reason for wanting to call on her, Theona Orr appeared mystified why someone she didn't know would come all the distance to Big Rapids to offer sympathy.

"It really isn't so far," Mercy said. "I can see why Charlie didn't mind the drive."

"Once a year he drove to Ossning."

Mercy nodded at the correction. Was Theona establishing the point, in the event Mercy didn't know, that Charlie never returned to Big Rapids once he had set up his summer camp in Rainbow Run? That she had been a fishing widow, in other words, long before becoming a real one?

"It wasn't any trouble," Mercy said, deciding to change the subject, "finding you."

"Big Rapids isn't large."

"But a lovely town. And you have a lovely home."

It wasn't, really. Lovely at least wasn't the word that came first to mind. It was a plain ranch-style house set on a neatly landscaped lot on a tree-lined street. Ordinary was a more accurate word. Or sensible.

The house was no more remarkable inside—exceedingly clean, a woman's house more than a man's, but nothing fussy about it: an ordinary, sensible interior. The only thing that suggested Charlie's presence was bookshelves on either side of a fireplace in the room in which Mercy and Theona now sat. Mercy reminded herself that Charlie's wife, a former school librarian, might be as omnivorous a reader as Charlie had been.

"I won't stay. I know how you must be feeling. And you'll have plans to make. If there's anything I can do, anything the DNR can do, anything Charlie's friends on the river can do, please just—"

"I believe not."

Mercy tried to wait, to say nothing, letting Theona respond to the silence. It might have been unwise to mention the river, to bring into the open that Charlie had had another life on the Borchard, one his wife never shared. Theona might not wish to be reminded of that in the setting of her own home.

"What I mean," Theona said finally, "is no plans will be made until my daughter arrives."

"Oh," Mercy said, "I'm so glad someone's coming."

Theona kept her hands rigidly folded on her lap. "My only child. She lives in California. Her husband's work will prevent him from coming."

"May I ask if you have grandchildren?"

"I'm afraid not."

"Will there be relatives coming?"

"No."

"Listen," Mercy said, and leaned forward, holding Theona's eyes. "Is there anything I can tell you about what happened? I realize the state police have spoken with you, but maybe there's something I can add. My office, the DNR field office in Ossning, is working closely with the Tamarack County sheriff's office. If it's something I don't know, I can try to find out for you. So if there's anything—"

"The police officers who came were quite thorough."

"Everyone around Ossning," Mercy went on, "is broken up. Everyone who knew Charlie. He had a lot of friends, close friends. Nobody can understand why something like this would happen."

"Nor can I," Theona said, but there was no puzzlement in her voice, let alone outrage. Or grief. Struck once again by its absence, Mercy decided to push a bit deeper—try to—out of curiosity. And there was still something else on her agenda, the job to perform for Willard Stroud.

"It wasn't a case of robbery. Nothing was taken from the tent. In fact, there's no evidence the tent was entered."

Theona nodded but didn't respond.

"It may be that whoever did this didn't know Charlie was inside the tent. I mean, he knew someone was, but it didn't matter that it was Charlie. It could have been anyone."

"The officers suggested it might have been a random attack."

"But if it wasn't, if Charlie was singled out, it was someone who knew him."

"Knew him to some degree."

"I realize that," Mercy said. "It could have been a casual acquaintance as well as someone who knew him well. Can you think of anyone, in either category, who might have had something against Charlie?"

"I was asked," Theona said, "by the officers."

"Anyone Charlie might have worked with at the post office? Any relatives? Any former friends? Any enemies?"

"I told them I could think of no one."

Did the state police also ask, Mercy was tempted to add, about you? A wife, an aggrieved one, was certainly a possibility. And the way the shooting was done, from outside the tent, without a confrontation, might be considered the way an aggrieved wife would do it, wishing her husband dead but preferring to avoid witnessing the process. But one look at Theona Orr would immediately dismiss the possibility. You couldn't imagine someone of her age and delicate appearance driving to Ossning, locating Rainbow Run, pulling out a shotgun, blasting the walls of a tent.

But there was something else, it occurred to Mercy, that would cause Theona to be eliminated at once as a suspect. She wasn't interested enough. Interested enough in Charlie. That realization had been at the edge of Mercy's mind since she entered the house, since she had noted Theona's resistance to grief. It wasn't resistance so much as lack of interest. Theona didn't reveal any grief because she didn't feel any.

Mercy shook her head, trying to clear away the thought. Perhaps when the daughter arrived, Theona *and* Charlie's daughter, perhaps then grief would surface. Perhaps grief always hit, really hit, later. It didn't, though, seem likely. Although she had never let herself dwell on it, Mercy had always assumed that Charlie's domestic life must be . . . well, not entirely fulfilling. Why else would he spend an entire summer living by himself in a tent in the woods? The fishing on the Borchard River was the answer, but fishing, as much as she wished to believe otherwise, couldn't be the sole answer. Putting some distance between a sensible wife and a sensible house on a sensible street could be another.

"No one at all?" Mercy asked.

"No."

"Does the name Alec Proffit mean anything to you?"

There was no change of expression on Theona's face, but neither was there an answer. Silence held in the air. Then Theona said, "Would you excuse me?"

"Sure," Mercy said, and felt her heart accelerate.

"I won't be a moment."

\*     \*     \*

WHEN SHE RETURNED to the room, Theona Orr carried a large black-bound notebook binder, the sort school children use. She sat down, knees pressed together, the notebook on her lap, and began leafing through the pages. When she came to the one she was looking for she methodically ran a finger down the length of the page.

"No," she said finally.

"You don't know the name?"

"For a moment it seemed familiar. I had to check my roster." Theona closed the binder, folded her hands on top of it. "My Elderhostel experiences."

"Sorry," Mercy said. "I don't understand."

"During the summer months I attend Elderhostel courses with a group of former school teachers, all cherished friends. We travel extensively. Next will be Stratford."

"England?"

"Ontario. In conjunction with the Shakespeare festival. I've kept rosters over the years of those attending the courses, in the event we might meet again. All my Elderhostel experiences are recorded here." Theona softly tapped the notebook binder with a finger. "No such name is indicated."

"But at first it struck you as familiar?"

"I was mistaken."

"I was thinking more of somebody who might have come to your home. Alec Proffit might have done that. He might have come here about Charlie."

"No."

"No one came around, asking about him?"

"Why would they? He was in Ossning."

Mercy nodded, aware of the slow deceleration of her heart. At length she stood, smiled faintly, preparing to leave. One last time she asked Theona if there was anything she could do for her, anything at all.

"Perhaps one thing."

*　　　*　　　*

FROM THE LIVING room, Mercy was led along a hallway to the kitchen, a room so ferociously clean it was hard to believe it was ever used. Theona opened a door off the room and over her shoulder advised Mercy to mind her step.

The basement was purely that: cement walls and floor, windowless, unconverted into added living space. When Theona touched a switch, suddenly filling the area with fluorescent light, Mercy blinked, then understood the reason for what seemed like excessive illumination. The cool, dank basement had served as Charlie's tying room.

One wall was dominated by a long table—an old unfinished door, actually, supported by a pair of two-drawer filing cabinets—above which were shelves arranged with plastic boxes of tying materials. The chair set in front of the table before an Abel vise was a high-backed wooden swivel chair, the kind you only saw now in old movies. The chair brought Charlie back to mind with a rush, as did an assortment of smoke-darkened pipes hanging from a rack and, leaning against a wall beside the tying table, an orderly row of rod cases that no doubt contained rods Charlie wrapped from blanks, rods he seldom—if ever—used, wrapped for the sheer pleasure of the craft. Thinking of Charlie in his basement workshop, tying flies and wrapping rods through the endless Michigan winter, caused Mercy to release a long, sad sigh.

"I'm wondering," Theona said, "what might be done with it."

"With what, exactly?"

"All of it."

"Eventually, you mean?"

"It should be put to some use. It shouldn't go to waste."

Mercy looked at Theona, who was looking steadily at the tying table. There was no expression on her face, nothing in her eyes. No sense of urgency. And no sense of loss.

"There's no one in your family, no friends, anyone who might . . . ?"

"I was thinking of someone you would know. Up there."

Mercy waited, but Theona said nothing more. "There's one thing. The Trout Unlimited chapter in Ossning has a silent auction each year to raise funds for river restoration projects. Items are donated: rods, flies, equipment, books, paintings. Anything of Charlie's would be greatly valued."

"Yes," Theona said.

"You'd like me to see to it?"

"When would it be?"

"The auction? It takes place over the winter."

Disappointment crossed Theona's face.

"Let's leave it this way," Mercy said. "I'll get in touch with you later. In the fall. You can let me know if you still like the idea. In the meantime, something else might occur to you."

"It won't," Theona said, and led Mercy back to the stairway.

*       *       *

AT THE ENTRANCE door of the house, Mercy took one of her DNR business cards from her handbag, used a ballpoint pen to add the telephone number of the A-frame, handed the card to Theona. "In case you want to get in touch. Or your daughter does. I'm at the office number during the week, at the other one evenings and weekends."

Theona smiled blandly. "Thank you for coming."

"I wish there was something more—" Mercy stopped herself. There was no use going on. Theona had made it perfectly clear: The only help she needed was getting rid of Charlie's fishing things. Mercy reached out, lightly grasped Theona's hand. It seemed an awkward thing to do, but she couldn't imagine leaning forward, kissing the woman's pale, tearless cheek.

"Goodbye." She took a step in the direction of the street, then turned back, feeling the void, needing to fill it one last time. Try to. "Will you be all right?"

"Of course."

"I'm sorry about Stratford. Having to miss it."

Theona looked back with eyes as mystified as they had appeared when Mercy first arrived, driving the distance from Ossning to Big Rapids. "But I won't. Elderhostel courses are firmly scheduled. Our group will go as planned."

Mercy tried to smile, to say it was good that Theona had her cherished friends to console her, but what came out was another long, sad sigh for Charlie.

# 11

"THOUGHT YOU WERE dead," Hoke Harkness said.

Fitzgerald smiled into the phone, told him no, just living in the north woods on the Borchard River near the town of Ossning.

"Same thing."

"You ought to come up," Fitzgerald said, "see the real world. We've got a spare bedroom."

"We?"

Harkness, an assistant managing editor of the *Free Press*, was a fat man with nimble feet and a quick mind. Beginning with sloppy syntax, not much slipped by him. Fitzgerald could imagine him now, leaning into the phone over a surprisingly neat desk, brow furrowed, trademark yellow suspenders straining against a soft mountain of chest.

"I'm living with a woman I met up here. You'd like her."

"Why?"

"She's got a weak spot for journalists."

"Any others like that up there?" Then Harkness said, "Tell you the truth, I'd heard over the grapevine you were writing a novel. Assumed you'd slit your wrists by now."

"I'm working on it," Fitzgerald said. "The novel, that is."

"So you're calling because you need a ghost writer, a shoulder to cry on, your job back, what?"

"Help with a name."

"You can't make one up?"

"It's not a name in the novel. I'm trying to locate someone as a favor for the sheriff up here. There's been a killing in a state campground on the river."

"An AP story came through."

"In the campground at the same time was a fellow named Alec Proffit with an address in Norwich, Vermont. There's reason to think he might be a journalist of some sort. I'm wondering if you could poke around for me, see what might turn up."

"More than you can find yourself?"

"If there is more."

"And this sheriff up there is using you as his gopher?"

"He's got his reasons," Fitzgerald said, but didn't explain.

"Give me some time. See what I can do."

"I'll owe you one, Hoke."

"You figured I wouldn't keep track?"

*       *       *

TWO HOURS WENT by before Hoke Harkness called.

"Seems your man belongs to the American Society of Journalists and Authors. He's a freelance writer with a specialty in outdoor stuff. He also turns out a regular column in a magazine called *Angling World*. Heard of it?"

"Yes," Fitzgerald said. "I subscribe. It's a quality publication."

"If fishing magazines qualify."

"But I don't recall seeing the name Alec Proffit in there."

"Try Will Woodsman."

"Sure. He has a regular column."

"Then here's something maybe you couldn't have found out. The column's written by Proffit. Woodsman's a pen name."

Fitzgerald said, "The column's got an edge to it. Will Woodsman's opinionated, outspoken. He's always going after some rascals who've broken the rules—sporting rules, environmental rules, his own personal rules. He's not big on humor or light touches. Half the time he irritates me, but I always read him."

"Thought that was the point if you're a writer. Here's something else," Harkness said, "that'll make your day. As Will Woodsman the guy's published two collections of essays—outdoor stuff, apparently. And— get this—a half-dozen novels, suspense variety, under the name Peter Allston. Not written, you understand. *Published.*" Harkness paused. "Probably got himself a blonde bombshell wife, too."

"No doubt."

"So what now?"

"I'll tell the sheriff what you found out. It's his baby from here on."

Harkness paused again before he said, "Writer you read in a maga- zine happens to be in a campground where a killing takes place, you're living in the area, you've got the info before anyone else, but you just pass it on to the local sheriff? C'mon, Fitzgerald. You think I believe that you must think *I'm* dead."

"Something else I might do?"

"It ever cross your mind? Write something for the paper."

"I forgot to tell you," Fitzgerald said. "Proffit's missing. Even so, his presence in the campground at the time of the killing might only be a coincidence. He might have been out here for the fishing."

"From Vermont? Stick to your novel," Harkness said, "you think that."

*    *    *

IT WASN'T THAT he doubted what Hoke Harkness had told him. Hoke was a stickler for getting things right. It was that he wanted confirma- tion about another matter, and Hoke couldn't help with that. Mercy probably could, but Mercy was on her errand for Willard Stroud in Big Rapids.

Fitzgerald drove from the A-frame to the Kabin Kamp, hoping to find Calvin's pickup parked in front of the fly shop. When it wasn't there, he stopped anyway, went inside. Verlyn was on the phone, red faced, enjoying himself. Fitzgerald, trying not to listen, searched through the shop's shelves of sporting books in an alcove next to a display of fishing vests.

"I told him," Verlyn said happily when he hung up the phone, "he's not running a police state. He doesn't decide who can offer a reward."

Fitzgerald said over his shoulder, "Stroud, I take it."

"Said it would cause his office too much work. I said, 'You'd have to answer the phone, you mean, work like that?' He got hot, some reason. When he simmered down, I told him, 'Give us a couple days, we know how much we got, we'd put an ad in the *Call*, announcing the reward.' He said we couldn't do that without the okay of his office. We'd be interfering in a murder investigation. So I said, 'How'd it look if Gus Thayer ran a story saying the sheriff was blocking a reward? Like he was trying to hide something, that's how.' Stroud got hot again, some reason."

"Listen," Fitzgerald said. "You ever have books in here by Will Woodsman? Collections of outdoor essays?"

"Don't recall."

Fitzgerald left the bookshelves and crossed the shop to the cash-register counter. "I was thinking Calvin might be around. He reads a lot."

"He and Kit, they're off somewhere." Verlyn turned, studied the black-lettered sign beside the display of tippet spools. "Fellow staying here put himself in for five hundred."

"He knew Charlie?"

"Only heard me tell about him. Somebody who knew Charlie ought to be good for that much."

"You know the writer I'm talking about?" Fitzgerald asked. "He has the column in *Angling World*."

"An eco-freak," Verlyn said. "Why I like him."

"Will Woodsman's a pen name. Alec Proffit's his real one. He writes novels under another pen name."

"Never heard of him."

"Me neither. But I thought Calvin might have."

"He's got a head full of trivia, that's so."

Fitzgerald asked, "Who had more? More information. Because he read all the time, knew all kinds of things?"

Verlyn straightened behind the counter. "What's Charlie got to do with this?"

"Probably nothing. But it just struck me: Charlie might have known Woodsman was really Proffit, picked that up somewhere. He regularly read *Angling World*. I know that much. Up here he probably went to the library, read it among the magazines."

Verlyn cocked his head, peered at Fitzgerald. "You trying to change the subject? It's the reward we were talkin' about."

Fitzgerald shrugged. "I don't know. Stroud could have a point. A reward might complicate the investigation."

Verlyn waited, still peering at Fitzgerald, before he said, "You just got yourself put down for five hundred."

\*       \*       \*

FROM THE KABIN Kamp, Fitzgerald took the South Downriver Road into Ossning, planning on stopping at the sheriff's office and telling Stroud what he had learned from Hoke Harkness about the missing camper in Rainbow Run. But when he reached the main drag and was passing the Borchard Hotel in the direction of the city-county building, he changed his mind. He decided to rendezvous first with Mercy, see what she had learned in Big Rapids. Together they could go to Stroud with their information.

In the meantime, there was the Ossning public library.

*Woodsman, Will* brought up on the computer catalogue the two collections of essays, both checked out. *Allston, Peter* brought up nothing.

Fitzgerald considered asking Wanda Voss, the librarian, if she had ever heard of novels by a writer of that name. And of course he could himself use the library's Internet connection, seeing what Amazon listed. But he decided to do neither. He didn't want to lose the sense of relief he felt, unbecoming though it was, in learning that whereas Alec Proffit himself had arrived in the Michigan woods, his string of novels hadn't.

The shelves of the Ossning public library remained wide-open territory for a fiction writer.

# 12

K IT KNEW WHAT was coming. Calvin hadn't asked him to drive
over to the cabin on the South Branch, stop in for lunch, simply to
pass the time of day. What was coming was a lecture about Gwendolyn
Underwood.

Kit was on the screen porch of the cabin in one of Calvin's beat-up
wooden rockers, Calvin inside working on the lunch. Through the tangle
of cedars and spruce in front of the cabin, Kit could barely glimpse the
river, a flash of silver in the sunlight. Calvin thought you shouldn't be
able to see cabins from the river, the bank left natural, and Kit agreed. It
wouldn't be bad, though, sitting on Calvin's porch, rocking away, with
a full view of the water.

When Calvin brought out the lunch, handing Kit his plate, Kit asked,
"What this?"

"Tuna salad, cottage cheese. You want crackers to go with it?"

"I was thinking about a sandwich."

"Naw," Calvin said, "this is better for you. You got to learn to eat
right. Junk food's all you eat around the Kabin Kamp."

Kit nibbled at the tuna salad, letting it go at that. He didn't want to
get into a big discussion of food with Calvin. Calvin was a nut about
food. He whipped up a terrific shore lunch when he was guiding—small
steaks, fresh morels, cooked carrots, red wine—but on his own he was
practically a vegetarian. A fly-fishing guide who didn't smoke, didn't
drink, didn't eat meat—Kit figured you could scour the country and
wouldn't find a clone of Calvin. All he wanted to learn from Calvin, he
had decided long ago, was what he knew about the river.

"I go out with Gwendolyn tomorrow," Kit said, trying to sound off-hand. "You got any suggestions?" He decided he would get to the point of the lunch rather than let Calvin circle around it. Calvin could be as slow as Mercy when he was planning to lecture you. Only Verlyn came right out with what he had to say—maybe the only trait, it occurred to Kit, he shared with his father.

"You got some brookies to hit. Go back there." Calvin didn't seem terribly interested, except in his food. He was chewing away like it was real food.

"I was wondering about going upriver, trying around the TU access. She might pick up a rainbow in the riffles."

Calvin shrugged. "Your dad might not want you driving her anywhere. I think he wants her fishing around the lodge."

"There's no fish around the lodge she can catch."

Calvin shrugged again, uninterested. Kit didn't get it. He had given Calvin an opening, but Calvin hadn't taken it. The lunch was shaping up as a long siege. Was until Calvin said, "You want a beer to go with the food?"

Kit gave him a look before he said, "You don't have any."

"I picked up a couple six-packs at High Pines on the way back from the fly shop. People stop by, good to have something on hand."

Kit didn't believe that for a second. People didn't stop by at Calvin's since the cabin was a long way in from the highway along a rutted dirt road that wasn't much better than a two-track. And Calvin wasn't the kind of host who stocked his place with what he didn't eat or drink himself. So what was going on? If a lecture wasn't coming about Gwendolyn Underwood, what was?

*    *    *

KIT SIPPED A can of Budweiser while Calvin, settled in his rocker with a glass of lemonade, finished off his tuna salad. Kit let him take his time, there not being any other choice. Minutes dragged by.

Calvin was looking out from the porch in the direction of the river when, out of the blue, he asked, "You still fooling with pot?"

Kit nearly choked, a mouthful of beer rising into his nose. He ran the back of a hand across his face before he could say, "What?"

"You used to. Do you still?"

Kit waited, wondering what had happened to Calvin's roundabout way of lecturing him, before he asked, "How come you want to know that?"

"Charlie Orr used to smoke pot, fishing the river at night."

"He did?" Kit found himself saying.

"Way back, when I first knew him. Your dad, too. Lots of fishermen did then, way back. Not me."

"Verlyn did?"

"Don't tell him I told you. What I'm asking is about Charlie."

Kit said, "Slow down, Calvin. You're asking me if I'm smoking pot, then you're saying Charlie Orr did. Way back. What're you getting at?"

Calvin kept looking out at the river, sipping his lemonade, acting as if they were talking about the weather. "You got any idea who'd want to kill Charlie? Harmless old guy camping in Rainbow Run, and somebody blasts his tent with a shotgun. Why would they? You got a guess?"

"Somebody didn't like him."

"That's a possibility," Calvin said, sounding thoughtful. "Another is somebody wanted his stash of pot."

"You said Charlie smoked a long time ago. So what stash?"

"I thought you might tell me."

Kit nearly jumped out of the rocker, the plate of uneaten tuna salad teetering on his lap, beer splashing from the can. "You got it in your head *I* killed Charlie for his stash?"

"Naw," Calvin said. "I know you wouldn't."

Kit tried to settle down, to sound as calm as Calvin sounded. "Then why'd you ask if I still used pot? Not that it's any of your business."

"You do, it's bad for your health. You ought to know that, smart kid like you. But what I was thinking, you aren't so smart, you still use it, you've got to buy it off somebody."

"That's good thinking," Kit said, trying now to sound sarcastic. "The only thing grows up here are pines. So you'd have to buy it."

"So where?"

Kit gave Calvin a long look before he said, "Let's get straightened out. I smoked some down at school, I got caught with some in my dorm room, they were going to bounce me out, so I quit before they could. And then Mercy and Verlyn blabbed it all over town."

"Naw, they were disappointed you left college, is all."

"Keep listening, Calvin. Since I came home, I haven't smoked once. And not because of my health. You know why? All pot ever did was give me a headache."

"So does beer, you drink too much."

Kit said, "We're talking here about pot. I'm telling you I don't smoke it. Haven't since I was in school. End of story. Got it?"

"Good news," Calvin said, and looked pleased. Then he aimed a finger in the direction of Kit's beer can. "You need another? Most of that one you spilled on my floor."

\*        \*        \*

HOW WERE YOU supposed to deal with older types like Calvin and Verlyn and Mercy?

Kit never knew for sure, because they wouldn't stay in focus, wouldn't behave the way you expected them to. Take Verlyn, who had Jan yet was mooning over Gwendolyn. Take Mercy, who had gotten free of Verlyn yet moved in with Fitzgerald. Take Calvin, his nose usually out of joint about beer yet buying six-packs at High Pines. Sometimes Kit felt that they must have a different sense of logic than he did. Or none at all, logic being among the inevitable losses of age.

So how should you deal with them? All you could do was go with the flow, ride the tide, seize the breeze, which at the moment meant lapping up the Budweiser Calvin had been illogical enough to provide.

But that wasn't quite right, writing Calvin off as illogical. Old Calvin could be devious, or try to be. The way he would figure—*his* kind of logic—was that beer would soften Kit up, get him to say something he wouldn't say otherwise, cold sober. To get the information he wanted, Calvin could ease up on health matters for the time being. But Kit had straightened him out: There wasn't any information to get.

"So what I'm asking," Calvin was saying, "is where you'd buy it."

Kit stared at him, startled. "I *don't*. That's what I *told* you."

"But where would you? If you did."

Kit said, "That's what you want to know?"

"I'm not making myself clear?"

Kit sighed and said, "You're not talking about me? Where anyone would buy pot, you mean? Where Charlie Orr might have?"

"Around here," Calvin said. "Ossning."

Kit took a long swallow of beer, leaned back in the rocker, tried to glimpse the river again through the wall of pine beyond the porch. "I'm going to say this, then I'm heading back to the lodge."

"You don't have to rush."

"I don't know where you'd buy pot around Ossning. I don't know because I don't buy it. Maybe you can't buy it. If you can, it's probably out at the Keg O'Nails. Some dude hanging around there."

"Charlie never went to the Keg."

"Where I bought it was down in Mount Pleasant. You could buy it there right and left. Half the people in town where pushing pot."

"Because it was a college town."

"You could buy it in the Student Union, you wanted."

"What I figured all along."

Kit turned from the flash of silver that was all he could see of the river, looked at Calvin. "You figured what all along?"

"That where you'd buy pot was in a college town."

"That's what you wanted to know? Then why didn't you ask me, straight out?"

"I thought I did."

Kit stood up, headed toward the cabin's kitchen with his plate and beer can. "Thanks for lunch," he said over his shoulder.

"You have enough to eat?" Calvin asked from his rocker.

Kit wanted to say something back, sarcastic as all hell, but knew it would be a complete waste of breath.

# 13

A DRINK WAS ready, John Jameson with a splash of water, when Mercy came in the back door of the A-frame. She kissed Fitzgerald, took a sip of the drink, handed it back, said she wanted to get out of the uniform she had worn to Big Rapids.

Fitzgerald was in a sling chair on the deck jutting out from the glass front of the house and overlooking a thick stand of woods, the river circling beyond in the early-evening light, when she reappeared in shorts, a tank top, bare feet. She sighed as she took the drink from him, eased herself into an adjoining chair.

"Long day?"

"Let's just sit here, enjoy this."

"All right."

After another sip of her drink, Mercy said, "We're lucky, Fitzgerald. You know how lucky?"

"You just want to sit here, I thought."

"That's what I mean, sitting here, talking or not talking. Like this. We're so lucky."

"Being together."

"Not only that. Lots of people are together. It's how that matters."

Fitzgerald looked across at her. "You want to go to bed, you mean?"

"Of course I do. Only not now."

Fitzgerald lifted his drink, examined the caramel color against the sky. "Maybe you ought to tell me about your day."

"It was hell. I stopped at the office before I came home. Verlyn had left messages with Fern Lax, all just alike, wanting me to call. So I did.

He thought I'd have all sorts of inside information about Charlie, about what happened, and wouldn't believe I didn't. I didn't tell him about the missing camper."

"Neither did I. I was over to the shop for a while."

"Apparently, Verlyn and Calvin are going ahead with the reward. Stroud notwithstanding."

"Apparently." Then Fitzgerald said, "Talking to Verlyn made the day hell?"

"Added to it. It was meeting Charlie's wife. I can't imagine Charlie and Theona ever sitting down like this, having a drink, talking over the day. Let alone planning on bed. They must have, there's a daughter, but I can't imagine it."

Mercy sighed again, launched into an account of the meeting for Fitzgerald, going through it step by step, including a description of the house, the street, the entire town of Big Rapids. "Charlie and Theona lived together, at least part of the year, but judging by the way she acted, they didn't have a thing in common. All that seems to interest her is attending Elderhostel courses."

"All that interested Charlie was fishing the Borchard."

"I know. It was a two-way street. It always is. Still and all, you would think she'd express a little feeling for Charlie, especially dying the way he did. Good Lord, Fitzgerald. Her husband was murdered, and she doesn't show a ruffled feather. She didn't seem to understand why I was there."

"So she's not an angry wife."

"If you mean was she angry enough to kill Charlie, no way. You have to have some interest before you can be angry. Anyway, she's a tiny old woman. She couldn't have come up here with a shotgun."

"And she knew nothing about Alec Proffit?"

"Nothing. And she didn't have anything to say about relatives or friends or coworkers of Charlie. Or enemies. Theona's a dead end. Stroud doesn't need to waste time with that side of Charlie's life."

When the phone rang inside the A-frame, Fitzgerald unfolded himself from the sling chair, left the deck. When he came back, he told

Mercy he was going to freshen their drinks before he told her who the call was from.

*     *     *

"CALVIN. WITH A worry he's got." Fitzgerald paused, examined again the satisfying color of Jameson against the light of the sky. "A wacky worry."

Mercy said, "Are we talking about Charlie's murder or what?"

"Sort of."

"Tell you what," Mercy said. "Let's sit here quiet, one whole minute, enjoy the evening. Then start over, tell me what Calvin called about, make some sense."

"He remembered Charlie used to have some pot in his pipe. When he was on the river, fishing at night. Charlie would sip whiskey from his flask, smoke pot, hook big browns. He's right."

"Of course he is. But that was way back then—a sixties thing."

"Seventies and eighties, too."

"You did?"

"Except I didn't inhale."

"Very funny. Verlyn used to, and not only at night on the river. I didn't want to run the risk, not with my job. Calvin and I were about the sole holdouts." Mercy turned, looked at Fitzgerald over the rim of her glass. "I didn't know you back then, a pothead."

"It didn't amount to anything. Nothing to excess. It was just part of night fishing on the river, a little pot, a little whiskey, big browns, break-fast the next morning at the Black Duck in Kinnich."

"So what's Calvin wondering about?"

"If he tells Stroud about Charlie, Stroud might put two and two together and realize Charlie's friends on the river, meaning me and Verlyn, were smoking, too. He'd know Calvin wasn't, Calvin being Calvin. Point is, Calvin doesn't want to get us in trouble with Stroud."

"What trouble? Stroud wasn't the sheriff back then. And he wouldn't care anyway. For all we know he was smoking himself."

"But you know Calvin. You look at him, you could believe he's an outlaw. In fact, you exclude his views on private property, he's probably the most law-abiding citizen in Tamarack County. He doesn't want to get us on Stroud's bad side."

"That's just dumb. He knows Verlyn's *always* on Stroud's bad side."

"There's more. He's got it in his head—from the reading he does—that every crime these days is drug related. So he assumes Charlie's killing must be. And he thinks he knows where Charlie got his pot. Down at Ferris State. Big Rapids is a college town, and in college towns you can get drugs anywhere you want. So Calvin thinks Charlie brought a stash up from Big Rapids, smoked on the river at night, somebody noticed, killed Charlie for the stash."

"Good Lord."

"I told Calvin there's one big flaw in his reasoning: Charlie didn't smoke pot anymore. All he did at night on the river was sip whiskey, puff on his pipe. Plain tobacco. If Charlie was still smoking pot, we'd all know because we fished with him."

"What did Calvin say to that?"

"That we're all getting old. We don't remember so well."

"Good Lord."

"Anyway, I told Calvin that if it made him feel better, he doesn't have to worry about getting anyone into trouble with the law for smoking in the past."

"So now we've got two," Mercy said, "dead ends. Theona Orr had nothing to do with Charlie's death, neither did drugs. That leaves Alec Proffit."

"Now I'll tell you what I learned," Fitzgerald said.

\*     \*     \*

FIRST THEY ATE at the trestle table in the kitchen—Spanish omelets, garden salad, half a bottle of chilled Sauvignon Blanc. Fitzgerald made coffee afterward, and they took their mugs out to the deck, the light purple-shadowed over the dark tips of the pines.

"I never knew Will Woodsman was a pen name," Mercy said after Fitzgerald told her what Hoke Harkness at the *Free Press* had learned about Alec Proffit. "No reason I would, I suppose. And I've never heard about Peter Allston as a novelist. You'd think I might, given all the books he's published."

"Maybe they didn't sell well. But Charlie might have known about Proffit," Fitzgerald said, "given the amount he read."

"So you think there's some connection? Because Charlie would have known?"

"I don't know. All we know is that an outdoor writer and novelist comes here from Vermont, camps near Charlie, takes notes about Charlie, even goes down to Big Rapids, then turns up missing the moment Charlie is killed."

"But he didn't just vanish. The tent, all his things, they're still there. Even the notebook was." Mercy paused. "There's another possibility, you know. Maybe Proffit hasn't vanished. Maybe he's dead, too."

"But why?"

"No idea. But with his camp still there, it makes you wonder. Maybe he and Charlie were both killed and it's just that Proffit's body hasn't been found yet."

"Charlie's body was inside his tent. Why would Proffit's be elsewhere?"

Mercy waved an impatient hand through the darkening air. "This is silly, Fitzgerald. All we know for sure is that Proffit made notes about Charlie and now he's missing. We don't know another thing."

Fitzgerald gazed into the black pine wall below the deck and said, "We know how much Proffit has published."

"What difference does that make?"

"None as far as Charlie's death is concerned. A helluva lot, tell you the truth, to me." Fitzgerald meant to go on, bare his nonwriting writer's soul. It seemed a good time to do so: on the deck, in the darkness of a soft evening, disabusing Mercy of any misconceptions she had about his prospects as a writer. All his writing had been done for newspapers, which in a way wasn't writing at all—what people ordinarily thought of as writing. It was just words. It wasn't writing that ended up in public libraries, the way Alec Proffit's did, even though his novels hadn't made it into Ossning's. Fitzgerald was about to confess to Mercy the relief he had felt discovering that, when the telephone rang inside the A-frame. "Big night," Mercy said as she left the deck.

*     *     *

"You won't believe this. *I* don't believe it." Mercy slid heavily into the chair beside Fitzgerald. "You know what time it is?"

"I can't see my watch."

"I saw inside. Half past ten. That was Theona Orr."

"What about?"

"You won't believe this. She took me down in the basement of their house, showed me Charlie's tying table, all the rods he'd wrapped. She wanted to know what to do with everything, meaning how to get rid of it. I suggested she could give it all to the TU chapter for the auction. Charlie's friends would be honored to have something of his."

"Sure."

"I didn't tell you. It seemed too sad seeing Charlie's things stuck down in the basement, Theona not giving a damn. It gave me the shivers, frankly, two people living together like that, not caring."

"All marriages are mysterious."

"Oh, I know. Maybe it wasn't the way it seemed. Maybe it was even worse. Anyway, Theona agreed when I suggested giving Charlie's things to TU. Now it seems her daughter's arrived from California, they've discussed it, and the daughter thinks it would be better to have a garage sale. That way, Theona said, they wouldn't have to wait for the auction in the winter. The truth is, you ask me, the daughter wants to *sell* Charlie's things rather than let Theona give them away. She wants the money. Talk about sad."

"And Theona was calling at this hour to tell you?"

"While it was on her mind, she said. And before she went on her next Elderhostel trip. Good Lord. Charlie isn't even buried yet."

"When they have the garage sale, we ought to go down, buy up the whole lot, donate it to TU."

"Get Calvin to go with you," Mercy said. "Or Verlyn. I couldn't face it."

"I understand."

Mercy reached through the darkness, took Fitzgerald's hand, drew it to her. "Now, Fitzgerald. Now we go to bed."

# 14

"So how come you dropped out of college?"

Startled, Kit said, "How'd you know I did?"

"You told me," Gwendolyn said. "Don't you remember?"

"No."

They were moving side by side down the center of the river, heading to the spot where Gwendolyn had cast for brookies the day before. Ordinarily, Kit would fish his way downriver, taking his time, drifting an Olive Stimulator with a small Pheasant Tail nymph on a dropper, seeing what he might pick up against the wood piles, but he wanted Gwendolyn to have some action right away. She wasn't likely to have any in the heavily fished-over water just below the Kabin Kamp.

Verlyn, leaving earlier in the morning for a float trip on the South Branch with Gwendolyn's father, had been too preoccupied to instruct Kit on where to fish. He had managed to sneak a look at Gwendolyn, though, and Kit had noticed the high school haze reappear in his eyes. If it weren't for the float trip with Gwendolyn's father, he probably would have put Kit in charge of the fly shop, rushed off on another strange drive into Ossning. As it was, Kit guiding Gwendolyn, the shop had to be left for Jan to run, which brought a different look, sour, into Verlyn's eyes.

"Well, you did."

Kit could feel Gwendolyn glance at him, feel the sudden thrust-out angle of her chin beneath the blue cap. The look reminded him of

Mercy: stubborn, independent. Gwendolyn might be quite a woman when she grew up. "I must have forgot. I've been hanging around old people too much."

"What?"

"It wasn't working for me," Kit said, "that was the main reason. I wasn't ready for college. I should have waited a year or two before I went. I might go back."

"Where?"

"Where I was, probably. Central Michigan. I wouldn't want to go as far as East Lansing or Ann Arbor."

Gwendolyn was silent for a while. When they passed the spot where Calvin had positioned her to cast to the big brown, she didn't seem to notice, and Kit didn't call her attention to it. They were nearly around the bend, coming up on riffle water, when Gwendolyn stopped in the middle of the river and faced him.

"When will you?"

"Go back? It takes dough."

"You can't get some from your mom and dad?"

Kit smiled at the assumption behind Gwendolyn's question. She was a rich kid whose parents would send her off to a rich kid's college, so naturally she thought that was how the world turned for everyone. "Maybe. But I want to go on my own."

To his surprise, Gwendolyn didn't ask him why. She merely nodded. When Kit looked at her closely, he could see that something was on her mind, something narrowing her eyes, tightening her mouth. It was something that had been there, he realized, since she had brought up the subject of college.

"How come you want to know?" he asked her.

Gwendolyn ignored him. "I saw the sign in the fly shop about the reward. Did my dad give?"

"I think so."

"Have other people?"

"Probably. Lots of people knew Charlie Orr."

"Why don't you find out how much they've given?"

Kit looked at her again. "Why?"

"Just because." Then Gwendolyn said, "This is where the brookies were."

*     *     *

MERCY GOT TO the office later than usual, but it was still surprising to find Burt Berry waiting in the outer office with Fern Lax. According to Billie, Burt usually slept in during the mornings.

"That's so," Burt said when Mercy asked him about it, "after I'm night fishing. Not last night, the way Billie is."

"It's good of you to stay with her."

"Had to come to town for supplies," Burt said. "Thought maybe I should stop in, have a talk."

Mercy brought him into her office, got him settled in a chair across the desk. "About Billie?"

"Campground. The sheriff won't let us open up yet."

"He's still investigating."

"I was thinking we could open the first loop, keep the second closed off. Deputy out there says to keep the whole thing closed."

"It's in the sheriff's hands," Mercy said.

"He's in charge of the campground?"

"Until the investigation's complete."

Burt nodded, looked up at the tiled ceiling, made no movement to leave. "Something else?" Mercy asked him. She still hadn't figured out why he'd come here. She vaguely wondered if it was to confess. For Billie's sake she hoped not. She'd been through enough.

"Doesn't feel right, campground shut down like that, nothing for Billie and me to do. The sheriff let the old couple and the young family leave. It's empty out there."

"I suppose," Mercy said carefully, "the campground will be kept closed until the missing camper is found."

"No sign of him."

"So I understand."

"Deputy out there won't say a thing."

"Sheriff's orders, no doubt."

"They figure he's the one broke into the cabin, shot Charlie with the stolen gun?"

Mercy said, "How do you know about the break-in?"

"It's in the *Call*. Paper's out this morning."

"I haven't seen it. But naturally the sheriff wonders why the camper's missing. It's strange."

"You bet," Burt said, "fellow all that way from Vermont."

Mercy said nothing, letting Burt hear the silence in the office. He kept looking at his hands, then the ceiling tile, back to his hands. "The *Call*," he said finally, "has it a reward's out."

"So I hear."

"Didn't say how much."

Was that what was on Burt's mind, Mercy wondered, the possibility of earning the reward? If so, he would have to come up with something more useful than the sound of firecrackers on the night of Charlie's murder. "The amount probably isn't settled yet."

"Paper says Calvin McCann and Verlyn Kelso are getting up the money. Probably won't be much."

"We'll have to see."

Burt nodded. "Billie and me, then, we go on like before?"

"I don't understand, Burt."

"Nobody around, but we keep on as hosts?"

"Is that what you came in to ask? Of course you do."

"We weren't so sure, place empty that way."

Mercy looked closely at Burt. After Shroud's initial theory, he seemed not to have kept Burt very high on his list of suspects. But here was an opportunity to explore Burt's frame of mind. She decided to take advantage of it.

"So how's Billie doing, Burt? Really doing."

"Oh, about the best you could expect."

"She must have been close with Charlie to be taking it so hard," she pushed on. "You know, beyond being the campground host. Did she know him well?"

"She told you about her visits with him?" Burt asked.

Mercy nodded. She waited for Burt to go on.

"She didn't think I knew she had coffee with the Odd Fellow in the morning, but I did." Burt gave a sad smile. "I think she kinda had a little thing for him. Put a little spark in her day. She'd be in a great mood by the time I woke up. I'll miss that about him."

"Well," Mercy sighed. That was hardly the confession of a jealousy-crazed spouse. So much for the love-killing theory. She'd never liked it anyway. "It's a big loss for both of you then."

Mercy stood up behind the desk, waited until Burt rose from his chair. "It's an awkward time for everyone, but we have to follow the sheriff's orders, which means the campground won't reopen until he says so. In the meantime, nothing's changed for you and Billie as the host couple. Soon enough campers will be arriving. You'll have your usual duties. Everything will be back to normal."

It was a pointless thing to say—Rainbow Run would never be back to normal, not as far as she was concerned—but Burt was clearly relieved. His long browned face relaxed.

"All right?" Mercy asked him.

"You bet," Burt said.

*       *       *

WHEN CALVIN FINISHED, Willard Stroud leaned back in his chair, looked across the desk, said, "Let me clear up something for you. What you read in the newspapers isn't the way it is. You read about an armed robbery, fellow needs money to buy drugs, he panics, ends up killing the person he's robbing. That happens, but it isn't the typical situation. Most drug killings are disputes about territory. Drug dealers kill other drug dealers."

"How do you know?" Calvin asked.

"Not from experience," Stroud admitted. "We don't get many drug killings up here. What I'm telling you is what I hear at law enforcement meetings."

"You take their word for it?"

"Dammit, Calvin, that's not the point. All I'm saying is drugs aren't behind every killing you run into."

"I think they're behind this one."

"And the evidence is that Charlie Orr smoked marijuana at night on the river way back when? Even if he still did, there's no indication the tent was entered. No indication it or the body was searched."

"Goes to show you."

"Show what?"

"You didn't look so good."

Stroud said, "We're chasing our tails. Let's leave it that you made your point. We'll keep in mind your drug killing theory." Stroud stood up behind the desk. "You've been a great help, Calvin. You might earn that reward you and Verlyn are getting up."

"Naw."

"You're too much an insider?"

"Naw."

"What, then?"

"Charlie was a friend."

# 15

"GOING OUT," STROUD announced from his office. "Stretch my legs. Call if anything comes up."

"Where?" Elsie answered.

"Maybe the bakery. Try there first."

"Bonnie will be 'round with rolls."

"Always is," Stroud said. "But I don't feel like waiting."

What he felt like was fresh air, a touch of sun, the smell of pine and river carried on a soft breeze. Or just banter with Bonnie on her own turf rather than his. It wasn't yet ten o'clock, and already he felt as if he had put in a full day at the city-county building. After Calvin left, Zack Cox had brought in reports from both the Michigan and Vermont state police, then Mercy and Fitzgerald arrived together. Finally, Slocum Byrd phoned with a summary of the findings in his medical report— and the information that Charlie Orr's body had been released to an undertaker from Big Rapids. But the weariness he was feeling, Stroud realized, wasn't the result of having been busy that morning. It was that he wasn't a step closer to solving the case than he had been before.

"No way," Mercy had said when Stroud told her of Calvin's theory that marijuana was involved in Charlie's death. "We'd know, someone would, if he was still using it. He couldn't keep it secret even if he wanted to. Besides, that was the whole point in the old days, smoking with your friends, everyone getting a little high together."

"How do you know?" Stroud asked her.

"I just do. Anyway, pot's a dead end, Stroud. Unfortunately," Mercy added, "so is Charlie's wife."

As far as Mercy could tell from her trip to Big Rapids, Charlie and Theona Orr lived entirely separate lives. The only thing they had in common was that, for a portion of the year at least, they were cooped up together in the same house, if not on its same levels. But there was no suggestion, on Theona's part, of any anger or bitterness, any sense of resentment—anything, in other words, that might be considered a motive for murder. There was only indifference.

"Besides, she's a little old lady. She could never find her way to Rainbow Run, let alone handle a shotgun."

"Another method," Stroud pointed out, "is having it done."

"A hired gun? Not Theona. It would have to be somebody else in Big Rapids. Somebody who had it in for Charlie."

But that wasn't likely, either. Stroud checked off the information that had come in from the Michigan police: Charlie had no police record, not even minor traffic violations; his work record with the post office was exemplary; and there was no hint of irregularities on the financial side. "Nothing," Stroud added, "about marijuana use, either."

"There's no police record," Mercy said, "so there wouldn't be."

"The point is that nothing about Charlie's home life, as far as we know about it, indicates a motive for murder."

"Big Rapids's a dead end."

Stroud sighed, patted his shirt pocket, sighed again. "Think you could use another expression?"

"All I'm saying is that Charlie's killer seems more likely to have come from up here, not down there. Charlie's past holds no clues."

"Neither does the Berrys'."

Mercy straightened in her chair.

"Just routine. Like I say, nothing there. Only thing that sticks out is after they retired, down in Battle Creek, they sold everything, bought themselves that big fifth-wheeler, took off. They've been living on the road ever since."

"That's a crime?"

"Just a fact. Tell you the truth, I think I envy them. Taking off, stopping where they want. I might do that when I retire."

"You might discuss it with Elsie first. And we might solve this murder first."

"What I had in mind," Stroud said.

Fitzgerald said, "So we write off the Berrys and anything in Charlie's background. That leaves the missing camper. Looks like he's the key."

"Maybe," Stroud said. "The Vermont police say his record is as clean as Charlie's. He lives by himself, out in the country a ways, and is a loner as far as his work goes. Doesn't employ a secretary or assistant of some sort. Nobody out there has spotted him or his vehicle in several days."

"I've got some more about him," Fitzgerald said, and went through what he had learned about Proffit from Hoke Harkness, including the fact that he was a published author of novels under a pen name as well as writing a column in *Angling World* as Will Woodsman.

"Had him figured all along as a writer," Stroud said when Fitzgerald finished. "From that notebook. But I didn't know about Will Woodsman. I've seen the magazine around, but I never paid attention to the column."

"Depending on where you stand," Mercy said, "it can seem pretty extreme."

"He's aggressive," Fitzgerald said. "And unpredictable. A few issues ago he raised holy hell with the Nature Conservancy in Florida. Something about plans for restoring an area of wetland around Kissimmee. The whole thing struck him as overly complicated and elitist. But, as I say, you can't predict him. At times he's a way-out elitist himself."

"Generally speaking," Mercy said, "I like the column. It's not the usual hook, line, and sinker stuff. He's someone with a point of view."

"All right," Stroud said. "Proffit writes novels under one name and an outdoor column under another, and the column's pretty good. But what's he doing up here, camped at Rainbow Run, making notes about Charlie? Why'd he take off after the murder but leave much of his stuff behind? Why can't my men or the state boys locate the vehicle he's supposedly driving? Or has he ditched it and is roaming about some other way? Tell me that?"

"If we could," Fitzgerald said, "we might have the case figured out."

"But we can't," Mercy said.

"The questions," Stroud said, "were rhetorical."

\*      \*      \*

"LIKE THIS PAIR?" Bonnie asked, and turned from side to side, giving him a good look. Her earrings this morning were bursts of golden sun the size of half-dollar pieces.

"They're you," Stroud said.

"You always say that."

"It's always true."

Their ritual morning exchange out of the way, Bonnie filled Stroud's mug with coffee, then remained beside his table, one arm angled sharply from a hard hip. "I was coming over with the rolls," she reminded him.

"I needed a walk. Helps me think."

Bonnie kept looking down at him, her eyes serious. "About Charlie, huh?"

"The main thing."

"Slocum Byrd was in earlier. Said they were taking the body down to Big Rapids for burial. That's awful."

"He let me know, too. Nice of him." Then Stroud asked, "Why awful?"

"Couldn't he be buried up here?"

"He has a wife in Big Rapids."

"Yeah, but friends here."

Stroud nodded, and Bonnie moved off with a swishing sound of her uniform to freshen the coffee of other customers in the bakery. There was a newspaper on the table, and Stroud slid it in front of himself, hoping to give the impression he was reading in the event one of the customers decided to strike up a conversation. That was the risk he ran stopping at the bakery, encountering a voter who thought he knew more about policing Tamarack County than the sheriff did. In the case of Charlie Orr's murder, Stroud thought bitterly, the voter might be right.

Bonnie Pym had brought Slocum Byrd to mind, and Stroud tried to concentrate on what the medical examiner had told him on the phone.

The only thing new was that Slocum had narrowed the time of death down to between midnight and three o'clock in the morning. Charlie had definitely died, died instantly, of two .16 gauge shotgun shells fired from the same gun, fired from outside the tent, and striking him in the head and upper torso. Slocum thought it certain that, at the moment of the shooting, Charlie had been stretched out on the cot, reading, the tent illuminated from inside by the neon lantern. The shots, in Slocum's view, hadn't been fired at random into the tent. The killer had stood only a step or two beyond the tent wall, aimed deliberately downward at the reclining form.

"Like shooting fish in a barrel, Willard," Slocum had said, the image inexact—and tasteless—but telling nonetheless. The killer had intended to kill. But knowing that didn't clarify the more important question: Was it Charlie Orr he had meant to kill or just somebody in a tent?

Stroud was thinking about that when his attention strayed to the newspaper in front of him, the weekly issue of the *Call*. Dominating the front page was Gus Thayer's account of the killing. Despite himself, Stroud scanned the columns of type, looking for errors. Surprisingly, Gus had most things right. And one thing Stroud didn't have at all.

Gus had managed to locate in Montana the owner of the log home on the mainstream that had been broken into around the time of Charlie's death. The owner, staying at a ranch through July and August and fishing private water on the Ruby River, told Gus he kept shotguns for upland bird hunting in the fall, the only period in which he was regularly in residence in his home on the Borchard. The owner couldn't be exact about the number of shotguns he owned, so he could say nothing definite about the missing gun until he arrived at the home in the fall. Even then he might not be able to recall for certain.

Stroud pushed the newspaper aside. When he got back to the office, he would ask Zack Cox if he had read Gus's story. Then he would ask him how the hell it was the *Call* had located the owner of the log home before a deputy sheriff of Tamarack County had. Maybe, he would add, Gus Thayer ought to be appointed a deputy sheriff.

Giving Zack grief would make him feel better, Stroud knew, but it wouldn't advance the case. Until he returned in the fall, the owner of the shotguns was another dead end. Even if he was compelled to come back to Michigan now—and maybe, Stroud conducting a murder investigation, he could be—there was no way of tying in the missing gun, assuming the owner identified it as a .1 gauge, with the gun that killed Charlie. The gun had to be found before that could be done.

Gus Thayer, of course, wasn't inclined to wait for the evidence. The *Call* story assumed a link between the shotgun taken in the break-in and the gun used to kill Charlie—and more, a link between the hell raising by young people from Ossning that had taken place in the past at Rainbow Run and the killing. Mercy Virdon, of the DNR field office, was quoted to the effect that the campground was regularly patrolled now, but the unavoidable conclusion of the story was that Charlie Orr's murder had been a thrill killing by young hoodlums looting private homes along the river and running amok in public campgrounds.

The further conclusion, there in the *Call* between the lines, the sheriff's office and the DNR equally incompetent, was that citizens of the county had ample reason to feel uneasy in their beds.

*　　*　　*

"BAKERY SUBSCRIBES TO this rag?" Stroud asked when Bonnie returned with a pot of coffee. He jabbed a finger toward the newspaper he had pushed to the side of the table. "Or some litterbug just leave it?"

"Got your goat, huh?"

"You ought to get some decent papers in here."

"We get the *Free Press*."

"I was thinking out of state," Stroud said. "Maybe Chicago."

"You want more coffee?" Bonnie asked.

Stroud shook his head. "Better be getting back."

"Maybe, long day ahead, you should have some." Bonnie waited beside the table. When Stroud gave her a look, she said, "Elsie called. Someone's waiting to see you."

"She say who?"

"Just someone."

Stroud sighed, got up to leave.

"The reason I said about coffee," Bonnie said, "is something else. A deputy saw a vehicle pull into the city-county building parking area. He told Elsie to tell you. The vehicle's got a Vermont license plate. The guy you're hunting for, huh?"

Stroud was nearly out the bakery door when he turned, came back to Bonnie. "How'd you know about that?"

"The old fellow who runs the campground out there. He was in."

"Burt Berry?"

"Said a camper, all the way from Vermont, was missing. Said he was the one probably killed Charlie." Bonnie glanced down at the newspaper on the table. "Only thing Gus Thayer doesn't know, huh?"

# 16

THE MAN ROSE from a chair, extended his hand. "Alec Proffit."
Stroud ignored the hand. "Get Zack down to the interrogation room," he instructed Elsie. Then he glanced at Proffit. "Follow me."

In the windowless, gray-walled room, waiting for Zack Cox, Stroud inspected the man. Big, tanned, with thick brown hair that could use cutting, wearing khaki trousers and a wrinkled blue fishing shirt with a Royal Coachman stitched above the pocket. His eyes, Stroud noticed, nearly matched the color of the shirt—eyes in a strong-featured face that gave off no suggestion of alarm. On the contrary, Alec Proffit appeared wholly at ease. He didn't look like a man who had just turned himself in for murder.

When Zack arrived, Stroud said, "I'd like this conversation recorded. All right with you?"

"Certainly," Proffit said.

Stroud nodded to Zack to start the machine. "Why don't you tell us why you're here. How'd that be for a start?"

"I understood you were looking for me."

"How'd you know that?"

"I didn't. Not exactly. But I knew you had reason to be." Proffit leaned forward, braced his elbows on the metal table separating him from Stroud, looked with level gaze into Stroud's eyes. "We could save ourselves time, sheriff."

"Fine," Stroud said.

"I didn't kill Charlie Orr. But I know who did."

Stroud shot a glance at Zack, beside him at the table. Zack was looking back at Alec Proffit with a fixed stare. Stroud satisfied himself that the machine in front of Zack was running. He hoped to hell it was also recording. He had resisted getting a new digital outfit, deciding an old Panasonic cassette recorder was just fine for Tamarack County. Too late for second thoughts now.

He tried to keep his voice flat, off-hand. "We'd like to hear about that."

"I don't mean I have a name. I know the types who had reason to kill him."

"Oh?" Stroud said.

"Poachers, for one." Lines tightened around Proffit's mouth. "They run wild on the South Branch of the Borchard."

"Poachers," Stroud repeated.

Proffit leaned back in his chair. "I've got to tell you how I know that. I write a column for an outdoor magazine called *Angling World*."

"You're Will Woodsman."

"I expected you'd done some checking by now. Charlie Orr was a regular reader of the column. I know that because he wrote me a letter— early part of the summer—about the poaching situation on the South Branch. He didn't know me, just knew the column, and thought I might be interested. I was. Charlie said that poaching was the main reason for a decline in the river's population of big fish, but the poaching wasn't taken seriously enough by the DNR. It was always put at the bottom of a list of factors causing the decline. He believed it belonged at the top. Now you have to understand that I get letters all the time from readers. Often they're complaints about something in a column, but occasionally they give me ideas for a piece. Charlie's did. I'd never thought bait fishing on flies-only water accounted for as much fish-kill as he was arguing. It accounted for some—that was obvious—but it never came in for much mention in studies of fishery decline. So I decided to look into it, see if it might be worth a column."

"This letter," Stroud asked, "how'd Charlie know where to send it?"

"It was sent to the magazine's editorial office in New York. The envelope was forwarded to me."

"Anybody else read it?"

"No reason they should."

"But you kept it?"

"For a time I did."

"For a time," Stroud repeated.

Proffit nodded. "I realize an explanation is needed. I let the letter remain on my desk, rereading it now and then, mulling over its possibilities for a piece. That's how I operate—letting ideas percolate, seeing if my interest holds up. I've learned over the years not to trust immediate enthusiasms. With Charlie's complaint about poaching, my interest eventually waned. I burned the letter. I always do with letters from readers. I don't want my correspondence ending up in a public landfill."

"So if your interest didn't hold up, I don't suppose you answered the letter."

"I didn't."

"Yet here you are—out in Michigan. Now why's that?"

Proffit offered a fleeting smile. "Try to understand. I burned the letter but remembered it perfectly. It was gone, but I couldn't get it out of my mind."

"Your interest returned."

"Exactly. You think you've dismissed an idea, but it stays with you. You reach a point where, almost despite yourself, you have to pursue it. So I got in my car and drove out. I had to see if I really had a piece to write. That's one of the marks of the column. I don't stay glued to a word processor, describing what other people have seen. I came here to find out if Charlie knew what he was talking about. He said he camped through the summer at a place called Rainbow Run, fished mostly at night, and that was how he knew about poachers. It seemed unusual, camping the entire summer, so I wanted to check that out too. I needed to get a firm fix on Charlie, make sure he wasn't a crazy of some sort, before I went fishing with him, saw his evidence. So I set up camp for myself at Rainbow Run."

Stroud put a hand to his chin, looking at Proffit, silent. Finally he said, "That's very interesting—how you work and all. But it leaves a problem. Charlie's not here to tell about this letter, and you can't produce it. I'm left to take your word for it."

"There's absolutely no reason, sheriff, not to."

"Is that so?" Then Stroud said, "Let's move on. You're in the campground and you're making notes about Charlie."

"I assumed you'd find them. I didn't plan on leaving my camp so soon."

"And went down to Big Rapids, made more notes."

"I investigated Charlie's background before I left Vermont. I knew the town he came from. I went there, looked around before I came up here. As I say, I wanted to make sure Charlie wasn't crazy."

"All right. You were at Rainbow Run and checking on Charlie because of this letter he wrote you about poaching. Go ahead."

"When he went out fishing in the evening, I followed his pickup from the campground, ended up on the wilderness stretch along the South Branch, all flies-only, catch-and-release water. I knew about the Borchard—I had read about it—though I'd never fished it. I wasn't entirely lost on the South Branch. I saw where Charlie left his pickup, parked myself at the next access point, fished the river in the general vicinity of where he was fishing. A couple times I passed around a wader I thought might be him. In the dark I couldn't tell for certain. But I could tell about the poachers."

"Wait," Stroud interrupted. "You never spoke to Charlie?"

"I never had the chance. I observed him, made notes, but—"

"He was killed before you could?"

"Yes."

"But you found out about poachers?"

"There on the South Branch at night you nearly stumble over them. Flashlights on, threading worms on hooks, brazen about it. I saw stringers of fish. They'd sit on the bank, toss out lines with spinning rods, start campfires, drink beer. You could come up on them, stay back in the pines, watch. Charlie was right on target. Poachers are savaging the Borchard."

"And you think one of them killed him?"

"Don't you?"

"Until now," Stroud said, "I didn't know Charlie was worked up about poaching on the river."

"He was enough to write me. Look, it stands to reason a poacher killed him. He observed them on the river—same way I did. He'd been observing them for a long time. Someone could have noticed."

"Charlie wasn't killed on the river."

"I know where he was killed. But what difference does it make? Poachers had reason to kill him. He knew what they were doing. It's against the law."

"So is driving over the speed limit. Someone sees you do it, that adds up to reason for murder?"

"Charlie was doing more than watching. He was blowing the whistle by writing me a letter."

Stroud said, "A letter you didn't show to anybody else."

"But Charlie might have told someone about it—and that got back to some poachers. What's more likely is that poachers knew nothing about the letter. They probably noticed him watching them, watching them night after night. Then one of them put two and two together."

"And concluded he needed to get rid of Charlie."

Proffit settled back in his chair. "We're not talking, sheriff, about sensible people. We're talking about total scum."

*       *       *

STROUD TOLD ZACK Cox to switch off the recorder. Then he told Alec Proffit he needed to speak with his secretary. He wouldn't be gone long.

"Get Mercy on the phone," he said to Elsie. "Tell her I want her over here quick as she can make it. Put her in my office when she comes." He was moving back down the hallway when he said over his shoulder, "Fitzgerald, too, if you can find him. Tell him the same thing."

In the interrogation room, Stroud resumed his place behind the table, indicated to Zack to start the machine. Alec Proffit was in the same position in his chair, the same confident look on his face. It was a face, Stroud realized, that contrasted with his wrinkled shirt: It had the sheen of a fresh shave. Proffit had been missing from his campsite, but he obviously hadn't spent the time wandering in the wilderness along the South Branch.

"Go back. You were at Rainbow Run and keeping an eye on Charlie. You wanted to make certain he wasn't a mad man of some sort before you talked to him about his letter. That right?"

"Yes."

"But you said you left the campground before you planned to. And you left gear there and your notes about Charlie. Now why was that?"

"The night he was killed was the third night I'd followed him around on the South Branch. I knew his routine now on that part of the river, and I knew he was right about the extent of the poaching. The next day, at the campground, I was going to introduce myself to him. The way I was thinking about the column I'd write, it would be a personal narrative—a night of fishing with Charlie, seeing poachers at work on the same water, the next day the two of us going together to the DNR, asking why they weren't cracking down. The whistle-blower, in other words, would now have some clout behind him."

"Will Woodsman."

"Exactly."

Stroud said, "But that doesn't sound like Charlie, wanting himself written up in a magazine."

"He sent me a letter, remember. It was his initiative. He wrote to call attention to the poaching problem."

"Call attention to himself, I meant."

"Yet that was the whole point of the letter. One man taking action when the DNR wouldn't."

"All right," Stroud said. "We're talking about why you left your camp."

"The night I'm talking about, the third night, I got into a couple decent-sized fish. I wasn't fishing seriously, just going through the motions. I wanted any poachers who were noticing to take me for just another fisherman. One of those oddballs who used flies, released fish, obeyed the regulations. You know how it goes. You aren't serious, but you have good luck. After I hooked a pair of browns, I got more serious and largely forgot about Charlie and the poachers. The next thing I knew, the sky was lightening up—and I was hungry. Driving back from the South Branch I found a café that was open, a place called the Black Duck, and I stopped in. The place was full of fishermen who'd been out all night, some still in waders. I had a big breakfast—eggs, bacon, toast, the works—and by the time I got back to my car, the sun was up. The combination, big breakfast, sun . . . Well, I leaned back in the seat, closed my eyes. The next thing I knew, it was the middle of the morning."

"Somebody would remember you in the Black Duck?"

"A waitress would. Maybe one of the fishermen."

"Go on."

"When I got to Rainbow Run, the campground was closed off, your people were there. I asked a deputy out on the road, he told me Charlie Orr had been shot to death in his tent. That was when I made a mistake."

"Oh?"

"I should have told the deputy I was camped there, gone in, told you what I'm telling you now. Frankly, all I could think about was my column. Now with Charlie dead, it had suddenly gone up in smoke. I needed his cooperation, and now I couldn't get it. I'd wasted my time in Michigan. I wasn't thinking about why he had been shot, about who had done it."

Stroud let himself smile. "You were thinking about yourself."

"And something else. I remembered the notebook in my tent, what I'd written about Charlie. I knew your people would be searching the campground, that they'd likely find it, that it wouldn't look good."

"For you."

"Yes."

"But you could have come in, explained about the notebook. Like you're doing now."

Proffit lifted his hands in a gesture of agreement. "What I did was get back in the car, leave. I can't explain why—except that it had something to do with disappointment over losing the column about Charlie. You get wrapped up in those things. They take you over. And there was something in the back of my mind, something—right then—I couldn't quite get a hold on. At any event, I left the campground, drove into Ossning. I needed a shower and shave. And time to think. I stopped at the first motel I saw, the Wolverine, and got a room."

"Somebody would remember you there?"

"The desk clerk would. And I can show you a receipt. I meant to stay long enough to get a toothbrush and razor, clean up, then—I stayed until this morning, as it turned out."

"We were looking for you. All the time you were there, in the Wolverine, vehicle parked outside your room?"

"Yes."

Stroud glanced sharply at Zack Cox, then looked back at Proffit. "Why'd you come in now?"

"Because I finally realized what was in the back of my mind, trying to get through the disappointment I felt over losing the column. Actually, Charlie's death would make for a better column. I wouldn't have his cooperation, but I'd have a hotter story than either he or I had bargained on."

"How do you figure that?"

"Think about it. Charlie believed poachers were destroying the quality of fishing on the Borchard—and he was right. That was the column I was going to write. Then Charlie is murdered before I can do the column, and that ups the ante, poachers going so far as to kill him to cover up their activity. But the story, I realized, gets even better. Charlie's letter to me was about the DNR as well as poachers, about the unwillingness to crack down. So—"

"So you're saying what, exactly?"

Proffit said evenly, "What I said when we started. I know the types who had reason to kill Charlie Orr. Poachers, for one. DNR types, for another. If he complained to me about poaching on the river, he must have done so to others—others here in Michigan. You'd think writing to me would come only after he'd complained locally. He told me, remember, that the DNR wasn't taking the poaching seriously enough. That could get back to people in positions of authority. They could understand it as dereliction of duty. They could want to cover that up."

Stroud waited a moment before he said, "That's what you figured out at the Wolverine motel?"

"Exactly."

"That Charlie Orr was killed by either poachers or the DNR?"

"Imagine Will Woodsman saying that in *Angling World*."

"I'm trying to," Stroud said.

# 17

"HE DO IT?" Mercy asked the moment Stroud entered his office. "Who's that?"

"Oh, for goodness sake. The guy from Vermont. Elsie said he turned himself in."

Stroud slowly released his breath, shook his head. "You know those big electronic bulletin-boards signs? We should stick one in front of the building, keep the town up-to-speed on law enforcement."

"It's our fault," Fitzgerald said. "We quizzed Elsie. We wondered why you wanted us over here."

"Well?" Mercy said.

Stroud closed the office door, eased himself into the swivel chair behind the desk, absently patted a shirt pocket that once held cigarettes. "Any possibility we could keep this conversation among ourselves?"

"Bonnie just went through with rolls from the bakery. What do you think?"

Stroud shook his head again. "No point having a sign, not when we've got Elsie and Bonnie."

"Come *on*," Mercy said.

"Alec Proffit hasn't been hiding out. He's been staying in the Wolverine motel, presumably eating in some restaurant in town, driving a big Toyota Land Cruiser with Vermont plates, in full view of everybody except my deputies and the state police looking for him. This morning he waltzes in here, tells his story. We got it recorded on a cassette." Stroud paused, looked at Fitzgerald before settling his gaze on Mercy. "Story about poachers."

"What?"

"Proffit came out here because he claims Charlie wrote him a letter saying poachers were ruining fishing on the Borchard. He sent the letter to *Angling World*, and the magazine forwarded it to Proffit."

"Charlie read the magazine," Fitzgerald said. "He'd know Will Woodsman."

Stroud held Mercy's eyes. "You didn't tell me Charlie was worked up over poaching on the river."

"I never thought about it," she said.

"Think about it now."

"He was concerned about it, yes, but I never made a connection between that and—" Mercy paused.

"His murder?"

She nodded and continued, "Every now and then he sent me a note in the mail about some poaching he'd seen. And he'd collect those empty worm containers along the river. When he had a plastic bag full, he'd leave it by the trash containers in the campground for the maintenance people to pick up. It was sort of a thing between us. The containers were evidence of what he was telling me in his notes, the poaching going on.

"When I'd see him, I'd tell him I knew there was poaching—there always is—and our enforcement people were doing the best they could. We never *argued* about it. But we did have a difference of opinion. Charlie thought bait fishing in regulated water was a big reason fewer big trout were being caught. At best, it's part of the reason. I agreed with him that there's probably more poaching going on these days. More worm containers showing up, our enforcement people making more arrests. I don't know why that is. Maybe it's just more lawlessness in the country, especially in regard to government regulations. But the bottom line is that poaching isn't the huge deal Charlie believed."

"Wait," Stroud said. "Why would Charlie send you notes? Why didn't he call or come to see you?"

"He didn't have a cell phone, though I told him he ought to. He shouldn't be alone all the time without one. And it wasn't his way to make a fuss directly. You know how soft spoken he was. He had opinions, but he wouldn't push them on you. A note in the mail was Charlie's way. Other people got them, too. The canoe liveries in town, for example. Charlie would send the owners notes suggesting they space out rentals at longer intervals, reducing congestion on the river. You know what Charlie was like. He was a natural-born riverwatcher."

"Okay. But when you and Charlie talked about poaching, what would he say?"

"He'd hear me out, smile, turn the conversation to something else. A couple weeks later I'd get another note, and there would be a bag of worm containers in the campground. It was almost a running joke between us." Mercy paused, glanced at Fitzgerald before looking back at Stroud. "At least I thought it was."

"According to Proffit, Charlie was serious enough to write to him. And Proffit took it seriously enough to come out from Vermont, camp at Rainbow Run, look into it. He says he decided Charlie was right about the poaching."

"Then Proffit's wrong, too. Look, I've gone the rounds with other people about this. Calvin, for one. Poaching makes me as mad as anyone. Maybe more so. I *know* the harm it does the river. All I've ever said is not to go overboard, blame everything on it."

"Charlie was a reasonable man. How could he be so mistaken?"

"He wasn't mistaken. Not from his own perspective. Fishing at night, usually in the wilderness section of the South Branch, he saw poaching going on. He really *saw* it. But that, his closeness to it, got in the way of drawing back, putting poaching in the context of the entire river system and the fishing that takes place. From that perspective it's not a major matter. That's all I'm saying."

Stroud nodded, rubbed his chin, said, "Proffit's got the notion some poacher killed Charlie. Charlie was blowing the whistle on the activity. The poacher wanted him stopped."

"But Charlie had been complaining about poaching for a long time. That's what I've been telling you."

Fitzgerald said to Mercy, "If the complaint appeared in Will Woodsman's column, think of the attention it would draw. There might be a big crackdown."

"That makes it sound like a conspiracy—poachers out to suppress magazine stories. Poachers aren't an *interest* group. And how would they even know Charlie wrote Proffit? If he really did. Where's the letter?"

Stroud held up a hand. "I'd like you to hear about that in his own words. Zack can play the cassette in the interrogation room."

"Now?" Mercy asked.

"Elsie can get you coffee. You'll need some."

\*　　　\*　　　\*

STROUD USED THE time they were gone to instruct a deputy to verify Alec Proffit's story about eating breakfast at the Black Duck, then taking a room at the Wolverine motel. Another deputy was to inspect the contents of Proffit's vehicle parked outside the city-county building—the big gray Toyota, Stroud emphasized, with Vermont plates. In the meantime, he intended to keep Proffit cooling his heels in a waiting room just beyond the interrogation area. If his story checked out and the Toyota was clean, there would be no reason to detain him any longer. Stroud would tell him, though, to remain in Ossning for the time being, at either the motel or the campground. If he chose the latter, a deputy would go out there first to inform the host couple that he was returning to his site.

Finished, Stroud asked Elsie to bring him one of the sweet rolls Bonnie had delivered to the office and a fresh coffee. He nibbled on the roll, sipped coffee, watched the clock. Ten minutes went by before Elsie peeked in the office.

"They're coming back. She's steamed."

"Wouldn't be surprised," Stroud said, and pitched what was left of the roll into his wastebasket.

\*　　　\*　　　\*

THE FIRST THING Mercy said was, "I want to see that bastard. He's under arrest?" Her face blazed with anger.

Stroud asked Fitzgerald to close the office door, motioned the two of them back into chairs in front of his desk. Then he said to Mercy, "Why would he be under arrest?"

"For killing Charlie."

"What makes you think he did that?"

"I don't know. But why else would he make such a wild accusation? He's covering up for something."

"Let's try to be calm," Stroud said. "Proffit's story is that he came out here to look into what Charlie wrote in his supposed letter, that poachers were messing up fishing on the Borchard and the DNR wasn't doing enough about it. After a few nights on the river, he comes to the conclusion Charlie was right about the poaching. Then, before he can talk to him, Charlie's murdered. So Proffit jumps to the conclusion that poachers or the DNR must be responsible. They wanted to stop Charlie from making complaints. And he sees this as a bombshell he can write up in *Angling World*."

When Stroud finished, Mercy waited a moment before she said, "You're done being calm? Fitzgerald and I listened to the cassette. We know what he said. You don't need to give us a summary. I'm responsible for everything the DNR does in this district, so when he says the DNR could be involved in a murder, he's talking about me. You understand? *Me*."

Fitzgerald leaned over, touched Mercy's arm. "We may be forgetting something. Proffit's a writer. What really interests him is his column. Not Charlie, not poachers, not the DNR, but the column. With Charlie's death, he thought he lost it—lost the column he was planning. He said that on the cassette. Then he realized that Charlie's death actually handed him a better column. Charlie's point, in his letter, was that poaching was a big problem on the river, but his murder reveals how big. Big enough to kill over. When Proffit charges poachers or the DNR with the murder, he's really hyping his column—hyping it for himself, enriching it. Writers do that. They create enthusiasm in themselves for what they're going to write."

Mercy jerked her arm away, glared at Fitzgerald. "You think that makes a difference?"

"Only that, maybe, we shouldn't take Proffit too seriously."

"Oh, really?" Mercy turned from Fitzgerald, directed her glare to Stroud. "I don't care that Proffit's a writer or what he's got in mind.

There's a cassette back there on which he says the DNR could have had something to do with Charlie Orr's murder. I take that damn seriously."

"I don't," Stroud said.

Mercy blinked but held him with her eyes.

"You didn't have anything to do with Charlie's death. Let's put that to rest right now. That you wouldn't like a subsequent story in *Angling World* blasting the DNR is another matter entirely."

"Right," Mercy said warily.

"No outfit likes bad press."

"Not bad, Stroud. *Wrong*. Charlie was simply wrong about lack of enforcement against poaching. That's what I've been telling you. We've got a RAP program throughout the state—Report All Poaching—with a toll-free, rapid-response number to call. Now and then rewards are offered. Just now there's a two-thousand-dollar reward for information about a gray wolf shot in the Upper Peninsula. I've tried to get all the guides on the river to carry cell phones, report any abuses they see, including poaching. I used to tell Charlie I'd buy him a cell phone if he'd carry it on the river, immediately report any poaching he saw. That's the thing—you have to catch them doing it, seize the trout they've killed. You can't just go around picking up worm containers. But you know Charlie. He went as light as possible as far as gear was concerned. He wasn't about to carry a phone is his fly vest."

Mercy stopped. "You know about our enforcement programs. You're briefed about everything we do."

Stroud nodded. "It's your people I don't know much about."

"What?"

"Look, I know you had nothing to do with Charlie's murder. But I'll need to talk to your enforcement officer responsible for the southern district of the county."

"Vic Lanski? Why?"

"See what he says about poaching activity on the South Branch. See if it matches what Proffit believes."

"I can show you the records. Vic's arrests, citations, everything he's done."

"I'd like something more personal."

Mercy's eyes narrowed. "You think Vic's involved in this?"

"I don't think anything. I just want to talk to him. He's in a position to know what's been going on along the South Branch."

Mercy seemed to rise from her chair, hover between sitting and standing. "And he's on the river at night armed with a service revolver—and a shotgun in his patrol car. Oh, no you don't, Stroud. If you talk to Vic, I'm present. He's my responsibility."

Stroud tried to keep an edge out of his voice. But sometimes, with Mercy, you simply had to lay down the law. "A murder," he said, "is mine."

# 18

"WHEN I GET mad," Mercy said, "I get hungry. I'm starved now."
"We could stop at the hotel," Fitzgerald suggested, "grab a bite."

"I have to get back. There's a pile of work. And I want to talk to Vic Laski before Stroud does."

"Be careful what you say."

"Don't worry. I won't obstruct justice. Besides, what have I got to lose? I've already been charged with Charlie's murder."

"Not quite."

"Well, that's damn well how it feels."

They separated in the parking area of the city-county building, Mercy in her Suburban, Fitzgerald in his Cherokee. He drove through the main drag of the town, crossed the river at the canoe liveries, headed out along the South Downriver Road to the Kabin Kamp. It was Verlyn he wanted to talk to, but when he arrived it was Kit he found behind the fly shop's cash register.

"You missed him," Kit said. "I got in from guiding, he took off to town."

"You're guiding now?"

"There's a girl staying at the lodge with her dad, learning to use a rod. Calvin worked with her for a while, now me. We tried for some brookies downriver. No big deal."

"Nice looking girl?"

"She's still in high school."

Fitzgerald grinned and said, "I seem to remember some knockout high school girls."

Kit grinned back. "Calvin says, guiding, never mix business and pleasure."

"But you know Calvin."

"Yeah." Then Kit erased his grin and said, "You come in for anything else?"

Fitzgerald sat at the fly-tying bench, angled his head to examine a finished caddis fly still in the vise. It had a pale yellow body, blond elk-hair wing, and ginger hackle—a cheap, simple pattern favored by river-boat guides who had clients who left batches of them attached to bushes and trees. "Your dad guiding?"

"Later this afternoon, if he gets himself back from town."

"What's in town?"

Kit shrugged. "You tell me."

Fitzgerald said, "I was with your mother this morning at Stroud's office. The fellow missing from Rainbow Run turned himself in."

"I heard." When Fitzgerald looked up from the tying vise Kit said, "The guy who trucks bread from the bakery was out here. Bonnie told him."

"Stroud's right."

"What?"

"Nothing. The fellow's name is Alec Proffit. He's got the idea Charlie was killed by a poacher. Maybe a poacher Charlie saw or confronted on the river."

"I thought it was a nut case after his pot stash."

"That's Calvin's theory. Proffit thinks it was a poacher."

"How about Proffit himself? He took off from the campground after Charlie was killed. Why'd he do that?"

Fitzgerald got up from the tying bench, crossed the shop to where Kit stood behind the counter, fly reels displayed beneath the glass. "A long story, one Stroud wants to keep under his hat for the time being. If Bonnie hasn't already broadcast it."

"The bread guy didn't say anything."

"Proffit believes there's widespread poaching on the no-kill, flies-only section of the South Branch. Late at night. Somehow or other Charlie got mixed up in it. I wanted to ask your dad what he knows about the extent of poaching down there. I fish that stretch but not as often as Charlie did. Or through the night."

Kit said, "There's poaching, sure. Slobs go in there, toss out gobs of crawlers, haul out monster fish."

"But how widespread is it? That's the question. Apparently, Charlie thought it was so bad it was seriously harming the river. I never heard him mention it. But he did to your mother. He mailed her notes about it. And he used to pick up empty worm containers, leave them for the DNR."

"That's useless. You've got the containers, so what? You've got to nail the slobs themselves."

"Charlie was hoping the DNR would crack down more. That's why he contacted your mother."

Kit leaned toward Fitzgerald, elbows on the counter. "If Mercy wants to nab poachers, she should ask me. You hang around the Keg O'Nails, is how. Those slobs—it's not fish they're after. They load up their freezers, sure, but the big thing is talking about what they've done. They get together, bull about how they pulled one on the DNR, pulled one on big shots using fur and feathers and taking six-inchers. You hear them out at the Keg, laughing their asses off. Flies-only water only means better fishing for them. Places like this"—Kit's eyes swept the fly shop—"they think it's total bull. All you need is a Wal-Mart rod, crawlers, and to hell with the river."

"You know any of them," Fitzgerald asked, "by name?"

"Slobs like that? I keep my distance."

"It wouldn't help anyway. As you say, they have to be caught poaching. Talking about their exploits isn't enough." Fitzgerald drummed his fingers on the counter. "Maybe I'll see what Calvin knows. Is he guiding this morning?"

Kit shook his head. "This afternoon. He's probably fooling around at the cabin. Or hunting drug dealers."

Fitzgerald smiled, pointed at the reward sign by the display of tippet spools. "How's it doing?"

"Verlyn or Calvin, you think they'd know? But Jan's keeping tab. The dough's coming in."

"Let's hope it helps." Then Fitzgerald grinned and said, "Nice-looking girl, huh?"

*       *       *

ON THE WAY back along South Downriver Road, heading to Calvin's cabin, Fitzgerald thought about Kit. Mercy's son was warming up to him, slowly but surely. At first, Kit camping out at Danish Landing and coming over to the A-frame now and then for meals at Mercy's insistence, he had barely said a dozen words all evening, and those to Mercy. He had examined Fitzgerald's books and CDs and looked over the materials on his tying bench, but otherwise he acted as if Fitzgerald wasn't there.

It was understandable. Fitzgerald was from Detroit, rich by Ossning standards, living in a plush house on the river and fishing through the seasons while he wrote a novel. All that made Fitzgerald odd enough from Kit's point of view, but the major oddity was that Mercy, suddenly, had rented out her place in town, moved in with Fitzgerald, and they acted like an old settled pair. Kit was bound to be puzzled. And wary.

Fitzgerald's strategy had been to do nothing—certainly nothing to suggest he wanted to be Kit's buddy, let alone surrogate father. It was a tricky situation. Mercy would never agree to marry him without Kit's approval—tacit approval, at any rate—yet that would have to come on its own, without any striving on Fitzgerald's part. Kit was as independent as Mercy. He would warm up to Fitzgerald on his own terms—or he wouldn't. Fitzgerald could only wait.

So he had, and it seemed to be working. Now he and Kit talked when they were together. Kit stopped, uninvited, at the A-frame, even when he knew Mercy wouldn't be there. Now and then he asked Fitzgerald about one of the books he saw in the A-frame, and he listened half-seriously to the CDs Fitzgerald played. He said that Van Morrison wasn't too bad and Vince Gill was okay if you liked that kind of music. Fitzgerald was encouraged but careful not to push things. He still had to let Kit come to him.

The best sign yet was Kit telling him about poachers boasting among themselves at the Keg O'Nails. If Mercy knew her son was hanging around the Keg, she would blow her cork. Kit knew that—knew Mercy considered the Keg the place where everything disreputable in Ossning took place—yet he had talked openly with Fitzgerald, man to man, a font of information about the Keg. Either he trusted Fitzgerald to repeat nothing to Mercy or hadn't, at the moment, stopped to consider that he might. It seemed, whatever the interpretation, a step forward in the relationship.

Which caused Fitzgerald to think about his relationship with Mercy. He disliked the word. What they had was a love affair, not a relationship. The only issue between them was marriage. Fitzgerald said he wanted to marry her, and Mercy said she wanted to marry him, and both knew they were only trying out the idea, seeing how it felt. Marriage wasn't confirmation that they were in love; they were. Marriage meant, or ought to, that they were in love for the long haul. That expression, the long haul, would give anyone pause, especially if they had each failed, once before, to live up to it.

Kit, it dawned on Fitzgerald, was a reminder to Mercy of that failure. She couldn't help but see Verlyn in him—Verlyn who was now with Jan while she was with Fitzgerald and so much for the long haul of marriage. Kit's warming up to Fitzgerald might not, finally, make any difference as far as Mercy was concerned. He was still her son with Verlyn. And Fitzgerald was still someone she loved but couldn't risk marrying.

When he came to the abrupt turn off the highway, Fitzgerald had to brake hard, at the same time felt a sense of relief. He could stop thinking, concentrate instead on negotiating Calvin's rutted road.

*       *       *

HE FOUND HIM in what Calvin called a garage, a rough-sawn wood structure where he kept tools, canoes, and fishing equipment but not his truck. It never seemed to occur to Calvin to put the truck in the garage.

He was cleaning and oiling a fly reel at the workbench when Fitzgerald entered and pulled up a stool beside him. "Busy?"

Calvin examined the reel in his hands as if that answered the question. "Naw. Thinking."

"Very dangerous."

Calvin nodded his agreement. "About drug dealers." He wiped excess oil from the reel, used the rag to clean his fingers.

"We've been through this," Fitzgerald said.

"They could run a test on Charlie's pipes, check for traces of pot. I told Stroud that."

"What did he say?"

"Nothing. So I've got a better idea: Go down to Big Rapids, go out to the college, ask around if a guy matching Charlie's description was buying pot. Recently."

"Stroud should go down, you mean?"

"Naw. Who'd talk to him? He looks like a sheriff."

"I get it. You're thinking of going down yourself, talking to drug dealers hanging around Ferris State." Fitzgerald looked at Calvin, grinned. "Might work. You look like a left-over pothead from the sixties."

"What I figured," Calvin said seriously.

"Before you go," Fitzgerald said, "you might want to consider another theory about why Charlie was killed. The camper missing at Rainbow Run turned himself in to Stroud this morning."

"Stroud toss him in jail?"

Fitzgerald shook his head. "I'll tell you why not."

He related to Calvin what he and Mercy had heard on the cassette recording of Stroud's interview with Alec Proffit. And that when Proffit's story about where he'd been since the murder checked out, Stroud told him to remain in the local area. He'd decided to go back to his site at Rainbow Run.

"Poachers," Calvin said. "Never thought about them."

"Neither did Mercy. Charlie used to send her notes about poaching activity and collect empty worm containers from the river. But she never made a connection between that and the killing."

"Charlie must have been ticked off big time with Mercy to write to Proffit."

"It was Will Woodsman he wrote to. He didn't know Proffit's real name. But you're right. It wasn't like Charlie to go over someone's head, and writing to Woodsman was way over. Apparently, Charlie was hoping Woodsman would concentrate on how poachers were harming the river, but an article was bound to make the DNR look bad. Mercy would have taken a lot of heat."

"Charlie was spot on about the poaching."

"He talked to you about it?"

"Now and then. Charlie fished at night more than anybody. He knew what was going on. Poachers take big fish. Big fish are survivors. That's the problem, stripping the river of the top of the gene pool."

"Charlie never said anything to me."

"Yeah, well, he knew you and Mercy were hooked up together. He wouldn't."

"But that's what I'm saying. If Charlie was concerned about Mercy's feelings, why write to Woodsman? It's odd."

"So Proffit thinks Charlie recognized some poacher, the poacher wanted to cover his tail, he went up to the campground, blasted away through the tent?"

"In a nutshell, yes."

Calvin placed the oiled reel in a cloth bag, cleaned his hands again. "I got an idea."

"Go down to Big Rapids, find Charlie's drug source."

"Naw, forget that. This makes more sense. We know Charlie was hot about poachers."

"So what's your new idea?"

Calvin said, "Let's take a hike, look at the river."

*       *       *

A PATH FROM Calvin's cabin ran for a hundred yards or so through thick pine, then emerged onto a grassy bank above a tight bend in the river. The current braided around a small island thick with alders and outlined at the water's edge with trout iris.

"Nice spot," Fitzgerald said.

Calvin lowered himself to the grass, propped his back against the stump of a poplar downed by beavers. "It's got a point. One night, 'round about here, Verlyn put an arrow this far from Stanley Elk's ear." Calvin held up a hand, showed the gap between his thumb and forefinger. "He got Stanley's attention."

Fitzgerald settled into the grass beside Calvin. "Don't think I know the name."

"This goes back before your time up here. Verlyn and I were still high school kids. Those days, there wasn't much DNR enforcement of fishing regulations, so we used to prowl the river on moonlit nights, enforce them ourselves. One night we ran into this Ojibway, kid about our age, fishing with worms and killing big browns right and left. There wasn't any flies-only, catch-and-release water then, but there was a bag limit.

"So Verlyn released an arrow, it zipped past Stanley's ear, stuck in a tree on the island. Verlyn was just getting into archery then, and he liked the challenge, sizing up a target in the river under moonlight, seeing how close he could come with a miss. Man, did it work. You're out at night, breaking the law, you hear that rush an arrow makes going past, then the plunk into a tree—you get the hell out of the water, never come back. We figured, an arrow, poachers would think it was a bunch of Ojibways letting them know this part of the river was already staked out for poaching. They'd think it was an Indian attack. Next thing, they didn't get out of the water, they'd get scalped.

"The night I'm talking about, Stanley, Ojibway himself, didn't think that way. He didn't move a hair after the arrow zipped by. We thought maybe Verlyn had screwed up, nailed him with it, so we waded out to where he was. That was how we first met Stanley."

"You really did that?" Fitzgerald said. "You fired off arrows at night?"

"The DNR should try it. With poachers, fines are a badge of honor among thieves. Stark fear is the only thing that works."

"So what happened with Stanley?"

"Like I say, he was about our own age, kid from around Roscommon. He was used to horsing around with bows and arrows, so getting shot at was nothing special. He thought it was kind of funny, in fact, two palefaces trying to scare off an Ojibway with an arrow. Anyway, we got to talking, telling him he was screwing up the river by killing fish, telling him it was more fun fishing with flies and a fly rod. Stanley was interested, so we agreed to meet over the next nights, start him in on a fishing education.

"We went through everything: different fly rods, different line weights and tippets, dry flies and wet flies, nymphs and streamers. All the black magic of fly fishing. Stanley took to everything except the catch-and-release part. He said Ojibways lived off the land, so they had to kill fish. We got him down to killing only a couple at a time, still using his spinning rod and worms, but that was as far as Stanley would go. He wouldn't buy a license, either. Claimed there was some treaty with the government about it, way back. Otherwise, Stanley ended up a fly fisherman."

"That's two rather large exceptions."

"True. But you've got to remember how we found him, a kid who didn't know anything but spin fishing with bait, hauling out stringers of fish. Stanley's a schoolteacher now. In Roscommon."

"A success story."

Calvin shrugged, looked out at the island ringed with iris. "He still lives off the land on the side, fishing the South Branch at night, killing a couple fish, no license. What I'm thinking is we get Stanley working for us. We get him talking to poachers, see what they're saying. The poachers know Stanley, know he's an Ojibway killing fish, so they tell him their war stories."

"Kit told me poachers like to boast about their exploits."

"The kid's right. Stanley might learn who it was recognized Charlie."

"But would Stanley do it? It's risky. He wouldn't just be talking with poachers. One of them—that's the theory—is a killer."

Calvin nodded. "You got a point. So I'll give him some incentive, tell him about the reward. Stanley could have a shot at it."

"I don't know," Fitzgerald said. "You'd have to see what Stroud and Mercy think."

"You kidding? I know what they'd think. They have to play by the book. I'm hunting up Stanley, seeing if he's interested. If Stroud or Mercy get wind of anything, I'll say I'm dangling the reward around, seeing what develops."

"All right," Fitzgerald said. "But watch your step. The reward's for apprehending a killer."

"Dead one," Calvin said, "you want my preference."

# 19

BURT BERRY WAS sitting at the picnic table under the awning of the fifth-wheeler when Mercy arrived at Rainbow Run. After she parked and leaned out the window, he hurried over to her.

"Just about getting ready for my chores."

"There are any?"

"Will be." Burt inclined his head toward the campground road. "No deputy at the entrance, you notice? Sheriff's letting us open is why."

"News to me," Mercy said.

"Campers just allowed on the first loop road. Sheriff wants the second kept closed a while longer. Deputies went over Charlie's campsite again, took more pictures. Now they're loading the tent and gear in a van. They're sending the whole batch to Big Rapids. The pickup too, pulled along behind the van."

"Stroud might have told me."

"Deputy said they called Charlie's wife, asked what she wanted done with his things. Said she wanted everything. She's the one sent the van up."

"More for the garage sale." When Burt looked at her, Mercy shook her head, said, "Are there any? New campers?"

"I'm thinking it'll take a while," Burt said, "given what happened. But August's coming up. People got to camp somewhere. No reason not to camp here."

"Some people might take murder as a reason."

"That's so," Burt said. "But safest airline to fly is one just had a crash. Here, the sheriff's going to double campground patrols. One of the deputies told me."

"I should keep checking in with you. You're way ahead of me."

"We'll be the safest place in Michigan."

"Let's hope. The reason I'm here," Mercy said, "is to see Alec Proffit. He's at his campsite?"

"Hasn't left since he came back. I've got a lookout on him."

Mercy started the Suburban, then leaned out the window again. "Billie still doing all right?"

"About the same."

"And you?"

"Can't complain. About back to routine."

"That's fine. We all are," Mercy added, "trying to get back."

*       *       *

WHEN SHE CAME up the path from the loop road, Alec Proffit rose from a folding camp chair beside the fire pit, ballpoint pen in one hand, stenographer's notebook in the other. "Mercy Virdon," she announced briskly. "From the local DNR field office in Ossning."

"Ah," Proffit said, drawing out the sound. "I assumed I might be hearing from you. But—"

"You didn't expect a woman."

Proffit smiled—a long, deep smile. "I hadn't really thought about it. But I suppose not." He looked down at the camp chair. "Would you?"

"This isn't a social call. Sheriff Stroud let me hear the recording of your interview with him. I want to talk about that."

"Of course." Proffit placed the notebook on the camp chair, sunk his hands into the pockets of his khaki trousers. "Could I make you a coffee first? I have a little espresso machine. It works off the car lighter."

Mercy ignored him. "What Charlie Orr wrote you about poaching on the Borchard was totally exaggerated. We have problems, sure. Every river does. But poaching isn't a primary cause of the Borchard's decline as a fishery, if there's a decline. It's one part, a small one, of a complex of problems. Charlie knew that."

"I'm sure he did," Proffit said evenly.

Mercy raised an eyebrow.

"I'm sure he understood the complexity."

146

"But that isn't what you claim he said in his letter."

"He wished to make a point, so he embellished the role of poaching. I understood that."

"But on the recording you repeated what Charlie told you. And you were going to put it in an article."

"Writers get carried away. Myself, I'm afraid, as well as Charlie."

Mercy stared across the fire pit. "You're saying you didn't believe what Charlie told you—told you about poaching—yet were going to write it up anyway?"

Proffit smiled again. "As you heard, I came out here to check what he told me. His letter was only a starting point."

"What I heard was, following Charlie around on the river, you came to agree with him about the poaching."

"There was some going on. One couldn't help noticing it."

"And from that you jumped to the conclusion that a poacher killed Charlie."

"I believed that a possibility."

"Or the DNR did."

Proffit drew a hand from his pocket, ran it through his hair, shrugged sheepishly. "I expected we would get around to that. Listen," he said, "it's awkward standing here. Couldn't we at least sit at the picnic table?"

*　　　*　　　*

THE MOMENT SHE did, she regretted it. Sitting just across the picnic table, its top a mosaic of carved initials, he was too close to her, too physically present. Mercy squirmed on the bench, unable to gain more separation.

Alec Proffit was somewhat older than she had imagined from hearing his voice on the cassette, fifty-something perhaps, though his hair was still dark brown and his tanned skin was strikingly smooth. The eyes looking back at her were clear and unblinking. She found herself turning away, concentrating on the Royal Coachman stitched above the pocket of his blue shirt. She could dislike that—dislike it as something excessive, perhaps even false—and so maintain her anger.

A genuine fisherman would never parade his obsession that way. The angling equivalent of a drugstore cowboy would.

"You have to bear in mind," he was saying to her, "that Charlie Orr's death took me by surprise. I was evaluating his account of poaching on the river. Then, like that, he was gone. Under the circumstances, it seemed sensible to conclude that an angry poacher had killed him. Just as sensible that an angry DNR officer might have. Charlie's complaint was twofold: Poachers were harming the river, and the DNR wasn't doing enough about it. So both parties had a motive for getting rid of him. It was incredible."

Mercy said, "And incredible material for Will Woodsman's column."

"I admit that. I got carried away. I'm only asking that you understand the situation—the shocking nature of Charlie's death, how disorienting it was."

Mercy forced herself to meet Proffit's gaze. "There are people around here, people who actually knew Charlie, who were shocked as well. They didn't accuse the DNR of killing him."

Proffit lifted his hands from the table. "What can I say?"

"You could apologize," Mercy said sharply, "to begin with. Then you could go to the sheriff, tell him what you said on the recording is complete nonsense."

"Certainly."

Mercy stared at him.

"I'll clear it up. It still seems likely that a poacher killed Charlie, but of course the DNR wasn't involved. Not unless there's a rogue agent who had a particular grudge against Charlie. You would know about that."

"Exactly," Mercy said. "I'd know and you wouldn't. And I know there are no rogue agents in the Ossning district."

"So I apologize. Heartily so." Proffit smiled, showing off teeth that seemed excessively white—all of a piece, somehow, with the stitched Royal Coachman on his blue shirt. "I'm glad we've got that settled."

"You're going to tell Sheriff Stroud you didn't mean what you said about the DNR. And he's going to record what you tell him. That's what we've got settled."

"Of course."

"The other matter is what Charlie told you about poaching. The importance of it on the Borchard. He was wrong about that."

"If you say so."

"Dammit," Mercy said, "don't be so agreeable. Just listen. I'd like to have Will Woodsman halfway informed, in case he decides to write something about the river. Charlie thought people should play by the rules, the legal rules and the rules of good sportsmanship, and he was right. But one of the first things you learn working for the DNR is people don't. Not all of them, not all the time. And you learn there's nothing, ultimately, you can do about it.

"People moan that fishing and hunting aren't what they used to be, but never seem to realize they contribute to the situation when they violate game regulations. I don't know what it is—maybe a continuing black urge to conquer nature by completely eliminating it—but some yahoos have a compulsion to kill anything that moves or swims. When we catch them breaking the rules, we hit them as hard as we can. The judges have come around on this. It used to be like drunk driving—there but for the grace of God go I. But now we're getting some serious sentences.

"Recently we got a repeat offender fined a thousand dollars and jailed for six months. And we're getting more cooperation from citizens, people as outraged as we are about violators. But it's not going to end the violations. That's my point. Enforcement isn't the problem, though we can always do better with it. Human nature's the problem."

Proffit dipped his head. "Well put."

"I'm not finished. Where Charlie and I really disagreed is about the specific harm poachers do the Borchard. There's no doubt they kill some big fish, but our river shocking surveys indicate the number of large fish has remained fairly stable. Charlie's evidence, on the other hand, is entirely anecdotal, plus his own fishing records indicated fewer big trout taken on a fly. So we went back and forth, scientific findings against personal experience. That's the rub the DNR always has with the public. Charlie and I simply agreed to disagree. It was all perfectly civil. There was no bigger supporter of the DNR, and of me personally, than Charlie Orr. That's why I can't understand why he wrote to you. It wasn't like him."

"Well," Proffit said, "it's water over the dam now."

"Not to me."

"With Charlie gone, I meant. We will never know what motivated him."

"Still and all."

"It might have been nothing more than seeing a trophy trout killed one night. That can be a sickening experience for someone dedicated to catch and release. Something of the sort might have triggered Charlie's reaction."

"Possibly," Mercy admitted.

Proffit paused a moment before he smiled and said, "Now could I interest you in an espresso?"

"I have to be getting back. I just wanted to speak my piece."

"You did. Eloquently."

"Just remember to talk to the sheriff and have him record it."

"Absolutely."

Mercy extricated herself from the picnic table, a graceless movement when someone on the other side was watching and smiling. She had taken a few steps away, heading toward the Suburban, when she turned, came back to Proffit.

"You had a notebook out when I came. Does that mean you're going to write something about Charlie?"

"I wouldn't think so."

"Unless you get carried away again?"

Proffit again ran a hand through his hair, then rose from the picnic table—more graceful about it, Mercy noticed, than she had been. "I was merely thinking. Old habit. I think best with pen and notebook in hand. Will Woodsman won't be writing anything about Charlie Orr. I assure you."

"But you'll be staying in the campground?"

"I believe that's what your sheriff has in mind."

Mercy nodded, turned away.

"Nice to have talked with you," Proffit called out from behind her.

\*　　　\*　　　\*

FOLLOWING THE LOOP road from Alec Proffit's campsite took her past Charlie's. When she came to it, Mercy parked the Suburban and walked up the incline on the path through the pines. She didn't know what she had been expecting to find, but it certainly wasn't this—a void, utter emptiness, every trace of Charlie Orr's presence removed.

She sat on the edge of the picnic table to steady herself. Burt Berry had told her deputies were removing Charlie's things from the campsite, but to be so quick about it—and so thorough! It took her breath away. Where she remembered Charlie's white tent standing, the dirt was no more hard-packed than elsewhere in the campsite. In the fire pit were no charred remains. Even Charlie's stacked firewood had been removed. Mercy ran a hand across the rough surface of the table, aware that Charlie had sat here, taken his meals here. At least the table hadn't been carted away.

The state parks people in Lansing would be pleased that Rainbow Run was returning to service, the murder put behind, business as usual. But she wouldn't forget. And neither would the maniac who had crept up to the campsite, fired a shotgun into the white tent, crept away. Charlie was gone, but not the terrible reality of what had happened to him.

Mercy left the table, crossed the campsite, followed a path that led in the direction of the river. How many times had Charlie come this way? In recent years he had rarely fished the stretch of the Borchard mainstream along the campground, driven off by heavy canoe traffic, preferring the wilderness water of the South Branch. But this is where he first fished the river, camping on the high banks when Rainbow Run was an angler-only campground—where he continued to take walks on trails deep into state-forest property. In some ways there were more reminders of Charlie here, in the thick growth and downed timber, than in the swept-clean campsite she had just left.

But it wasn't Charlie she wanted to think about here. It was Charlie's killer. She hated to admit it, but Alec Proffit might be right. It might be a poacher. Charlie *was* concerned about poaching, and he spent his nights fishing the no-kill section of the South Branch, prime water for poachers. If he saw poachers at work, it wasn't like Charlie to confront them, threaten to turn them in. It had been a point of mild contention between them, Mercy arguing that citizens had a duty to actively support the DNR by reporting poaching, Charlie agreeing but at the same time resisting the role of informant. Writing her notes and collecting empty worm containers was as far as he would go.

But maybe, his concern over poaching deepening, he had changed. Maybe one night he confronted a poacher, announced he was reporting him. Or maybe it happened another way, a poacher seeing Charlie observing him, assuming Charlie would report him. So . . . But going to the extreme of killing Charlie would imply—wouldn't it?—that the poacher had a lot to lose if he was turned in.

The loss had to be more than the prospect of a stiff fine and jail sentence. And more than the public shame that would follow, or should follow, from seeing yourself written up in the *Call*. Still, she recalled the word that had come to her before, thinking about Charlie's killer. He was a maniac. How could you reason your way into the mind of someone like that?

Mercy followed the path through the woods until it veered alongside the river. Through the tops of pines she could see the water below, dark, quick-flowing, shimmering in patches of sunlight. Ahead of her was a broad grassy clearing, wild blueberry and seedling pines taking over yet not fully erasing the scars of old campfires. It was probably the area where Charlie had first camped on the Borchard. Farther ahead were the remains of an old log stairway, nearly hidden now in hemlock, leading from the high banks down to the water. It was probably the route he had first taken to fish the river.

When she came to the edge of the clearing, Mercy sat on a downed log, hearing the deep quiet, letting herself stare into the encircling woods, trying to think. Confronted with a maniac, reason might be of little help, but it was all she had. And reason told her that if Charlie's killer was a poacher, he wouldn't have killed simply because, Charlie reporting him, he faced a fine and jail and shame. Poachers were used to all that. It was part of the cat-and-mouse game they played out with authority.

So it had to be something more, a greater loss. But what? What would matter so much to a poacher?

# 20

~~~

"YOU'RE NOT GUIDING me now," Gwendolyn protested. "We're having lunch, is all."

"Yeah," Kit said, "but you're supposed to eat in the lodge."

"I asked your mom for two box lunches and—"

"Jan's not my mom."

Gwendolyn nodded. "I forgot. Anyway, your dad and my dad won't know. They're floating the river."

"And I'm minding the fly shop."

"You can see from here if anybody comes in."

"That's not the same as being there."

"Oh, come on," Gwendolyn said. "Eat."

They were sitting on the peeled-log bench beyond the stand of white birch at the river's edge, box lunches on their laps. Beyond, under the noonday sun, tiny trout rose in the middle of the stream, dimpling the surface. Gwendolyn had waited until her father and Verlyn left for the South Branch, one of the Kabin Kamp's riverboats towed behind Verlyn's Land Rover, before entering the fly shop and telling Kit she wanted to eat together by the water. There was something she wanted to tell him in private.

"The reward," she said now. "Did you learn how much it is?"

Kit bit into half of a smoked-turkey sandwich, shook his head.

"I did. I asked Jan." Gwendolyn nibbled on a dill pickle. "Over five thousand dollars."

"No kidding," Kit managed to say with his mouth full.

"That's a lot, huh?"

"Not bad."

"So?"

"So what?"

"Just eat," Gwendolyn said, "and listen. I thought maybe you'd figured it out for yourself by now." She put the pickle back in the box, began nibbling on a carrot. She didn't seem interested, Kit noticed, in her sandwich. "What does it cost at Central Michigan for a year?" Before Kit could answer, Gwendolyn said, "Forget that. I'm sure it's more. But five thousand would be a start. You know, one step at a time."

Kit finished the half sandwich, wiped his mouth with a napkin. "I'm earning money here. I don't need the reward. Besides, who said I'm going back to college?"

"You said you might."

"Yeah, might."

"Let's think about it. To get the reward, you need to tell the sheriff who killed Charlie Orr. That's how it works, right?"

"Yeah, but I'm not interested."

"Of course you are," Gwendolyn said, and pointed to the other half of the sandwich in his box lunch. "Just eat."

Kit stared at her but picked up the sandwich. Gwendolyn was beginning to remind him of those bossy girls, usually the good-looking ones, of his own high school days. One minute you were helping them out, like teaching Gwendolyn the basics of fly fishing, the next thing you knew, they were running your life. Or trying to. Kit told himself that listening to Gwendolyn was one thing, doing what she said another. The distinction had thus far kept him a free man.

"So we've got to figure out the killer, is all. Jan says the sheriff hasn't a clue. But we've got to hurry. Other people will be trying for the reward. That's why I wanted to talk outside."

Kit kept eating, let her go on. "Jan said Calvin thinks Charlie Orr was killed for his hash. He smoked while he was fishing, somebody noticed, went to his tent to steal his supply, killed him in the process. Calvin's on the lookout for people around here smoking hash."

"Hash?" Kit edged out.

Gwendolyn seemed surprised. "What we call it at school."

Kit finished chewing, wiped his mouth again, looked at her with a cocked head. In some ways Gwendolyn wasn't as young as she appeared, and her pricey school might not be as cut off from the real world as he imagined. "Here we call it pot." Then he said, "That was yesterday's theory. Today's is he got nailed by some poachers who didn't want Charlie blowing the whistle on them."

"Poachers?"

"Slobs using worms and keeping fish on flies-only, no-kill water."

Gwendolyn seemed to ponder the explanation for a moment before she asked, "What's Calvin think?"

"It doesn't matter what he thinks. Calvin knows about fish, not everything else. There's another guy involved, name of Alec Proffit. He was camped in Rainbow Run near Charlie. The sheriff's keeping the details under wraps, but this guy has reason to think Charlie got mixed up with poachers. Like I say, it's today's theory. Who knows about tomorrow."

"But could it be?"

Kit picked his pickle out of the lunch container, tried a taste, found it too sour. "There's poachers on the river, sure. And they're slobs. I don't know if they'd kill anybody."

"How could we find out for certain?"

"We?"

"C'mon, Kit. You can't get the reward otherwise. How can we find out?"

Kit dropped the pickle back in the container, gave Gwendolyn a brief smile. He was back on his territory now, instructing her again, Gwendolyn paying attention. "You hang out at a place called the Keg O'Nails. All the slobs in the county turn up there, poachers included. You listen to them talk. If someone blew away Charlie, sooner or later he'll be bragging his head off about it."

Gwendolyn's eyes narrowed to a frown. "You'd think he wouldn't."

"You don't know poachers. They don't care about the fish they haul out of the river. Talking about it, that's the real game."

"Bullshitting, huh?"

Kit's smile returned, deepened. "You got it."

"So let's go to this place, listen in."

"You kidding? Your age, you wouldn't get a foot inside the door. Besides, your dad's going to let you hang out at some dump at night?"

"He wouldn't know. After a float trip he's sound asleep by nine o'clock. I could slip out of my room, go out the back way of the lodge, meet you."

Kit kept smiling. "You'd do that?" Then he said, "Forget it, Gwen. No way we're going to the Keg."

"So how else can we find out?"

"Hang out at night on the South Branch, pretend we're poaching, talk with the other poachers. They get as beered up on the river as they do in the Keg. They probably talk their heads off."

"You know that?"

"Not from experience. I keep my distance from those slobs. But I'm sure we'd learn plenty."

"Okay."

"Okay what?"

"Let's do it," Gwendolyn said. "Tonight. I'll meet you behind the lodge as soon as it's full dark. We'll go to the South Branch."

Kit stared at her. "You serious?"

"Weren't you?"

"No."

"You were just bullshitting?"

Kit stiffened on the bench. "I was telling you, theoretically, what could be done. I couldn't take you down on the South Branch at night. Your dad would kill me. After that Verlyn would. It's stupid. I shouldn't have said anything. And I shouldn't have let you talk me into this box lunch."

"Too late," Gwendolyn said. She was gazing at him, her eyes wide and dark, a broad smile on her face. She was about the best-looking girl, Kit realized, he had ever seen. He was still gazing back at her when Gwendolyn said, "Have my sandwich if you want."

\* \* \*

"Is HE UP yet?" Mercy asked into her cell phone.

"More than that," Angie Laski said. "The sheriff was here."

"Damn it all. I wanted to talk to Vic first. Prepare him."

"You should have prepared me. I had to chit-chat with the sheriff while Vic got out of bed."

"Sorry about that. I didn't think Stroud would barge in on you. Shows what I get for being a sensitive soul."

"Hold on, Mercy," Angie said. "He's coming."

On her way from Rainbow Run, Mercy had stopped at the High Pines convenience store for coffee and a sandwich. While she ate in the Suburban, she called Vic Laski's number, intending to give him warning before she arrived at his home in Kinnich. Earlier, calling from her office, Angie had told her Vic was still asleep. He had been on duty late into the night—something to do, Angie thought, with illegal tree cutting on state land—and Mercy had said not to wake him. She would phone again later.

"Sorry about that," she repeated when Vic came on the line.

"No matter." Vic's voice was weighted with sleep. "I didn't have anything to tell him."

"I should have forewarned you, anyway. Stroud's got this hot idea that Charlie Orr may have been killed by a poacher on the South Branch. That's why he wanted to talk to you." Mercy stopped herself. She was telling Vic what, now, he knew. "It went all right, then?"

"I told him I knew Charlie. You couldn't help it, the amount of time he spent on the river. But I wouldn't have figured a poacher killed him."

"Why not, Vic?"

Mercy could sense him shrug on the other end of the line. "Poachers kill fish, not people."

"Exactly."

"But you can't say for sure one didn't. Anyway, I told Stroud I didn't have any reason to think a poacher was the killer."

"What else did you talk about?"

"He wanted to know how well I knew Charlie. I said well enough to talk to when we met up on the river. No more than that."

"He ask you about the amount of poaching that goes on?"

"He brought it up. I told him there's always some, but it's up and down. Right now it's down. We got more problems with people hauling out pines than fish."

"Angie said you were on an operation last night."

Vic's voice cleared, gained strength. "We got lucky. Nailed a pair, both repeat offenders. We ought to get jail time."

"That's great, Vic. But Stroud wasn't interested?"

"Only about the river. He wanted to know if we talked about poaching, Charlie and me. If Charlie thought it was a big problem. I said Charlie never mentioned it that I recall. We talked about bug hatches and weather, that sort of thing."

"Great, Vic." When Vic didn't respond Mercy added, "If Charlie was killed by a poacher, it wasn't due to lax enforcement. It just happened. That's what I mean."

"Sure," Vic said.

"The killing couldn't have been prevented by the DNR. It wasn't anything under our control."

"Sure, Mercy," Vic repeated.

*     *     *

AFTER SHE FINISHED talking with Vic Laski, Mercy remained in the parking area of High Pines, her coffee cooling in the Styrofoam container. She knew how she was acting: defensive, circling the wagons, protecting her rear end—the knee-jerk bureaucratic reaction she professed to hate in others. It was all totally unnecessary. Alec Proffit had apologized for what he had said about DNR involvement in Charlie Orr's death, an apology he would repeat to Willard Stroud.

What rankled, nonetheless, was an implication that remained: that if the DNR had rid the river of poachers, one wouldn't have killed Charlie. That was absolutely mindless, of course. It would take the Navy Seals to end poaching, and even they might not be up to it. Still, if a poacher killed Charlie, the DNR came under a shadow, mindless or not. Actually, it occurred to her, a *second* shadow, the first being that the killing had taken place in a state campground under DNR supervision. She had ample reason, in other words, to feel defensive, though she might— with a little effort of self-control—be less out-in-the-open about it.

From the Suburban she phoned the sheriff's office. "Well?" she said when Elsie put Stroud on the line.

"I called," Stroud said, "you weren't in your office."

"I'm in my car, at High Pines, drinking lukewarm coffee. I just talked with Vic Laski. You hadn't arrested him, I found."

"Never intended to. Only thing I learned is Charlie didn't complain to him about poaching. Seems he only complained to you."

"I told you," Mercy said. "That was Charlie's way. I was a friend—and I was the boss. He wouldn't get on the case of an employee like Vic."

"All right," Stroud said. "But that doesn't square with Charlie writing to Alec Proffit, someone he didn't know, complaining about the DNR to him."

"I realize that," Mercy sighed.

"Other than that, Laski gave me the company line about poaching on the river. Admitted there's some, but it's not the be-all problem Charlie claimed to Proffit."

"It happens to be the truth, not the company line."

"Then how could Charlie be so wrong?"

Mercy sighed again. "I don't know."

Stroud said, "There's something else to tell you. You remember the report we had about the place on the river broken into, shotgun taken? Gus Thayer blabbed about it at the news conference. We got hold of the owner out in Montana, pushed him about his gun collection. Now he's saying he's pretty sure he doesn't own any .16 gauges. If a gun was taken, it's more likely a .410 or a .12 gauge. He told Zack Cox, on the phone, that he's partial to little guns and big guns."

"Oh, swell," Mercy said.

"He can't say for sure until he gets back from Montana. But the way it looks now, there's no connection between the break-in and the murder. No question, Slocum Byrd says, it was a .16 gauge used on Charlie."

"Another dead end, then."

There was silence on the phone before Stroud said, "Thought we'd agreed on another expression."

"Find me a better one. Anyway," Mercy said, "how come I wasn't notified about the reopening of Rainbow Run?"

"I tried to get you. Fern knows. People downstate keep calling, telling me it's time to reopen, August coming, all that. No use them calling you. I was the one had the campground closed. I made a deal with Lansing, let the first loop open."

"And I wasn't notified about the removal of Charlie's things."

"Ask Fern about that, too. Slocum was finished with his work. Things had to be removed sooner or later."

"I would have preferred later."

"I would, too," Stroud said, his tone suddenly grave. "But what good would it do?"

"Oh, I know."

"Zack went out there, told the host couple first, so they'd know we were clearing out the campsite. Said Billie broke down, cried." When there was more silence on the line, Stroud said, "Anything else to talk about?"

"I was trying to think of another expression for dead end," Mercy said.

*     *     *

BUT THAT HADN'T been entirely right. While she was talking with Stroud, she had been trying to think of something else as well, something that had held in the back of her mind since leaving the campground for High Pines. Stroud, mentioning Billie Berry, had brought it closer. Still . . .

Mercy considered stopping at the Kabin Kamp, lengthening the period before she had to get back to the office, allowing herself more time to think. She could see Kit, even Verlyn. Somehow that might help. But at the Kabin Kamp she was likely to run into Jan, and that, definitely, would not help.

A better idea was stopping at the Six-Grain Bakery, seeing Bonnie. Bonnie could talk your arm off, but she had a knack for listening, too, even when you were just chatting away, aimlessly. If anyone could help, Bonnie might.

Mercy was halfway back to Ossning, driving through long stretches of jack pines on the South Downriver Road, when she suddenly pulled onto the shoulder of the road, put her emergency signals on, left the engine running. The thought that had broken through was so startling that she needed a moment of calm, a moment to concentrate. She closed her eyes, squeezed them tightly shut, held herself still.

When she opened her eyes, she immediately reached for her phone, punched in the numbers of the A-frame. She wouldn't need Bonnie. Stroud had gotten her on the right track.

It *was* Billie.

# 21

I T WAS LATE afternoon when Mercy reached Fitzgerald in his Cherokee. She had first called him at home, then at the car, and Fitzgerald explained that, following a stop at Calvin's cabin, he had taken a walk in the woods along the South Branch, thinking about the case. Mercy told him he could stop thinking. She had figured something out. Something important.

But she didn't want to tell him about it on the phone, and she was tied up now, so she wanted to meet, the moment work was over, for a drink at the Borchard Hotel. She couldn't wait until they both were home.

When she arrived, Fitzgerald was at the bar, talking with Sandy. It took several minutes before Sandy, after serving them schooners of beer, drifted away. "What I figured out," Mercy said at once, leaning close to Fitzgerald, "was about Billie."

"Billie?"

"Not that she killed Charlie. Stroud had to consider her a suspect, simply because she found Charlie's body. But I never did. Lord, no."

"So why is she so important?"

"Because of Burt."

Fitzgerald took a long drink of his beer, wiped foam from his mouth, leaned back for a full look at Mercy. Her hair was more wind tossed than usual, except wind had nothing to do with it. It was the unruly nature of the hair itself, a perfect match for the dark, wild, unruly cast—at this moment—of her eyes. "You know something? You look terrific. Who would know you spent the day behind a desk?"

Mercy gave him a narrow-eyed appraisal. "You don't look so bad yourself. And it was only part of the day."

"Sorry?"

"At the desk."

Fitzgerald smiled and said, "Want to drink up, head home?"

"Not until I *tell* you this."

"So get started. I'm not sure how long I can last."

"I'm trying. This is serious."

"All right." Fitzgerald let the smile slip from his face. "It's serious, and it's about Billie because of Burt. I'm with you that far."

"It's what Billie told me about Burt."

"Told you when?"

"I've got to backtrack a bit. I went out to Rainbow Run after we left Stroud's office this morning. I wanted to confront Alec Proffit about what he'd said on that recording. I was going to really chew him out. But he turned out, big surprise, to be a pussycat. He didn't argue, took back everything he'd said, admitted he was wrong, said he'd set the record straight with Stroud. I said he'd damn well better set it straight on another *cassette*. And he agreed, just like that."

Fitzgerald said, "Wait. You and Proffit had this talk at the campground? Just the two of you?"

"That's what I said."

"It ever occur to you to bring me along? Proffit could be Charlie's killer."

"I doubt that. Anyway, I had to deal with him myself. You heard what he said about the DNR."

"You should have had somebody with you."

"Well, I didn't. And it didn't matter. He was perfectly agreeable."

"A pussycat."

"Yes."

"Good looking?"

Mercy pivoted on the bar stool, glared at Fitzgerald. "I'm trying to tell you about Billie and Burt. Alec Proffit's looks have nothing to do with anything."

"Except in a general way. Published writers shouldn't have good looks. They shouldn't have all the luck in the world."

"You've got nerve talking about luck. Now listen. After I left the campground, I spoke with Vic Laski from my car, then with Stroud. Stroud had gotten to Vic before I had, so we went the rounds about that. Then we talked about the fact that Lansing wants the campground available for August, so Stroud's allowing the first loop to open. And he's removed everything from Charlie's campsite. Theona said she wants it all. Stroud told me that when Zack Cox told Burt and Billie about Charlie's things, Billie broke down and cried. That's what got me thinking about Billie."

"You said Burt was the important one."

"He is. But you have to see how it comes around. At the campground, before I talked to Proffit, I talked to Burt, asked him how he and Billie were doing. He said they were getting back to routine. So that started me thinking, back in my head somewhere, about their routine. Not the work routine of campground hosts. Their other routines. For Billie it was talking to Charlie every morning, but that was something she couldn't do anymore. For Burt it was fishing in the evening, and that's something he could still do. Billie had told me how regular he is about it, fishing in the evening. And she told me something else. That's why Billie's the key."

"Keep going."

"You remember I went to see her right after Charlie's death? That's when Billie told me she and Burt called Charlie the Odd Fellow. But that isn't important. Something else is. That morning, before going out to see Charlie, Billie made coffee in the trailer. While she was waiting she took a cleaned trout Burt had caught, put it in a plastic bag, put the bag in the freezer compartment. With other trout Burt had caught. So you see?"

"Frankly," Fitzgerald said, "not a thing."

"Burt caught the trout. The freezer compartment has other trout in it, all caught by Burt. Trout, Fitzgerald. *Trout*."

"Trout?" Sandy had materialized in front of them, hands on her hips. "Special tonight"—she dipped her head toward the dining room beyond the bar—"it's rainbow stuffed with crab, you're so inclined. Shipped all the way from Idaho, if you believe that. You'd think Michigan would have plenty. Farm raised, of course," Sandy said, and winked at Mercy.

When neither Mercy nor Fitzgerald responded, Sandy turned away and moved down the bar. "You need another," she called over her shoulder, "yell."

"So you see?" Mercy said, and edged close again to Fitzgerald. "What Billie said made me realize Burt fishes at night and kills trout. I knew that, but I hadn't *realized* it. It might explain everything. Burt might be poaching, and Charlie might have found out."

"Wait," Fitzgerald said. "It doesn't follow that Burt's poaching. Not just because he's out at night and keeping trout. Not all the river is catch and release. Should be but isn't. So there's nothing necessarily illegal about a freezer full of trout."

"Sure, sure, sure," Mercy said. "I *know* that. But there's more."

"Go on."

"Let's assume Alec Proffit's right: Charlie was killed by a poacher. I *hate* that, but for the sake of argument, let's assume it. And assume Charlie was going to turn the poacher in. Maybe Charlie said he was, or the poacher just thought so. But there's a problem: Poachers kill fish, not people. So, in this case, the poacher had to be really worked up over Charlie turning him in. Worked up about more than a fine or jail. So what could it be, a big thing that would cause a poacher to kill to keep Charlie quiet?"

"You're going to tell me."

"Loss of your position as campground host."

"Oh, come on," Fitzgerald said after a moment.

"Just listen. Assume that Charlie saw Burt poaching on the South Branch in no-kill water. Maybe Charlie even said something to him about it, threatened to go public. But that doesn't matter. It's enough that Burt *knew* Charlie had seen him. If Charlie told me, Burt and Billie would be out on their ears in a flash. Burt would have known that, so he had to silence Charlie. Burt's the one, remember, who reported hearing shots in the campground. Firecrackers, he said. There's a good reason why he heard them."

"Because he pulled the trigger of the shotgun."

Mercy raised a hand, then let it fall back to the bar. "It all fits."

"Not unless Burt cares enough about the campground job to kill for it."

"I know," Mercy said. "All he and Billie get out of it is free camping. And there's some sort of status, I suppose, in being a host couple. Maybe it's only the campground itself. Rainbow Run is a great place on a magnificent river."

"It still seems a leap, killing for that reason."

Mercy swiveled on the bar stool, glared again at Fitzgerald. "I don't *like* what I'm saying. I'd already convinced myself that Burt had nothing to do with the killing—and it doesn't exactly put the DNR in a terrific light if one of our campground hosts *was* involved. Imagine what Gus Thayer would write in the *Call*. I don't even want to imagine what Alec Proffit might write. You, too. You'd be hearing from the *Free Press*, wanting something out of you. It would be a mess, and I'd be the one closest to it."

"I know," Fitzgerald said.

"So I'd leap at any other explanation if I could come up with one. I'm stuck with the fact that Billie might have unwittingly given me the key—that Burt killed Charlie to cover up his killing of trout, and all because he feared getting booted out as campground host. I know it's zany, but tell me something different."

Fitzgerald took a long drink of beer, wiped his mouth, slow about it, Mercy still glaring at him. At length he said, "There's a way of finding out."

*      *      *

THEY DECIDED TO eat in the hotel dining room, though neither of them felt like ordering the stuffed trout. When Mercy said, "At home, Fitzgerald, we're turning into health nuts," they decided on steaks, fried potatoes, and onion rings, with a bottle of red wine as hopeful counterpoint to the cholesterol intake. It was still early, the dinner crowd of tourists and locals not yet assembled, the old Finn everyone simply called Nils not yet perched on his stool at the head of the room, squeezing once-familiar tunes from his accordion.

"Well," Mercy said while they waited for the food, "how?"

Fitzgerald said, "By starting with your first assumption. We have to find out if Burt's a poacher."

"And?"

"And I'm the one to do it. I'll follow Burt when he goes out, locate the part of the river he fishes, see if it's no-kill water. It won't be hard following him, if he actually fishes at night."

"He does."

"So that's what I'll do. We'll go home, I'll get my fishing gear together, I'll drive out to the entrance to Rainbow Run, wait there for Burt's truck to come out. If it does."

"It might not," Mercy said. "When he came to the office, he told me he hadn't fished the night before. Because of Billie. On the other hand, out at the campground, he said they were getting back to routine."

"It's worth a try then. Tonight."

Mercy said, "You remember something, Fitzgerald? My seeing Proffit alone? You didn't think that was such a hot idea because he might be the killer. So how about you running around after Burt alone?"

"There's a difference. Burt won't see me. I'll just be keeping an eye on him."

"He *could* see you, just as he may have seen Charlie. I'm going with you."

"You can't. Burt knows you. Even if he spots me, he won't make anything of it. I'm just another fisherman on the river."

"You visited Charlie. He may remember you."

"That's possible. I had to pass by the host's trailer to get to the back loop road. Now and then I got a look at both Burt and Billie. So, yes, he may recall me. But it's a chance we have to take. There's no way he wouldn't be alerted if he saw you on the river. Just remind me about Burt's truck. Make and color."

"It's one of those big ones, enough to pull that fifth-wheeler. Chevy Silverado or something. All white."

"Good," Fitzgerald said. "Easy to follow."

When dinner came, they ate in silence. Afterward, when Fitzgerald asked if she wanted coffee, Mercy shook her head, told him she just wanted to finish the wine. They could make coffee at home. After

Fitzgerald refilled her glass, she said, "I still don't like it. Why don't we tell Stroud, let a deputy follow Burt?"

"There's a chance Burt would recognize him. Stroud's people have been in and out of Rainbow Run the last couple days. There's something else."

Mercy swirled the wine in her glass, looked across the table.

"If Burt isn't poaching, you wouldn't want it around that the DNR had any suspicion of a campground host as Charlie's killer. This way, me following him, we keep the suspicion between ourselves."

"I could ask Vic Laski. He'd keep it under his hat."

"Could you be certain of that?"

Mercy thought for a moment, said, "All right. But you don't confront Burt, anything stupid like that."

"I'll see if he's poaching, is all."

"Then?"

"Then we have to test the next assumption. If he was found out, would that be reason enough to kill."

"How do we do that?"

Fitzgerald filled his own glass with wine, leaned back from the table, grinned at her. "I'm the entire brains of this organization?"

Mercy didn't grin back.

"Don't worry. I'll be careful. If we're lucky, we'll know by night's end if there is a next step."

# 22

<hr>

THE TOUGH PART was convincing Gwendolyn she couldn't come with him. She had wanted to sneak out of the lodge as soon as her dad went to bed, join Kit in his Toyota truck, search along the South Branch for poachers who might know something about the killing of Charlie Orr, might even be boasting about doing it. Kit went through a list of reasons why she couldn't come along, but the only one that persuaded her was that poachers wouldn't say a word in the presence of a girl. All of them were male chauvinists.

She could believe that, Gwendolyn said, poachers being lowlifes in other ways.

What faced Kit next—how best to join up with poachers, overhear their talk—was comparatively simple. He considered canoeing the no-kill section of the river, stopping to shoot the breeze with poachers if and when he ran into them. He could cover the most water that way, but the canoe would be a dead giveaway he wasn't a poacher himself. A poacher wouldn't talk to a canoeist any more than to a girl. The only way with a chance of working, Kit decided, was to wade the river, stop when he found poachers, try to get them talking. It would probably take him three nights to cover the bulk of the no-kill water.

He thought he looked the part. He had put on patched-up waders, found an old spinning rod someone had abandoned at the lodge, bought a container of worms at High Pines. He didn't wear his vest with all the fly-fishing gadgets hanging from it—another certain giveaway he couldn't be trusted by poachers. As an added touch, he bought a stringer at High Pines, fastened it to the suspenders of his waders.

He had left his truck at Schoolcraft Bridge and entered the water just below, the upstream boundary of no-kill water. His plan was to wade as far as what locals called Frenchtown Flats, leaving the river there and hiking the DNR ski trail back to his pickup. He figured that would be a good night of detective work. When he returned to the lodge, he had agreed to signal by blinking his headlights three times in the parking area beside the fly shop. She couldn't wait for morning, Gwendolyn had said, to learn what he had found out.

Clouds now scudded past a half moon, the river a silvery path for a time, then a black void. Kit moved down the center of the stream, the unfamiliar spinning rod in one hand, on the lookout for bank fires or the sudden flare of a flashlight on the water. It surprised him, as it always did, how acutely he heard at night: the motion of the water, crests breaking against woody debris, birds in the pines, animals back deep in the woods, all the dark music of the river. It was always slightly spooky, especially when you heard, a few feet away, a big brown slurp a bug from the surface. You froze then, trying to fix on the spot as you stripped out line for a back cast.

Except, this night, he wasn't fishing. He was a one-man search party.

What Gwendolyn said about the reward had seemed, when she brought it up, far-fetched, but the more Kit thought about it the more he warmed to the idea. Somebody was going to get the reward, so it might as well be him. Gwendolyn thought the reward would be his ticket back to college, and he let her think that. It might, as a matter of fact. But the main thing was how teed off Verlyn and Calvin would be if the reward they got up was won by Kit. The appeal of that was enough to keep him on the river, searching, for three nights. If nothing turned up by then, to hell with the reward.

When the moonlight was strong he moved ahead quickly, keeping to the center of the stream but careful to make as little sound as possible. He hadn't seen another fisherman until, fifty yards or more downstream, he saw a light snap on, hold for a minute or two, snap off. He edged closer to the bank, shadowed here by the pines, and moved ahead. Finally he could make out the silhouette of the fisherman, using a fly rod, casting to a bend where the water deepened. He must have used the light to change flies. Kit was sure, given the way he cast, he was using flies.

When Kit got closer, he made a little noise in the water, alerting the fisherman to his presence, called out, "Doing any good?"

"Nothing," the fisherman called back.

It was the standard response on the river, and maybe even true. Kit decided the fisherman was the genuine article, not a poacher. "Okay if I pass around?" he called out.

"No problem," the fisherman replied.

Kit had gone on downstream, the river twisting sharply now through an area known as the Rollercoaster, when he saw the flickering light of a fire along the bank, then heard the sound—the distinct *plunk*—of lead striking water. Whoever was fishing from the fire wasn't casting flies in flies-only water. Kit felt a sudden flush of adrenalin. Then he cautioned himself: It might have been this way with Charlie Orr, coming up on a poacher who turned out to be a killer.

He decided he would seem more a poacher himself, less a fly-fishing purist like Charlie, if he left the river and came up to the fire through the woods. He had the look of a bait fisherman, more or less, but bait fishermen didn't wade the river at night, which implied familiarity with the nature of the bottom. They barged through the woods, noisy as deer breaking through to water.

One more thing, though, would have added to the picture. He had forgotten to buy a six-pack of beer at High Pines, stuff some cans in his waders. The best way to get a poacher yakking away was to offer him a free beer.

\*       \*       \*

THE FIRE HAD burnt down by the time Kit emerged through a tangle of deadfall into a small clearing at the edge of the river, only embers glowing. The night had cooled, but the fire was for warding off mosquitoes, not for warmth. The figure sitting beside it, his back to Kit, looked big and powerful, but beyond that and hair flaring out under a baseball cap, nothing was distinct in the weak light. The figure didn't shift, didn't look around at Kit's approach.

"Doing any good?" Kit asked.

He could see the figure slowly shake his head.

"Maybe too early yet."

This time the figure made no motion.

"What're you using?"

It was a stupid question—Kit's eyes had adjusted just enough to make out a Styrofoam container in the grass beside the figure—but he had, somehow, to strike up a conversation. It was evident the figure didn't have flies at the business ends of a pair of spinning rods propped in the crotches of sticks. Kit was pretty sure, too, that what looked like a rope running through the grass and into the water had a stringer attached at the end. All of which added up to the fact that the figure now hunched in front of him was a poacher.

Damned if he hadn't found what he was hunting for.

The poacher had inclined his head in the general direction of the container in the grass, which Kit took as an answer to his stupid question. On the other hand, nothing had been said directly, which was probably the way you handled yourself if you were poaching and a stranger came up behind you. The poacher, Kit decided, needed reassurance.

"I've got some fresh crawlers, you want to give 'em a try. Fat as hogs."

No response.

Kit rustled in the front pocket of his waders, drew out the worm container, extended it to the poacher's back. "Help yourself."

A few moments passed, during which the poacher might have been trying to make up his mind. Then he turned slowly, peered up at Kit. His face seemed broad and dark in the light of the embers, and Kit could make out a Gothic-style D in white on the front of his cap. The poacher kept looking him over, at the same time reached out for a handful of small sticks, dropped them on the fire, a gesture Kit took as encouraging. Or the need for more light.

The fire flaring, Kit again extended the container. After more moments passed, the poacher took it from him. He lifted the lid, held the container near the fire, the entangled nightcrawlers greasy in the light.

He replaced the lid, handed the container back. "Got some as good."

Kit nodded, leaned his spinning rod against a tree trunk, lowered himself—uninvited—into the grass across the fire from the poacher. "These come from High Pines," he said. "You got a better place?"

"Don't buy 'em," the poacher said. "Pick 'em myself."

Kit nodded again. "That's the way. Except, my place, we got more sand than dirt. Crappy for crawlers."

"Where's that?" the poacher asked.

"My place?" Kit shifted his weight, firelight gleaming from his waders. "In town."

"What town?"

"Ossning."

The poacher kept looking at him, studying him, which was probably to be expected. Poachers might like to talk, but they had to make certain they were talking to another poacher. Kit looked back, trying to give the appearance that he was sizing up the poacher, too. Facing him, the poacher looked even bigger, thick as a bull through the shoulders, but he had some years on him. In the dark skin around his mouth, there were deep lines.

He was about to ask the poacher where he was from, then decided against it. He didn't want to push too hard too soon. He took another tack. "You follow the Tigers?" he asked, and directed a finger at the poacher's cap.

"No," the poacher said.

"Just as well," Kit said.

"They got good caps, is all."

"Can't beat 'em, that's so."

"You want a beer?"

The poacher reached through the grass for the rope, pulled it toward him. What came over the bank at the end wasn't a stringer but a net bag heavy with beer cans. The poacher reached in, removed two, lowered the bag into the river. He handed Kit a dripping can of Milwaukee's Best.

"A life saver," Kit said. "I got crawlers at High Pines, forgot my brew."

"You old enough to buy?" the poacher asked.

"Sure."

Kit worried for a moment that if the poacher thought him too young to buy beer, he might consider him too young to poach. Most poaching seemed done by older guys. "Like I say," he said, "I forgot."

The poacher shrugged, popped open his beer can. Kit did the same. He drank off half his can before he said, "So you think it's too early or what?"

"Could be," the poacher said.

"I've been having some luck. Big browns."

"Where?"

"Upriver." Kit remembered his waders, said, "Got a place I get out to. Little island."

"With crawlers?"

"What?"

"What you're having luck with."

"What else? Big browns along here don't see many crawlers."

"Why's that?"

Kit looked back across the fire, decided it was time to push harder. The beer was encouraging, but he didn't want to waste the whole night before the poacher got around to talking. "You know why. The hot shots in here use only feathers and fur, is why."

The poacher seemed to indicate his agreement but kept studying Kit. With his free hand he tossed more sticks on the fire just at the moment the moon edged from behind the clouds, flooding the grassy bank above the river with light. The lines of the poacher's two rods were visible now, angled tightly to the water.

"Where'd you say you're from in town?" the poacher asked.

"Didn't say."

The poacher didn't appear to take Kit's response in the wrong way. He nodded, seemed to turn inward, thinking. "Come from in town," he said after a moment, "you'd know that campground."

Kit leaned back, tried to hold himself rigid, adrenalin again flushing through him. "Which one?"

"On the mainstream. Along them high banks."

"I know it," he managed to say.

"So you know about the old man got himself shot."

"Sure."

"I heard tell," the poacher said, "he fished the South Branch at night. Used them feathers and fur you were tellin' about. One of them hot shots."

"Yeah?" Kit said, his voice as bland as possible.

"Never ran into him myself."

"Yeah," Kit said again, and thought, So why'd you bring it up? Then he thought, Most things you plan in life don't work out. They fizzle, make you realize it's stupid to plan anything. But this . . . it's working. The poacher's being cagey about it, asking me about Charlie Orr, but he'll come around, blab what he knows. It's just the way I told Gwen. Poachers get beered up, they talk their heads off. If you find the one who killed Charlie, he'll end up bragging about it. So what happens? The first poacher I run into brings up, out of the blue, the killing. It blows your mind, a plan actually working like that.

"Another beer?" the poacher asked.

"Just waitin' for you to ask," Kit said, and realized he had crushed the empty can in his hand.

\*      \*      \*

THE POACHER HAD reeled in both his lines, added crawlers to the hooks, tossed out again into the middle of the stream, replaced the rods in the crotches of the upright sticks. He had thrown more wood on the fire, creating a decent blaze. And he had again pulled up the net bag from the water, removing a third Milwaukee's Best for each of them. Kit, edged away from the fire now, had found the limb of a downed tree to lean his back against.

Despite himself, he was half hoping the poacher would get a strike. It would take a monster brown to suck up the gob of crawlers resting on the river bottom, maybe the biggest brown Kit, a hot-shot fisherman himself, had ever laid eyes on. All he wanted, though, was a look at the fish. He didn't want a stringer run through its jaw, the brown dying slowly in the river.

"I've been having some luck," Kit said to the poacher, "but later in the night." The poacher, it occurred to him, might be wondering why he hadn't baited up, tossed out himself. Poachers didn't seem to mind fishing side by side. They weren't like fly fishermen, in a funk if another angler came within eyesight. "After midnight. Big browns start moving around then."

In the light of the fire, the poacher looked at his watch. "It's after midnight now."

"Yeah?" Kit tried to shift his weight, to check his own watch, but it took too much effort. He was feeling, he realized, a little mellow. "Soon as I finish this brew."

"You fished upriver, after midnight, maybe you ran into the old man."

Ah, Kit thought, back to that. Finally. He had been waiting, letting the poacher get around to it. It might take all night and a load of beer, but it was worth the wait. "What old man's that?"

"One got himself shot. Old man smoked a pipe."

"You see that," Kit said, "with old types."

"You ever run into him?"

Kit shrugged. "Could be."

"You'd know if you did. He'd give you grief."

"Why's that?"

The poacher looked at Kit through the firelight, studying him again, his eyes heavy lidded but alert. "Breaking the law, is why."

Kit looked back, meeting the poacher's eyes, smiling now. "The old man didn't like that, huh?"

"Hear he didn't."

"He bitched to the DNR?"

"Might have."

"But you never ran into him yourself?"

"What I said."

"You did," Kit said. "I remember."

Together their eyes held across the firelight. Minutes seemed to pass. Then the poacher reached into the pocket of his shirt, drew out a pair of wire-rimmed glasses. With them on, leaning forward, peering through the firelight, he had a different look. Kit experienced a moment of confusion. It didn't seem quite right, a poacher wearing wire-rimmed glasses.

"Hell!" the poacher blurted out, and in one motion rose to his feet, through the firelight looming twice as big as Kit had thought. The confusion cleared, replaced with a sting of fear. Then the poacher said, "You owe me three beers, kid."

"What?" Kit was able to say.

"Make it a whole pack," the poacher said, "for wasting my time."

Kit managed to get to his feet, clumsy in his waders. He felt better standing even though the poacher didn't look any smaller. "What're you talking about?"

The poacher seemed to release a stream of air through his nose, roll his shoulders. He stuck his hands in the pockets of his jeans. He wasn't angry, Kit realized, so much as mightily irritated. "Your cap I'm talking about. You noticed mine, I've been trying to read yours. Been sitting here, trying to. Didn't want to put on my glasses."

Kit narrowed his eyes, cocked his head. "Why not?"

"Poachers don't wear glasses."

"Ah, hell," Kit said, and seemed to feel air escape from him, too.

"You know Calvin McCann?" the poacher asked.

"Sort of," Kit said.

"That's how you know about the reward he's giving? Him and Verlyn Kelso."

"Heard about it," Kit said. "How'd you know?"

"Heard, too." The poacher lowered himself heavily back into the grass and reached for the rope. "What's it matter," he said. "Have another, you want."

Kit shook his head. "I got to be going." He turned away, grabbed his spinning rod, then looked back at the figure across the fire. "You really poaching," he asked, "or what?"

"It's a long story, kid."

"Yeah?" Kit turned back, eased himself down to the grass. "We've already shot half the night."

"You want a beer, then?" the poacher asked.

# 23

L ESS THAN AN hour had passed, the Cherokee pulled into a turnoff on the South Downriver Road below the entrance to Rainbow Run, when Fitzgerald saw a white truck emerge from the campground road, dark plume of dust in its wake. He replaced the top on the thermos of coffee Mercy had sent with him, switched on his headlights, turned onto the asphalt road. It wasn't full night yet. The truck, well ahead of him, was still in sight.

But headed in the wrong direction.

Burt Berry ought to have turned east out of the campground, headed toward Schoolcraft Bridge and the entrance to the wilderness section along the South Branch. He should have passed the Cherokee, giving Fitzgerald, slumped in the driver's seat, the opportunity for a positive identification that the white truck was in fact Burt's. Instead, the truck had turned west, headed for Ossning.

Burt might have an errand to run in town before he went fishing—or he might need to buy worms at a bait shop. Fitzgerald pressed down on the accelerator yet gained only enough ground to make certain the truck was the size of a Silverado. Wherever he was headed, Burt was in a hurry.

When he reached the stoplight for the state highway that ran through the center of Ossning, Burt made a left turn, followed traffic to the entrance of Glen's supermarket. Fitzgerald parked two rows away from the truck, kept the Cherokee's motor running, watched Burt cross the parking lot to the store. Seen under the high orange lights of the lot, there was no question of Burt's identity.

Ten minutes later, Burt left the supermarket, a sagging plastic bag in his hand. You could buy a lot of things in Glen's in addition to food, but Fitzgerald doubted worms were included. Nor would a container of worms fill a bag like the one Burt was carrying.

Burt's next stop, north edge of town on the old highway up to the Mackinac Bridge, was the F. O. E. lodge. Outside the low cement-block building, a blinking portable sign announced fish fries, spaghetti suppers, T-bone evenings, all open to the public. Was Burt planning to eat? And this time of evening? He left the truck in the jammed parking lot and hurried inside the building. He wasn't carrying the plastic bag from Glen's.

Another ten minutes went by. Fitzgerald unscrewed the top of the thermos, poured more coffee, kept his eye on the building's entrance door, ran through in his mind other possibilities. Burt might be getting a drink at the bar or rendezvousing with poaching buddies before heading out to the South Branch. More minutes ticked away and still no Burt. Fitzgerald decided finally on a plan of action. He would go inside, have a look around, avoiding Burt if possible. If Burt returned to the truck, on his way at last to the South Branch, he would follow close behind.

The bar of the Eagles club was darkly paneled, dimly lit, and oddly empty given the number of vehicles in the parking area. If he had been occupying one of the bar stools, Burt would have been spotted at once. Fitzgerald ordered a draft beer from the bartender, asked if meals were being served in the dining room.

"Were."

"But not now?"

"Bingo now."

"Tonight?"

The bartender seemed surprised by the question. "You don't know?"

"Know what?"

"It's Wednesday. Our night."

"Maybe you could explain," Fitzgerald suggested.

"Wednesday is always here. Other nights Moose, Elks, V. F. W., Knights of Columbus."

"For bingo, you mean?"

"What else?"

"So somewhere around here it's possible to play every night?"

"Except weekends. You should see what it's like come Monday. Two days off, the regulars got wild looks in the eyes."

"Withdrawal signs?"

"You got it," the bartender said.

Fitzgerald carried his beer through swinging double doors into a sizeable room as bright with fluorescent light as a hospital corridor. And as hushed. In long rows people sat tightly packed, heads bent to bingo sheets, hands with markers poised above, as a voice at the head of the room intoned numbers over a loud-speaker system. Fitzgerald blinked in the light, ran his eyes up and down the rows, located Burt seated at the very end of one—the poacher he had followed, playing bingo at the Eagles.

*　　　*　　　*

THE THING TO do was write off the evening and head back home. But a question would hang between them when he talked with Mercy. Had he just followed Burt on an off night, a bingo evening at the Eagles not necessarily overruling other nights of poaching on the South Branch? According to Billie, Burt went fishing nearly every evening. If he didn't play bingo that often, how did he spend his other evenings?

Fitzgerald waited through several games, the hospital-corridor hush alternating with shrieks and moans when cards were decided, until an intermission was declared. When Burt rose stiffly from the table and made his way in the direction of the bar, Fitzgerald intercepted him.

"Burt Berry?"

"Yup."

"Thought I recognized you from Rainbow Run."

Burt peered back

"Fitzgerald. Mercy Virdon and I—"

"Yup," Burt said. "Mercy's friend. You won the lottery."

"One of the small ones," Fitzgerald said. "A while ago now."

"Maybe you got some luck left. You want to move by me?"

"How about a beer first?"

"Now you're talkin'," Burt said.

In the bar, crowded now, they found a small table off to the side. Burt brought a bottle of Budweiser with him, Fitzgerald another draft. "Here's to you," Burt said, and tipped back his bottle. "Cheers," Fitzgerald said.

After he had wiped his lips, Burt looked closely at Fitzgerald. "Haven't seen you here before."

"First time, to be honest."

"Mercy won't let you out?"

"It's not exactly that."

"Is with me," Burt said. "Billie don't believe in gambling."

Fitzgerald couldn't hold back a smile. "It's only bingo."

"Had my choice, I'd feed the slots."

"There's the Indian casino in Traverse City."

Burt shook his head. "Too far. Couldn't get over and back without Billie knowing. Here's the best I can do."

"Bingo, you mean?"

"Yup."

"On Wednesday nights?"

Burt gave Fitzgerald a close look. "Between you and me?"

"Absolutely."

"Other nights, too."

"You move around town, you mean?"

"Yup."

"Monday through Friday?"

"Unless I'm under the weather. Or Billie is."

Fitzgerald sighed and said, "Get you another beer, Burt?"

"Now you're talkin'."

*     *     *

WHEN FITZGERALD RETURNED from the bar, a look of caution had appeared on Burt long face. He leaned close across the table. "Wouldn't want it getting back to Mercy."

"About bingo? She wouldn't care."

"Wouldn't want it anyway."

"I won't say a word."

"Wouldn't want her thinking I'm a booze hound, neither. Two or three's my limit. Have a sandwich and coffee before I leave. Come home snockered, I'd catch holy hell."

"Billie's against drinking, too?"

"Her book," Burt said, "one's same as the other. She was brought up strict. Lot of things got stuck in her head. When we was first married, she wouldn't even drink coffee. Not that I'm complaining. There's a lot I owe to Billie. She kept my nose to the grindstone."

Fitzgerald tried a smile. "Except for sneaking out for bingo."

Burt smiled back after a moment's indecision. "Got to sow a few oats."

"Trust me," Fitzgerald said, "I won't say anything to Mercy. But there's something I don't understand. This time of night, doesn't Billie wonder where you are?"

Burt kept smiling. "You hunting for tips?"

"I suppose I am."

"I'm out fishing, Billie thinks. Got my gear in the truck. Night fishing, when the big ones move around."

"My problem would be," Fitzgerald said, "that Mercy likes to fish, too."

"I got you there," Burt said. "Billie don't care for it. What I do is pick up a rainbow and some ice at Glen's, leave the fish in the frig when I get home, Billie figures it's one I caught. We got ourselves a freezer full of rainbows."

Fitzgerald nodded. "Idaho rainbows."

"Yup."

"Farm raised."

"Yup."

"And Billie believes they're Borchard trout."

"That's the idea."

"But the water along Rainbow Run is catch and release. Billie knows that. So how do you explain bringing home fish?"

"She thinks I'm below Stump Road. Creel limit's five down there."

"You've got everything figured."

"Yup."

Fitzgerald nodded again, finished what was left of his beer. "Tell me one thing, Burt. Do you ever really fish?"

"I get the urge," Burt said. "But not late night. Pitch dark, I got no interest being in the river. Evening rolls around, I haul into town."

"Clean, well-lighted places."

Burt looked blank.

"Bingo in Ossning."

*    *    *

WHEN FITZGERALD CREPT into bed, Mercy turned over and said, "I sent coffee. You smell like beer."

"It's a long story," Fitzgerald said.

"I was asleep. Give me the bottom line."

"We were lucky. Burt left the campground in his truck."

"And?"

"But we were wrong. He's a dead end."

"For sure?"

"Believe me. Burt had nothing to do with Charlie's death."

"So where does that leave us?"

"Where we were before."

"Nowhere."

Fitzgerald kissed her hair, rolled on his side. "Let's talk in the morning. Maybe things won't seem so bleak."

"You believe that?"

"No."

# 24

<br>

I<small>T WAS AFTER</small> nine o'clock when Fitzgerald rolled over, awake, a ladder of sunlight edging through the Venetian blinds. It took him a few moments to realize Mercy wasn't beside him, another to realize—whatever the weather beyond the windows—that looming ahead was a bleak day.

In the kitchen he found fresh coffee and a note on the trestle table. *Call me—office. Heaps of work.* Fitzgerald poured a mug of coffee, took it through the A-frame to the deck overlooking the river, settled himself in a sling chair.

It was a time of morning to be at work on his novel, the laptop balanced on his lap, concentrating, making progress. It was equally a time to be on the river, working an attractor pattern, alert as birds for the first trico lifting into warming air. The decision, in the normal course of events, would be difficult. Wrenching.

This morning the decision had been taken out of his hands, for which, admittedly, he wasn't entirely ungrateful. The decision, in any event, had been postponed. He had things to do, the first of which being to call Mercy. Then the two of them ought to confer with Stroud. Then... Fitzgerald sipped coffee, drew in the sweetness of the morning. Soon enough the bleak reality of the day would settle in.

With a second mug of coffee he called the DNR office from the phone in the kitchen. "She's been waiting," Fern Lax confided.

"Tough night," Fitzgerald said to her, trying for a breezy tone. "You wouldn't believe."

"She won't either."

"Well?" Mercy said when she came on the line.

"I slept in. Just got myself in motion."

"I meant last night. Why Burt Berry's a dead end."

"It's comic, in a way."

Mercy let silence hold between them before she said, "I've been *waiting*, Fitzgerald."

"I followed him—way we planned. Except Burt didn't head to the South Branch for a night of poaching. He went to Glen's in town, where he bought himself a fat farm-raised Idaho rainbow trout. Then he went to the Eagles to play bingo and drink beer. It seems there's bingo around here every weekday night. Billie doesn't believe in gambling or drinking, so Burt sneaks off, telling her he's going fishing down below Stump Road. The rainbow from Glen's—Billie believes it's one he caught. She believes Burt's one helluva fisherman. Now you don't think that's comic?"

"Good Lord."

"I gave Burt my word I'd keep his secret. He doesn't want you knowing, let alone Billie. You might not think it proper, a bingo-playing, beer-drinking campground host."

"Good Lord."

"That's why Burt's a dead end. If a poacher killed Charlie, Burt's not the poacher."

"I suppose," Mercy said without conviction, "Charlie could have learned about the bingo and beer. He might have discovered what Burt was up to."

"If he did, he'd have laughed his head off. Face it. We got it wrong. Burt Berry didn't kill Charlie."

"It just seemed—" Mercy sighed into the phone before she said, "Brace yourself, Fitzgerald. My guess is the whole poaching thing is a dead end."

\*　　\*　　\*

As soon as she had gotten to the office that morning, Mercy explained, there was a message from Calvin on her voice mail. Calvin had called at six-thirty. He always thought the rest of the world was up and functioning as early as he was. When she called him back, Calvin told her he'd had only a couple hours sleep. A visitor had come to his cabin in the middle of the night.

"You don't know him," Mercy told Fitzgerald. "The visitor was Stanley Elk."

"Say again?"

"Pal of Calvin's. He's an Ojibway from around Roscommon. Pal of Verlyn's, too. They all go way back together. You do know him?"

"Heard of him." Fitzgerald cleared his throat. He didn't like hiding things from Mercy.

"Stanley used to be a big-time poacher. Now he's small-time, a fish is all. Keeping his hand in, so to speak. Well, Calvin gets the bright idea of having Stanley scout around the South Branch, seeing if any poachers are talking about Charlie. Poachers will tell all to other poachers, especially an Ojibway poacher. That's Calvin's brainstorm. As incentive, he tells Stanley about the reward. So last night Stanley sets up shop on the river, and darned if he doesn't run into a poacher who knows about Charlie. Stanley grills him. And the poacher, he grills Stanley in return. All the while the poacher seems familiar, and finally Stanley figures out who he is. Ready for this, Fitzgerald?"

"Go ahead."

"Kit."

"Say again?"

"Kit was pulling the same thing Stanley was, and for the same idiotic reason. The reward. So he dresses up the way he thinks poachers do, buys worms, wades the South Branch. Kit forgot, though, one thing about his outfit. His cap, one Calvin brought him from New Zealand, said Slowdne Inn on the front. That's how Stanley got wind of who he was. He knows the Slowdne is an angling hotel on the South Island that Calvin guides from. Kit probably thought poachers would take the name for some new beer hangout. Anyway, there the pair were, Kit and Stanley, hunting for poachers and finding each other."

Fitzgerald sipped coffee, said, "Comic, you might say."

"*You* might," Mercy said in a rising voice. "I'd say frightening. You realize what could have happened? They were alone in the wilderness section of the South Branch looking for Charlie's murderer. Stanley's a grown man, so maybe he could have taken care of himself. But Kit? He could have been *killed*, Fitzgerald."

"You're right, of course."

"So as soon as I finished talking to Calvin I called Kit. I wanted to go over to the Kabin Kamp, give him a piece of my mind in person, but I didn't want Verlyn to know what he'd done. I called—and got Jan. She took her sweet time, but she found Kit and, believe me, he got an earful. Know what he told me? His excuse? He was trying to get the reward so he'd have money to go back to college. It's unbelievable. I've told him about a million times he already has the money if he wants it."

"I know you have."

"I made him promise to forget about the reward. He said he didn't need to promise. He'd already forgot. One night on the South Branch, wasting his time with Stanley, was enough. The reward wasn't worth the aggravation. Calvin told me Stanley feels the same way."

"That takes care of Kit and Stanley Elk," Fitzgerald said after a moment. "But you said, before, you thought poaching itself was a dead end."

"I know I did."

"So you think Alec Proffit's wrong? Charlie wasn't killed by a poacher?"

"It's the only thing we've got to go on," Mercy said. "I realize that. But it just seems, after last night, so—"

"Last night was a mix-up, Kit and Stanley Elk running into each other. A poacher still could have killed Charlie. Kit and Stanley might have been on the right track. One night just went wrong."

"So what are you saying? We suit up somebody else as a poacher, put him on the South Branch, wait to see what happens? Night after night?"

Fitzgerald nodded into the phone, said, "It's more nutty than comic."

Mercy sighed. "Proffit may be right. But doing anything about it, that's the dead end." Then Mercy said, "Hold on. Fern's got somebody on another line." A moment later she said, "I'll call you when I'm done. Stay exactly where you are."

\*     \*     \*

"Guess who that was? Theona Orr. Calling from Big Rapids."

"What about?"

"Charlie's things arrived from the campground, and Theona and her daughter were going through them. Planning a garage sale, I'll bet you anything. They found three books from the Ossning library. Theona was miffed I'd sent them to her. They should have been returned to the library."

"You didn't have anything to do with removing Charlie's things."

"But I was the one who came to see her. And I left her my card with the office and home phone numbers. She wanted me to drive right down to Big Rapids, pick up the books, return them to the library. She was a school librarian, if you remember. Library books floating around seem to bother her more than the loss of Charlie."

"What did you tell her?"

"To mail them, of course. I gave her the address of the library. By the time we were done talking she was mightily miffed."

Fitzgerald waited before he said, "Could you get away for lunch? I could grab a bottle of wine, make us some sandwiches. It's a terrific day, if you can forget everything else."

"I haven't done a thing yet except talk on the phone. I'll try to get home early this evening. Make me a huge drink."

"All right. But should I mention anything to Stroud?"

"Lord, no. He'd have a fit if he knew about Kit and Stanley on the South Branch. I told him, the last time we talked, I thought we'd hit a dead end. Nothing's changed."

Fitzgerald waited again before he said, "Just for my information, if Stanley Elk is a known poacher why haven't you—"

"Arrested him? Or why hasn't Vic Laski? We did, a few times way back. Now we leave him alone. Like I said, he only kills fish every now and then."

"In other words, Stanley's a special case with the DNR. Like Charlie was."

"Damned right. Charlie could camp at Rainbow Run and pay when he liked, and Stanley can kill fish. That's what running this office is all about—knowing when to bend, when not. It wouldn't be worth the trouble, clamping down on an Ojibway schoolteacher who is an ideal citizen in every other way. It would probably cause more people to take up poaching, as a protest."

"I'm convinced," Fitzgerald said. "But I doubt Gus Thayer would be."

"He knows. But if he ever prints anything in the *Call*, I'll wring his neck. He knows that, too."

"You're a tough lady."

"And," Mercy said before hanging up, "thoroughly tired of talking on the phone."

# 25

~~~

SOME MORNINGS FITZGERALD found it impossible to get through breakfast, alone at the trestle table, a mug of coffee, a defrosted bagel, a glass of orange juice set out before him. He would switch on the kitchen radio, listen to the news on NPR, but nothing could obscure the deep, burrowing silence of the A-frame. On such mornings he half wished he were back in the newsroom of the *Free Press*, aware of the muted music of computer keys, drawn out of his isolation. The rough equivalent, in Ossning, was the morning rush at the Six-Grain Bakery.

Ordinarily, he would have coffee and a sweet roll in the bakery, glance at a morning paper, chat with Bonnie, then drive back to the A-frame, clean the dishes from the breakfast he hadn't eaten, put some music on the CD player, turn the volume low, and get down to work on his laptop. Or go fishing. Either way, he could get on with his day.

But this morning was different. It wasn't the silence of the house that froze him over his breakfast—an agreeable silence, actually, after the long conversation with Mercy. It was something Mercy had told him, something that stuck in his mind yet refused to clarify itself. Burt Berry hadn't killed Charlie—and searching for a killer among South Branch poachers was a hopeless task. The only new development was what Mercy had said about Charlie's books. That Theona Orr was annoyed they hadn't been returned to the library.

But why couldn't he get that minor matter, library books, out of his mind? It seemed to have something to do with the fact that there were three books.

Fitzgerald left the kitchen, walked through the house, stepped out into the sunshine of the deck. He glanced down through the trees at the river, then turned his back to the view. If he watched the river he would only concentrate on it, wondering whether tricos were coming off the water.

When he wasn't fishing, Charlie was always reading, and always books from the Ossning library. Charlie didn't buy books, as far as Fitzgerald had ever noticed, which was probably understandable if your wife was a librarian—school librarian, as Mercy had reminded him—and it was natural to patronize the local library. So there was nothing unusual about Charlie having library books in his tent at the time of the killing, and nothing unusual about Willard Stroud's deputies not bothering to check the books, finding they were from the Ossning library, before sending them to Theona Orr. But there had been three books. Charlie had checked out three.

And that day at the library, when examining the computer catalogue, he saw that two Will Woodsman books had been checked out.

*       *       *

BACK IN THE kitchen he dialed Mercy's number. "She's stuck in a meeting," Fern Lax told him. "Some people over from the Traverse City office."

"It's important," Fitzgerald said. "At least it might be. Just ask her if Theona Orr mentioned the titles of the three books. Mercy will know what I'm talking about."

"No," Fern said when she came back on the line. "All she told Mercy was three books."

"Okay. Now this is important, too. Call Theona Orr in Big Rapids. Tell her you're Mercy's secretary, that Mercy wants to know if the three books have been put in the mail yet. If not, Mercy has changed her mind. She'll come down after them."

"Has she changed her mind?"

"It doesn't matter. I'll go down, get the books. But it will be better if you make the call to Theona, as Mercy's secretary. Theona wouldn't know who I was."

Fern hesitated.

"It'll be okay with Mercy. I promise you."

Fitzgerald had just poured more coffee when Fern called back. "Too late. Her daughter took the books to the post office. Should I call there now?"

He thought for a moment before he said, "No. Probably only Theona could get the package back. Going down to Big Rapids might have taken too much time anyway."

"For what?"

"Tell you the truth, Fern, I'm not sure. Have Mercy call me when she gets free of the meeting."

"Okay."

"On my cell phone," Fitzgerald added, "if I'm not at home."

*     *     *

ON THE WARM, sun-filled, high-summer morning, Fitzgerald approached the circulation desk as the sole patron of the Ossning public library. Wanda Voss, peering at him over the top of half-glasses, produced a welcoming smile. The smile broadened when he told her that Charlie Orr's library books were safely on the way to Ossning via mail from Big Rapids.

Then he told her what he wanted, and the smile changed to a frown.

"I know," he agreed, "there's confidentiality involved—a library member's circulation record. I wouldn't want mine handed around, not that it would reveal anything. I read a lot of junk fiction, is all." He tried a grin, sheepish variety, but the frown remained fixed on Wanda Voss's narrow face.

"This is different, Wanda. Charlie's dead. Murdered. The sheriff could require the circulation records be turned over to him. He might make them public. Who knows, they could get written up in the *Call*. This way, telling me, I can decide if they have any importance. If not, there's no reason to involve the sheriff."

"And it's only the last books Charlie checked out?"

"I don't need the whole record. Only the last three."

"Having books out like that—I was worried what might happen. I didn't wish to say anything to the sheriff. It's such a small matter under the circumstances."

"Of course."

"But—"

"But what?"

"One of the books is an interlibrary loan. From Michigan State University. It would be terribly costly to replace."

Fitzgerald said he understood that. But the two books from the Ossning library—could she look the titles of those up for him?

Wanda Voss still hesitated.

"Maybe we could do it this way. My guess is they're two collections of fishing and hunting articles by an outdoor writer named Will Woodsman. Could you confirm that?"

"How did you know?"

"You don't need to check your records? You're certain?"

"I checked earlier. People don't know, but librarians have an awful duty when someone passes away in the community. We must look to see if they have books outstanding, and if they do, make inquiries as to their return. Delicate inquiries. Charlie Orr was one of our best patrons. He was certain to have books outstanding."

"The interlibrary loan," Fitzgerald asked. "What was that?"

"It's rather involved. First Charlie took out the two volumes by Will Woodsman. Then he came back in, another book on his mind, one he believed he'd read in the past, and he wanted to check to make sure. But the exact title eluded him. He knew the author's name, though, and that was enough. So we put in an interlibrary loan request. We charge two dollars per request—in case you ever want to use the service. Anyway, there was a copy at the Michigan State library. We got it for him, then after two weeks he came back and said he'd like more time if that was possible. We checked with the library, and they were willing to renew it for another period."

"And?"

"Frank Forester was the name Charlie remembered. It was unknown to me. The book we sought, *The Warwick Woodlands*, is quite old. It was published in the 1840s."

"Frank Forester," Fitzgerald repeated.

"He's thought to be one of the founders of outdoor writing in this country. He was an Englishman, well educated, equally well versed in aristocratic sporting traditions. For financial reasons he began writing for the magazines, applying those sporting traditions to America. Frank Forester was a pseudonym first used, if I remember correctly, in a magazine called the *Spirit of the Times*. He thought the name sounded woodsy and democratic. Eventually, Frank Forester became widely admired, publishing numerous sporting books as well as articles."

Fitzgerald said, "How come you know all this, Wanda?"

"Charlie knew. He knew so much."

"And you're certain the name was a pen name?"

"Charlie was. The author's real name, Henry William Herbert, he reserved for publications he considered more serious. Under his real name he published several novels."

"He would have."

Wanda Voss dipped her head, examined Fitzgerald over the top of her glasses. "If you already knew, why are you asking?"

"I didn't know," Fitzgerald said. "But it fits. That's all."

*    *    *

THE WISE THING was to wait—wait for the books to arrive in the mail from Big Rapids, then do some hurried reading, making absolutely certain. He was operating entirely on a hunch. Charlie had checked out the two books of Will Woodsman from the Ossning library—that much of his hunch had been proven right. The third book was something new, something he hadn't known about. Now that he did, he thought he understood why Charlie had wanted it. It all fit together, he had told Wanda Voss.

But that, everything fitting, was another part of his hunch. He wouldn't know anything for certain until he had the three books in his hands. The mail from Big Rapids would take a couple days or so. And going through the books once they came . . . more time lost. He could have Wanda check with Traverse City, the nearest good-sized public library, see if they had the books, drive over there if they did. But Wanda wouldn't have contacted Michigan State if Traverse City had the interlibrary-loan book. It was fairly rare, she had said.

Fitzgerald sat in the Cherokee in the library parking lot, windows open to the warmth of the day, trying to decide. The wise thing was to wait. If he asked anyone for advice, that was what they would advise. Don't go off half-cocked. Go back to the A-frame, settle down with the laptop, work on your novel, wait for the books to arrive from Big Rapids. Or go fishing, waiting that way.

It was advice he couldn't take. He wouldn't be able to get his mind on anything but the books, on what they might reveal. He wouldn't be able to focus on his novel or the river. But that wasn't the whole of it. He had a nagging feeling he was pressed for time.

From the car he called Hoke Harkness at the *Free Press*. When Harkness came on the line, Fitzgerald apologized for what he was going to ask. He needed help. Again.

"Up there in the woods," Harkness said, "everybody's useless?"

"I'm in the parking lot of the public library," Fitzgerald said. "I could go in, ask the librarian to dig up the information. Or I could get on the Internet, find out that way."

"But you'd rather use up my valuable energy."

"I'm in a rush, Hoke. At least I think I am." After he told Harkness what he wanted, he said he would phone back within the hour.

"Hold on," Harkness said. "This is a different guy. You're sniffing out another story?"

"Within the hour," Fitzgerald repeated, and added, "I'll owe you one."

"It's two. You don't think I'm running a tab?"

*     *     *

"WHY?" WILLARD STROUD said when Fitzgerald asked to listen again to the recorded interview with Alec Proffit.

"I'm not sure. There was something . . . I'm not sure I'm remembering it right."

"Something about what?"

"I won't know until I hear the recording."

"Are you trying to be mysterious," Stroud asked, "or don't you really know what you're talking about?"

"Probably the latter."

Stroud called out to Elsie to get the cassette from the file on Charlie Orr, put it on the machine in the interview room. "Maybe I should listen with you," he said to Fitzgerald. "Except I've got things to do. So maybe you'll tell me if you remembered right. We're working together on Charlie's death. You, Mercy, me. You remember that much?"

"I do."

$$* \qquad * \qquad *$$

"Well?" Stroud asked when Fitzgerald returned to his office.

"What I remembered—I was right."

"And?"

"Proffit told you he came back to Rainbow Run when he realized that, Charlie murdered, he had a better story than the one he planned to write about poaching on the Borchard. It was a hotter story, he told you, than the one he'd bargained on. As Will Woodsman he was going to write it up in *Angling World*."

"Go on," Stroud said when Fitzgerald stopped.

"That's all."

"You wanted to remember he was going to write about Charlie's murder, pointing the finger at poachers?"

"And the DNR."

"I could have told you that's what he said."

"I needed to hear for myself."

Stroud looked hard at Fitzgerald. "You figuring on writing something? That's what this is about? You figuring on beating Proffit to the punch?"

"He's a big name as a writer. I couldn't do that if I wanted to."

"You could get something in the *Free Press*."

"But you know I won't. Not unless I tell you first."

"Then what the hell's going on here?"

"I was only trying to remember something," Fitzgerald said. "I told you."

$$* \qquad * \qquad *$$

"Short notice like that," Hoke Harkness said when Fitzgerald called from the parking area of the city-county building, "it's all I could pull up."

"It's enough."

"Don't suppose you could tell me why."

"It would take too long. It's just the last piece of information I needed. I'm pretty sure everything fits together now."

"Okay, play it your way."

"I'll let you know when it's over."

"You do recall we run a newspaper here?"

"But I don't work for it anymore."

"You're on leave, is all."

"I don't know," Fitzgerald said. "It's beginning to feel permanent."

# 26

H IS FIRST CHOICE was Calvin, but when Fitzgerald called him from the Cherokee there was no answer at the cabin, which probably meant Calvin was either guiding or out fishing himself. Verlyn was a possibility, but getting Verlyn involved would require a lengthy explanation—and might, in the process, alert Kit. Mercy would never forgive him, Fitzgerald knew, if any harm came to her son.

There was no reason to anticipate harm, or at least any he couldn't handle himself. But it was wise, all the same, to have a backup. He believed he knew now what had happened to Charlie Orr, and what was likely to happen next. But he couldn't be certain. A backup was needed in the event he was wrong.

Mercy would expect him to call on her, but she was in a day-long meeting, and he didn't want to draw her out, foolishly so if what they were doing turned out to be yet another dead end. Besides, Mercy would insist on even more of a backup: Stroud and his deputies, everyone armed to the teeth.

Fitzgerald wasn't that confident he was on the right track. He wasn't merely operating on his hunch. He was beyond that, thanks to what he had heard on the tape and what Hoke Harkness had told him on the phone. But he couldn't know definitely until he took the next step, which meant going out there, confronting him—with a backup hidden in the jack pines.

*       *       *

AT THE DOOR of the fifth-wheeler, Billie Berry told him Burt was inspecting campsites farther along the first loop road in preparation for campers who, so it was hoped, would soon be showing up at Rainbow Run. When Fitzgerald located him at site twelve, Burt came over to the Cherokee, leaned in the passenger-side window.

"Remember me," Fitzgerald asked him, "from the Eagles?"

"Yup."

"Billie told me you were here."

"She's fixing us lunch."

"I need your help, Burt."

Fitzgerald motioned Burt into the Cherokee. He still felt pressed for time, but he needed Burt to fully understand. What he was going to ask of him wasn't among the ordinary duties of a campground host.

"Yup," Burt said when Fitzgerald inquired, "I got one. Smith & Wesson .38. Don't like being in the woods with Billie without protection. Deputies asked what I had, I told 'em a handgun, they were only interested if it was a shotgun."

"I'm asking for another reason."

As Fitzgerald explained what he wanted, Burt nodded knowingly. "I've been keeping an eye on him for the sheriff," he said when Fitzgerald finished.

"This is something more, Burt. Can you get the handgun from the trailer without Billie noticing?"

"Yup."

"And make certain she stays inside?"

"She doesn't go around the campground much. Not after what happened to Charlie."

"Good. Now when you get to the campsite, hold back in the cover. Make totally certain he can't see or hear you."

"Had him sized up all along as Charlie's killer," Burt said. "He tries anything, I'll wing him."

"It's just a precaution. I don't expect a problem."

"Fellow who killed once can kill twice."

"That's why you're backing me up. But don't overreact. If I'm right, he has no reason to kill me."

"You figuring out he killed Charlie, that's a reason."

"I don't think so." Fitzgerald reached across the seat, touched Burt's arm. "You don't have to do this. We could get the sheriff out here."

"Give me five minutes."

"You're certain?"

Burt grinned. "Beats hell out of bingo."

\*　　　\*　　　\*

"You don't know me," Fitzgerald announced. "Mercy Virdon and I live together. You've met Mercy. She came out here to see you."

Alec Proffit had risen from his camp chair, lowering a stenographer's notebook to the ground beside him, when Fitzgerald stopped behind the Land Cruiser and came up the path into the campsite. He stood now across the fire pit, taller than Fitzgerald had imagined, well proportioned, better looking, hands sunk in the pockets of khaki trousers. The blue shirt he was wearing had a Royal Coachman stitched above the pocket. Only Orvis, the Berrys had called him.

"I'm disturbing you?"

Proffit smiled. "I was merely making notes."

"For a Will Woodsman article?"

"No." Proffit turned, motioned toward the campsite's picnic table.

"I won't be staying," Fitzgerald said.

"You're with the DNR as well? I confess I failed to live up to my agreement with your colleague. I told her I'd go to the sheriff, speak with him again. Earlier I made a rather baseless charge against the organization."

"I know."

"Oh?"

"I heard the recording with Mercy. I know what you said."

"Yet this isn't about that?"

"Mercy and I are together," Fitzgerald repeated, "but I'm not with the DNR. I used to work for a newspaper, now I'm trying to become a writer. I fish and I write." He paused, holding Proffit's eyes. "The other thing you should know is that I was a friend of Charlie Orr. We fished together—and talked about books. We talked a lot about books."

"Ah," Proffit said, releasing the sound in a long sigh. "You didn't, I suppose, come here to discuss your writing."

"No."

"You came to discuss books. I was expecting that—that someone would. The sheriff perhaps. He seemed an intelligent man, possibly a reader." Proffit again motioned to the picnic table. "Please. Humor me to this extent."

\*         \*         \*

FITZGERALD SAID, "THERE were three books in Charlie's tent: Will Woodsman's two collections and a book of Frank Forester's called *The Warwick Woodlands*. The books were sent back to Charlie's wife along with the rest of his belongings. She phoned Mercy, told her the books were library books. Two of them were from the local public library, the other was an interlibrary loan. The librarian told me this much."

"And you made the connection."

"Guessed it."

"Yes, a writer would. Very astute, nonetheless."

"Did Charlie really send you a letter?"

"He did."

"But it wasn't about poaching on the river."

"No. Not on the river." Alec Proffit folded his hands on the scarred surface, looked agreeably across the table. "I've often thought it could be a plot for a novel: committing a crime, knowing you would be caught out, wondering who will make the discovery. In this instance, one might expect a fanatic bibliophile, someone spending his life in a library, devoted to unmasking errors. In truth, I suspected it would be someone less obvious, though I hardly guessed it would be someone spending his summers in a tent in northern Michigan. When Charlie Orr wrote to me, the plot was completed."

"When he wrote to you about poaching?"

"Let's not beat about the bush. The proper term is plagiarism. Charlie had read Frank Forester as well as Will Woodsman. He realized I'd appropriated Forester's work, changing only some of the archaic phrasing and punctuation. In his letter he reproduced several parallel passages. It was quite telling."

"He meant to expose you?"

"He didn't say. He didn't even use the word—plagiarism. There was no indication he meant to contact the magazine or the publisher of the book collections."

"He wouldn't have. Not Charlie."

"Perhaps not. But that wasn't the point. He knew. I'd been found out."

Fitzgerald said, "As Will Woodsman, that pen name, you didn't go out of your way to disguise the connection with Frank Forester."

Proffit appeared to smile inwardly. "Don't criminals wish to be caught? Isn't there some psychological nonsense to that effect? The truth is I greatly admire Forester. Will Woodsman—I chose the name, to the degree that I'm aware, as a form of homage to a distinguished predecessor."

"So you came out here, to Michigan, to see what Charlie meant to do with his discovery of the plagiarism?"

Proffit shook his head. "That didn't matter. I came out of curiosity. The return address on the letter was a state forest campground. I doubted mail would even be delivered to such an address. When I looked up the town he'd given in the address, Ossning, I found it was located on a notable trout stream. As I say, I was curious."

"Yet you never, after you came out here, met with Charlie."

"There was no need. I observed him from a distance in the campground and possibly on the river. If he'd checked with the campground hosts, he wouldn't have associated my name on the registration form with Will Woodsman's column, nor would he have associated my novels, if he knew them, with the name. And he had no reason to be alerted by my license plate, since he'd written to me in care of the magazine."

"You went down to Big Rapids as well."

"To see how Charlie lived when he wasn't in the campground. That was all. I was filling in my curiosity."

Fitzgerald leaned across the table, again held Proffit's eyes. "So you satisfied your curiosity about the man who discovered you were copying Frank Forester's work in your magazine column."

"Yes."

"That's all you wanted to do, learn about Charlie."

"Yes."

"And you learned all you needed."

"Yes."

"Then why did you kill him?"

\*　　　\*　　　\*

WHAT REACTION DID he expect? Fear? Anger? A burst, for a second time, of uncontrollable rage? Alec Proffit's manner across the picnic table had been calm, measured, assured—yet now he was accused of murder. Fitzgerald searched Proffit's face, waiting for the reaction that must come, at the same time cocked his ear for any sound emerging from the wall of pine beyond the campsite.

How, out there, would Burt Berry react?

For several moments Proffit said nothing. Then, slowly, he swung his head from side to side. When he spoke, his voice was unchanged. "I shouldn't have. It was quite useless."

Fitzgerald repeated the word. "Useless."

"It changed nothing."

Fitzgerald felt his chest tighten. He forced himself to hold his hands clasped on the surface of the table, fingers clenched in a vise. "For Charlie it changed everything."

Again Proffit shook his head. "I was speaking of myself. Nothing was changed for me. I thought you might understand, a fellow writer."

"Would-be writer."

"For a deluded instant I tried to escape my fate. That sounds overly grand, yet it captures the way I felt. That night I came back late from following Charlie on the river. What I told the sheriff was true. I hooked some fine browns, allowed myself to become engaged in the fishing. When I returned to the campground, Charlie was here, light coming from his campsite. I felt drawn to it. When I approached the site, I could see a form clearly illuminated inside the tent, stretched out on a cot, reading by lantern light. Instantly, I decided to kill him. It was a thought that hadn't, at any prior point, entered my mind. It wasn't

Charlie himself I wished to kill. I had no feeling for him one way or another. It was what he represented—a man reading. I wished to rid the world of that."

Proffit's eyes shifted from Fitzgerald, seemed to penetrate the trees at the edge of the campsite. When he looked back, a faint smile had emerged on his face.

"A strange hope, wouldn't you agree, for a writer? In any case, it was totally irrational. Yet I acted upon it. I came back to my campsite, took a shotgun from my vehicle, walked back to the tent, fired both barrels at the reclining form. Charlie's life, I presumed, was instantly extinguished, yet his lantern was not. I stood there for some time, immobile, watching the light continue to glow. Continuing to mock me. Standing there, outside the tent, the light glowing, I understood the hopelessness of what I'd done."

Fitzgerald felt his fingers grow numb. He tried to ease his grip, to keep looking back steadily at Proffit, to repress fury from his voice. "If you didn't plan on killing Charlie, why did you have the shotgun?"

"A precaution when I'm camping. Nothing more. Until the moment I removed it, I'd nearly forgotten it was in my car."

"And afterward?"

"I replaced it."

"The sheriff searched your campsite. He found your notebook in the tent."

"I'd driven off, so the car couldn't be searched. I drove to a café, then a motel in town."

"From the motel you came to the sheriff's office. Why did you?"

The smile faded from Proffit's face. "You don't understand, do you? You really don't see."

Fitzgerald said nothing.

"I've already told you. Killing Charlie was an attempt to escape my fate. Going to the sheriff was another. And equally irrational."

# 27

FITZGERALD FORCED HIMSELF to hold his gaze on Alec Proffit's face, not let it shift in the direction of a sound that, this moment, appeared to come from the pines enclosing the campsite. Had Burt, shifting position, snapped a fallen branch? Looking, Fitzgerald knew he would notice nothing in the dense growth. He had to keep believing Burt was out there. And close enough, if the time came, to help.

Proffit gave no indication he had noticed the sound. His eyes across the table looked steadily at Fitzgerald yet seemed strangely unfocused. "You're right," Fitzgerald said to him. "I don't understand."

Proffit raised his hands for a moment before returning them to the table. "Perhaps you can't. Perhaps only a genuine writer can."

"Try me."

"In the motel I sought to concentrate my attention, yet my mind kept returning to Charlie's tent. I kept seeing the lantern light, seeing its glow. The light had been meant to illumine words on a page—and from that my mind leaped to the letter Charlie had written me. Had he, I began to wonder, kept a copy? In the handwritten letter Charlie had gone to the painstaking effort of copying out the parallel passages in Frank Forester and Will Woodsman. He might have made an equal effort to duplicate his letter.

"I knew I couldn't return to his tent, search to see if a copy existed. Charlie's body would have been discovered, the authorities would have sealed off the campsite. It occurred to me that the tent could be searched indirectly by turning myself in to the sheriff. I knew he'd be looking for me, someone who had been camping at Rainbow Run and was now missing. I assumed he might have entered my tent, discovered the notes about Charlie. By turning myself in I'd learn whether he had also found, in Charlie's tent, a copy of the letter—the letter contradicting the one I'd tell him Charlie had written.

"I left the motel for the sheriff's office, told him my story. He said nothing about a copy, asking only about the original, which I told him I had burned. That was the truth—I hardly wanted in my possession a letter demonstrating my plagiarism—but it had no importance. What mattered, so I chose to believe, was that the sheriff had no reason, from what he'd found in Charlie's tent, to reject what I had told him. I could return to the campground, remaining there until the sheriff released me. I had escaped my fate.

"It was impossible, of course. Eventually, someone else would find me out. I had given no thought to the books that might be discovered in Charlie's tent. I thought only of a copy of the letter. Yet it didn't matter. What Charlie had learned about me would be learned again. I knew that. There was no escape from myself, consequently no escape from my fate."

Fitzgerald said, "You keep saying that."

"And it keeps sounding overly grand, whereas the reality is merely sordid. That was what I was fleeing when I came to Rainbow Run in the first place. What I was fleeing when I killed Charlie and again when I left the motel for the sheriff's office. I was fleeing the sordid business that must be done." Proffit paused, looked closely at Fitzgerald. "You don't understand this, either?"

"I'm trying."

"Let me show you something."

Proffit rose from the table, easily swung his legs over the seat. Fitzgerald's impulse was to rise with him, follow. But Burt was out there, hidden in the pines, watching. If Fitzgerald moved as well, followed Proffit, Burt might overreact, might reveal himself. Or worse.

From the table, Proffit crossed the packed dirt of the campsite to his tent, removed from inside a long gun case. Fitzgerald froze. His hands were locked to the edge of the table, but he couldn't lift himself, couldn't move. He stared at Proffit, walking back toward him now, the case—brown suede, leather trimmed—already unzipped along its length and carried horizontally by a pair of handles. He placed the case on the table, carefully took from it a double-barrel shotgun and extended it outward.

Rapidly Fitzgerald calculated what Burt could see from the pines: one man seated, the other standing, looking down, shotgun in hand but holding it forward, displaying it. There was no threat—Burt could see that. Not yet there wasn't. At the same time, Burt could conclude what Fitzgerald concluded: from the already opened case and the cautious way Proffit handled the gun, it could well be loaded.

"Supreme craftsmanship," Proffit was saying to him. "In its way, a work of art. You're knowledgeable about shotguns? A Mossberg, .16 gauge, black walnut stock, used for upland bird shooting, the only hunting I do. A Sweet Sixteen, some call it. Yet this work of art left Charlie torn to pieces. It must have. I didn't see the body. I spared myself that. But I imagined the horror there beside that mocking light. You employ a thing of beauty yet the result is sordid. From that reality there is no escape."

Fitzgerald tried to rise, fell back against the seat of the picnic table. "Wait," he managed to say.

"I kept the gun in the car when I went to the café and then the motel. I knew this was a risk, but there was more use for it. Then I hatched the idea of going to the sheriff's office, telling him the story of the letter. It was possible the car would be searched while I was there. So I removed the gun to the motel room, concealed it, instructed the desk clerk not to make up the room until I returned. When I left the sheriff's office, I placed the gun back in the car. It was never, you see, Charlie I meant to kill."

"Wait," Fitzgerald repeated. "You copied Frank Forester in your columns. Okay. But not all the time. You couldn't have. Much of the time it had to be your own work. It was good work. And you wrote novels that didn't have anything to do with Forester. Right?"

Proffit nodded.

"So what's it really matter? Probably every published writer poaches some words now and then. Nobody gets upset these days with something like that. Besides, Charlie wouldn't have said anything. What he wrote you, it was between the two of you. That was his way. Charlie liked to organize the world, but he was always private about it. One on one. You could depend on Charlie keeping quiet."

"I told you," Proffit said. "That wasn't the issue. I knew."

"Hear me out." Fitzgerald spoke rapidly, filling the air with his voice. "If you have to get it out in the open, write a column, tell what you did. Make a public apology. In the end, readers will think more of you, a man able to admit a mistake. They'll forgive you."

"Possibly. But I can't. And you're forgetting something. I killed Charlie. That isn't forgivable."

Fitzgerald dug his fingers into the edge of the table, began forcing himself upward. "The thing to do is let me drive you in to the sheriff. Tell him what you've told me. You'll get legal counsel. You owe yourself that much."

Proffit shook his head.

"But why not? You can't just—"

"I've waited too long. You've done me a favor, coming here this way. There's no escape. Your presence makes that quite certain."

"I just wanted to talk. About the library books. That's all."

"A writer finally brought to his senses by books. Appropriate." Then Proffit repeated, "I've waited too long."

"Just do this," Fitzgerald said. "Put the gun on the table. We'll work from there. We'll talk some more."

He was nearly standing now, the position awkward, half bent over the table, trying to swing his legs free from the seat without making a sudden movement. He had to stand. He had to face Proffit, close to him, in position to reach out for the gun. He had to try.

He eased a leg over the bench, at the same instant heard the sound, certain this time, and caught the movement from the corner of his eye.

"Wait!" he shouted, too late. Burt had stepped free of the cover of the pines. He was stumbling toward them, handgun extended.

Fitzgerald saw Proffit's head snap toward Burt, surprise in his eyes yet the faint smile returned to his lips. Saw him draw the gun inward, toward his chest, twin barrels directed upward. Saw him open his mouth, with fluid motion lean forward at the waist. Saw one hand reach, unerringly, for the trigger.

Then Fitzgerald shut his eyes.

# 28

MERCY HAD INSTRUCTED Fern Lax to phone Fitzgerald at the A-frame at eight-thirty. During the night he had taken a sleeping pill at Mercy's insistence and was fast asleep when she left for the DNR office at seven. Mercy had turned off the answering machine, and Fern was to keep ringing until Fitzgerald picked up the phone. She was to remind him of the news conference Willard Stroud had scheduled. Fitzgerald wasn't required to attend, but Mercy thought it would be easiest for him if he did. Gus Thayer, for one, was certain to hound him for details of what had taken place at Rainbow Run.

"I'm supposed to get you up," Fern said when Fitzgerald answered on the first ring.

"On my second cup of coffee."

"Mercy said you were dead to the world—" Fern nearly bit her tongue. "You know, really asleep."

"Until she left I was. I can't sleep in an empty house."

"Some can." Fern was about to tell him about her husband, Luther, who once slept through a tornado that hit a trailer court they were living in at the time. But there was something in Fitzgerald's voice that stopped her. He sounded fully awake, yet he didn't seem his usual self, which certainly wasn't surprising given what he had been through. Mercy had given her some information about events at the campground, but she needn't have. The story was all over town.

"I'm supposed to remind you of the news conference." She tried for a business-like tone. "It's in the city-county building at eleven." When Fitzgerald didn't respond, she added, "There's already TV from Traverse

217

City here. A young woman came to the office, wanted to talk to Mercy. Mercy said there wouldn't be anything to say until the news conference."

When Fitzgerald still didn't respond, Fern said, "So you'll be there?"

"I will."

"Mercy said why don't you come by here first. You can go over together."

"No need. I'll meet her there."

"Good. I'll let her know." She knew she should end the conversation, but a question lingered, one she had wanted to ask the moment Fitzgerald answered her ring.

"Are you okay?" Fern asked him.

\*       \*       \*

THROUGH THE WINDOW behind the cash-register counter, Jan saw the Grand Cherokee pull into the parking area outside. She hurried to finish what she had started to do, removing the black-lettered reward sign from the fly shop wall. Fitzgerald didn't need any reminders of what he had gone through the day before.

When he entered, he smiled at her behind the counter, at the same time his eyes took in the rest of the shop. "Sorry," she said, and brushed back loose strands of hair, "everybody's out. You're stuck with me."

"Lucky me."

"You're sweet." She asked then if he wanted coffee.

"On my way to town. I thought I'd stop in."

Jan glanced at her watch. "You're early—for the news conference." She stopped herself. He didn't need any reminders of that, either. On the other hand, maybe he needed someone to talk with about it. She doubted that Mercy, hard-bitten as a nail, provided much of a sympathetic shoulder to lean on.

"C'mon," she insisted, "have some coffee with me." She went out the door behind the counter and came back into the shop with two plastic mugs. Fitzgerald was sitting at the fly-tying bench. She placed one mug in front of him, then went back behind the counter with the other, leaned her elbows on the glass top. "They were talking about the news conference on the radio. That's how I know. And Calvin was in, telling about it."

"He's guiding today?"

Jan shook her head. "He didn't have anything better to do. Verlyn had gone to town, and he and Kit were just hanging around the shop. So I told them to do something, go out fishing for a while, do anything. I'd watch the place. Calvin finally got in gear and took Kit downstream to a place where there's supposed to be a big brown. Kit's says it's probably there but nobody can catch it, not even Calvin. To tell you the truth, I was glad to get them out of here. Kit especially. He's down in the dumps. You know about Gwendolyn Underwood?"

"I heard about her," Fitzgerald said.

"She and her father left this morning for Ohio. Their week's up. Kit won't admit it, but he's got a crush on Gwendolyn. It seems they had a spat—something to do with his failure to keep some sort of planned rendezvous the other night. Anyway, she was upset with him. Kit apologized, and she came around to the extent of telling him she might think about Central Michigan as a college. But Kit claims that's just talk. He says her father will make her go to some school out east, that she probably won't even come back to the lodge again." Jan stopped. "Remember how gloomy the world could appear when you were Kit's age?"

"Just barely," Fitzgerald said.

Jan reached for her coffee, then left the mug resting on the counter. She was talking herself rather than letting Fitzgerald—and she didn't need to be talking about gloom. He knew all there was to know about that. She waited, looking across at him at the tying bench, studying him. He was looking back, but she could tell he wasn't seeing her. He wasn't paying attention. One of his hands idly twirled the arm of the tying vise.

"You okay?" Jan asked him.

\*     \*     \*

CROSSING THE STREET from the Six-Grain Bakery, Verlyn saw the Grand Cherokee parked behind his Land Rover, Fitzgerald sitting there, arm angled from the open window. He came over to him, stood beside the vehicle's door. "Killing time?"

It was a dumb thing to say, considering, but Fitzgerald didn't seem to notice. "Until the news conference," he said.

Verlyn dipped his head in the direction of the bakery. "Going in?"

"I was. Thought I'd pass the time with Bonnie, then changed my mind. Saw the Rover, so—"

"You did right. You go in there, they'll swarm all over you. You'll never get to Bonnie."

Fitzgerald was looking at him, smiling faintly. "You did?"

"Bonnie and I go way back," Verlyn said. "*Way* back." He went around to the other side of the vehicle, opened the passenger door, got in beside Fitzgerald. "She was the first girl I ever went around with in Ossning."

"I didn't know that," Fitzgerald said.

"You weren't here then. We were in school together, Bonnie a year behind me. We had serious hots for each other. Talked about getting married, all that stuff. Instead I hooked up with Mercy."

"Why did you?"

"Mercy had some sense, Bonnie didn't have any. Back then I didn't have any either, but I knew that much. Bonnie hooked up with the big jock in my class, Ernie Sheets. Her first husband. Slick Sheets, we used to call him. He works out at Weyerhaeuser now. Damned bait fisherman."

"I don't know him," Fitzgerald said.

"I've been coming in mornings, talking with her. Puttin' a little thrill in her life." Verlyn grinned across the seat. "That's bull. Bonnie's had too many thrills. I've just been thinking about when we were in school, both kids, seeing what she remembers." Verlyn paused, rubbed his stubble of beard. "Bonnie says I'm gettin' like all the old farts, digging up the past. That's not the whole reason. You know what is? Little girl's been staying at the lodge with her old man, taking some instruction from Calvin and Kit. She looks enough like Bonnie, that age, to be her own kid. That's what got me coming in, the girl a copy of Bonnie, bringin' to my mind our old stuff together. But I know—I got to get myself back in the real world. I've got Jan now, and that's pretty lucky for an old fart."

Verlyn stopped, looking at Fitzgerald, realizing he wasn't listening.

Why would he? Other things were on his mind. "You got some time before the news conference," he reminded him.

Fitzgerald nodded.

Verlyn kept looking at him, trying to read his face. "You gonna be okay?" he asked finally.

*     *     *

WHEN FITZGERALD CAME through the door, Elsie told him everyone was in the conference room, Mercy included. Then she told him there had been phone calls for him—three calls, to be exact—from someone at the *Detroit Free Press* named Harkness. He had been calling for Fitzgerald all over town.

Fitzgerald turned back to the door. "I'll call on my cell phone."

"No you won't," Elsie said, and aimed a finger at the phone on her desk. "Right here."

"It should be on my nickel."

"Call," Elsie insisted.

Fitzgerald nodded toward the sheriff's door before he picked up the phone. "Boss still breathing fire?"

"Afraid so."

"I deserve it."

Elsie leaned across her desk, whispered, "You just take care of yourself, that's all."

*     *     *

"I KNOW WHAT happened," Hoke Harkness said when he answered. "We got a wire story, couple grafs. Bad time, huh?"

"Bad enough."

"I figured you wouldn't write anything. You feel like talking to a rewrite man, I'm wondering? Feed him some inside stuff?"

"I don't think so," Fitzgerald said.

"Your deal with the local sheriff?" When Fitzgerald didn't answer, Harkness said, "We could send a reporter up there."

"You could."

"But I think we'll go with the wire story. Maybe all it's worth, north woods stuff like that."

"Your decision."

"Right." Then Harkness said, "Hang in there, boy."

\*     \*     \*

STROUD ASKED FITZGERALD to sit beside Mercy at the folding table, the three of them facing the media contingent. Mercy thought it wasn't right, Fitzgerald having to squint into the light of the television camera after what he had been through, but he said it was the best way, sitting up front, to respond to questions.

Gus Thayer sat directly before them, crew cut bristling under fluorescent light. Beside him the rail-thin blonde from WGTU in Traverse City kept glancing at her watch. On the other side the summer intern for the *Traverse City Record-Eagle* scratched his beard, with his other hand doodled in a spiral notebook.

"All right," Stroud began, "I'm going to give you a brief statement. Then you ask your questions. Yesterday morning Mr. Alec Proffit, Norwich, Vermont, died from self-inflicted shotgun wounds in Rainbow Run campground at approximately eleven twenty. An emergency vehicle arrived from Ossning shortly thereafter, but nothing could be done for him. The Tamarack County medical examiner, Slocum Byrd, has officially ruled Proffit's death a suicide.

"Prior to his death, Proffit confessed in the hearing of two witnesses that he was responsible for the murder of Mr. Charlie Orr. We have sworn statements to that effect from both witnesses, Mr. Donal Fitzgerald and Mr. Burt Berry. Proffit was a writer of magazine articles under the pen name Will Woodsman and a writer of novels under the name Peter Allston. It seems that Orr discovered Proffit was taking material for his Will Woodsman articles from an early nineteenth-century outdoor writer by the name of Frank Forester. Orr wrote to Proffit, demonstrating the plagiarism, which was the reason Proffit came here from Vermont. He killed Orr to try to cover up the plagiarism. Then he killed himself, using the same shotgun with which he killed Orr. The county attorney will make the final determination, but at the moment we believe that Proffit's suicide closes the murder case. The parks department in Lansing will be issuing a statement, but as far as my office is concerned, Rainbow Run is fully operational as a state forest campground."

When Stroud said the floor was open for questions, the television camera swung at once to Fitzgerald. "Would you explain," the TV reporter asked, "why you went to the campground to see Alec Proffit? Did you know then he was the murderer?"

"I believed so," Fitzgerald said. "Everything pointed his way."

"Because you learned—learned, too—that he was plagiarizing the work of another writer?"

"I guessed he was. Charlie Orr had two books of Proffit's—Will Woodsman's—and a book of Frank Forester in his tent at the time he was killed. They were library books. I learned about them when Charlie's wife said she was returning the books to the Ossning library. Proffit claimed Charlie had written him about poaching on the river—that's what made the connection for me. Charlie had written him about poaching, but poaching of words, not fish."

The intern with the *Record-Eagle* raised a hand, asked, "Proffit killed Orr because he found him out. Why didn't he try to kill you?"

"All I know is what he said, which is that he anticipated someone else would learn about the plagiarism. Others would discover it. Killing Charlie, he said, had been a mistake. He didn't want to kill anyone else."

"Except himself."

"Yes."

"You risked your neck," the intern went on, "out there alone. You couldn't know for sure Proffit wouldn't kill you."

"I didn't go alone. The campground host, Burt Berry, was back in the pines with a handgun. In case anything went wrong."

"How come he isn't here?" Gus Thayer asked.

"I'll answer that," Mercy said. "Mr. Berry hasn't been feeling well since—since what happened. I advised him to rest for the time being."

"It did go wrong," the TV reporter said, "at the campground. Proffit killed himself."

"Yes," Fitzgerald said.

"Would you describe the manner in which he did so?"

"I'll handle that," Stroud broke in. "Proffit put his mouth over the muzzle of a double-barrel .16 gauge shotgun, pulled the trigger."

"He could do that," the intern asked, "reaching down?"

"He did it."

Silence held in the conference room until the young woman asked Fitzgerald, "In retrospect, do you wish you had contacted the sheriff's department before you went to the campground?"

"I'll answer that one, too," Stroud said. "He should have. He knows that. We've talked about it. He shouldn't have gone out there with just the campground host. It was a mistake, and he knows it."

"Hold on," Gus Thayer said. "In town they're sayin' Fitzgerald's the one solved Charlie's murder."

"In town," Stroud said stiffly. "Not in this office."

"He didn't go out there," Gus pushed on, "confront Proffit about the library books, nothing would have happened. Proffit might have flown the coop. He might have hustled back to Vermont, and you wouldn't have known a thing. Fitzgerald got him to confess."

"And could have got himself killed in the process."

"That's what they're sayin' in town."

"I heard people calling him a hero," the intern joined in. "He risked his neck figuring out the murder."

The TV reporter glanced at her watch, said, "I understand there is a reward, Sheriff Stroud, for information about the murderer of Charlie Orr. Could you tell us who will receive it?"

"Fitzgerald," Gus Thayer said.

"Who else?" the intern said.

Stroud looked directly into the light of the television camera, announced sourly, "It's my decision, and I haven't decided."

# 29

~~~~~~~~~

"Let's agree on this," Mercy said to him in the parking area of the city-county building. They had gotten in the Cherokee, and Fitzgerald was about to start the engine. "We're not going to say another word about risking your life in the campground. You shouldn't have gone out there with just Burt as a backup. It was entirely stupid, but it's over and done with. Period. The end."

"Agreed."

"Next thing to settle is where to have lunch. Your choice."

"Anywhere with you," Fitzgerald said, "that's alone."

"Really? We could go to the hotel, though everyone would want to talk with you."

"Really."

"Then let's grab sandwiches and stuff at Glen's, have a picnic. There's a place I'd like to go."

"Where?"

"Rainbow Run."

\*　　　\*　　　\*

From Glen's supermarket Fitzgerald took the South Downriver Road, turned in at the campground, slowed as they neared Burt and Billie's fifth-wheeler at the entrance to the first loop road. "Don't stop," Mercy said. "I'll wave in case they're looking."

"What you said about Burt at the news conference," Fitzgerald asked. "It's true?"

"He cared for Billie after Charlie's death, now she's doing the same for him. He's pretty broken up. He thinks he should have done something different. Maybe tried to hit Proffit."

Fitzgerald said, "Coming out of the woods, he fired a shot in the air, trying to draw Proffit's attention. Trying anything. He didn't know what was going on, Proffit bending over the shotgun that way."

"How could he?"

"I could have told him. Warned him it might happen."

"Shooting at Proffit wouldn't have helped. I told Burt that last night when I came out to see him. He couldn't have stopped somebody hell bent on killing himself. Besides, he probably couldn't have hit him with a handgun."

"They'll stay on here, Burt and Billie?"

"We'll talk together later. But I'm thinking it might be good for them to leave for the rest of the summer. I can work out something—a temporary host couple. Next season it might be best to transfer to another campground, if they still want to serve as hosts. I can find a place for them nearly as nice."

"I hope you do. They've been through a lot."

"Billie can't get over the look of Charlie's tent, shot through the way it was. Burt can't get over Proffit. You know, how he looked afterward."

"It was a God-awful mess."

"And we're not going to talk about it."

*       *       *

ON THE SECOND loop road, Mercy told Fitzgerald to park outside campsite forty-three. From there, avoiding having to drive past Charlie Orr's campsite or Alec Proffit's, they could follow a pine-chip path through the jack pines in the direction of the high banks along the river.

They walked single file, silent, Fitzgerald carrying the plastic sack from Glen's. When the path turned, close now to the river, they could see patches of water below the pine and spruce. In a small open meadow Mercy stopped, pointed to a downed log. They could sit in the clearing among wild blueberry and seedling pines, prop their backs against the log, have their picnic.

"Charlie probably camped about here when he first came to the river. Before the campground was redesigned. You can still see where the old campfires were. Over there, the old steps, he'd have gone down that way to fish."

"Nice spot," Fitzgerald said.

"That day I went to see Proffit, I came out here afterward. I could really feel Charlie's presence."

Fitzgerald handed Mercy a sandwich and a can of beer, opened a bag of potato chips. "That's why we're here now?"

"In part."

"The other?"

"Tell me honestly how you feel."

"Not the way everyone seems to think. It's not because of how Proffit died, in front of me that way. Mostly I feel guilty."

"But why?"

"Did Stroud tell you what Proffit was writing in his spiral notebook?"

Mercy shook her head.

"A debate, I suppose you'd call it. Pros and cons of killing himself. What first put it in his mind is what Hoke Harkness told me about what happened to Henry William Herbert. One night, after a dinner party with friends, he'd shot himself with a pistol. His young wife had left him, and he was despondent, though no one thought he was suicidal. Proffit was suicidal for another reason—the plagiarizing he'd done from Herbert's Frank Forester work.

"In the notebook he put down a lot of reasons for not killing himself: He was still fairly young and healthy, he had money, friends, position. All the usual reasons. But he kept coming back to one thing. It wasn't just that he'd plagiarized but what he'd plagiarized—the work of a man who pioneered a code of ethical conduct in hunting and fishing. From Frank Forester came the idea of outdoor sportsmanship in the country, and that was what Proffit couldn't write off in his notebook. He'd become an important voice in environmental ethics by poaching words from the man who gave birth to such views. It was the hypocrisy of what he'd done that he couldn't get around."

Mercy said, "That day I came out here he was writing in a notebook."

"He was trying to write his way out of killing himself. Killing Charlie was another way. But he couldn't rid the world of people who'd learn about his plagiarism. The way Charlie's light stayed on after the shooting—that told him so. There would be someone else discovering the plagiarism. And he couldn't rid himself of his sense of hypocrisy. That was the main thing, an inability to escape himself."

"Okay," Mercy said, "I see that. But why should you feel guilty?"

"When Hoke Harkness told me about Herbert's suicide, I guessed that's what Proffit had in mind. Deep down, maybe I guessed that was why he'd come out to Michigan in the first place. To kill himself. But when I came to the campground, it wasn't to stop him. I wasn't thinking about that. I wanted to learn if he'd killed Charlie. If he killed himself first, we would never know for certain. We'd have the gun to run tests on. But we wouldn't have an admission of guilt. I was thinking about Charlie, not Proffit."

"So that's why you were in a hurry. It wasn't because you thought Proffit might run off. But you were right. You did learn what happened to Charlie."

"And in the process pushed Proffit over the edge."

"You said yourself he was bent on killing himself."

"I think so. But he was still writing in the notebook, still debating with himself when I showed up."

*       *       *

WHEN THEY FINISHED eating, Mercy leaned back against the log, said, "One thing I don't understand. Proffit said Charlie wrote to him about poaching on the river. But he didn't. He wrote about Proffit's plagiarism. Yet Charlie *was* concerned about poaching. He'd complained to me about it. How could Proffit make up a story that was so plausible?"

"He was a writer."

"So?"

"He wrote novels as well as outdoor articles."

"So?"

"Novelists tell plausible lies. Proffit was good at it. Maybe seeing poachers on the South Branch gave him the idea for the letter, or maybe he invented it from whole cloth. Remember that on the cassette—Stroud's recording—Proffit said that in the letter Charlie disclosed he camped all summer at Rainbow Run and fished at night, which was how he knew about the poaching? Proffit couldn't have actually known such things until he drove out to Michigan and started shadowing Charlie. And—"

"*And*," Mercy said, "Charlie would never have written anything so personal in a letter. He just wouldn't. Not to a total stranger. Why didn't we catch that on the recording?"

"Like I said—Proffit was good at telling a story. He had us believing Charlie wrote him about poachers."

"But at least one thing never rang true. It wasn't like Charlie to go over somebody's head. He'd complain about poachers to me, not to my superiors. And certainly not to a magazine writer. I said that all along."

"You did."

"So Proffit wasn't all that terrific at inventing things."

"I don't know," Fitzgerald said. "He published his novels. Six of the things."

*    *    *

"We came here because of Charlie," Mercy said after they gathered the remains of lunch into the sack from Glen's, "not Proffit. This was Charlie's place. I'll always remember him more here than in the campground." Then she looked over at Fitzgerald and said, "You'll get the reward, you know. Stroud will have to give it to you."

"I'll give it back."

"You can't do that."

"Give it away, then. Maybe to the library in Charlie's name."

"I've got another idea. For some of the money, anyway. Let's get a big stone, have it hauled in here, this clearing or maybe more toward the old stairs. Let's put a plaque on it—brass with Charlie's name, his dates. Something else about his life up here—angler, camper, riverwatcher, something like that. Maybe a quotation at the bottom. Is there anything from Thoreau?"

"Maybe."

"You could work on it. What should be on the plaque."

"All I'm able to write, you mean? No plausible lies?"

"What I mean," Mercy said, "is it's something you could do for Charlie's memory."

"I know," Fitzgerald said. "I'd like to."

"So let's do it. We'll have a dedication ceremony for the monument. All Charlie's old friends from around the river. They're the only ones who ever come this way, who really care for this place."

"You'd invite Charlie's wife?"

Mercy grimaced. "I don't think so."

Fitzgerald said, "How's this? 'I went to the woods because I wished to live deliberately, to front only the essential facts of life . . .'"

"That fits Charlie."

"I'll keep working on it," Fitzgerald said.

#

# Note to the Reader

The outdoor writer Frank Forester is not an invention but, as the story notes, a pen name of Henry William Herbert, a popular writer of the 1840s and 1850s who was an early champion of a code of ethics for anglers and hunters. His book *The Warwick Woodlands, or, Things as They Were There, Ten Years Ago* was published in Philadelphia in 1845. Herbert took his own life in 1858.